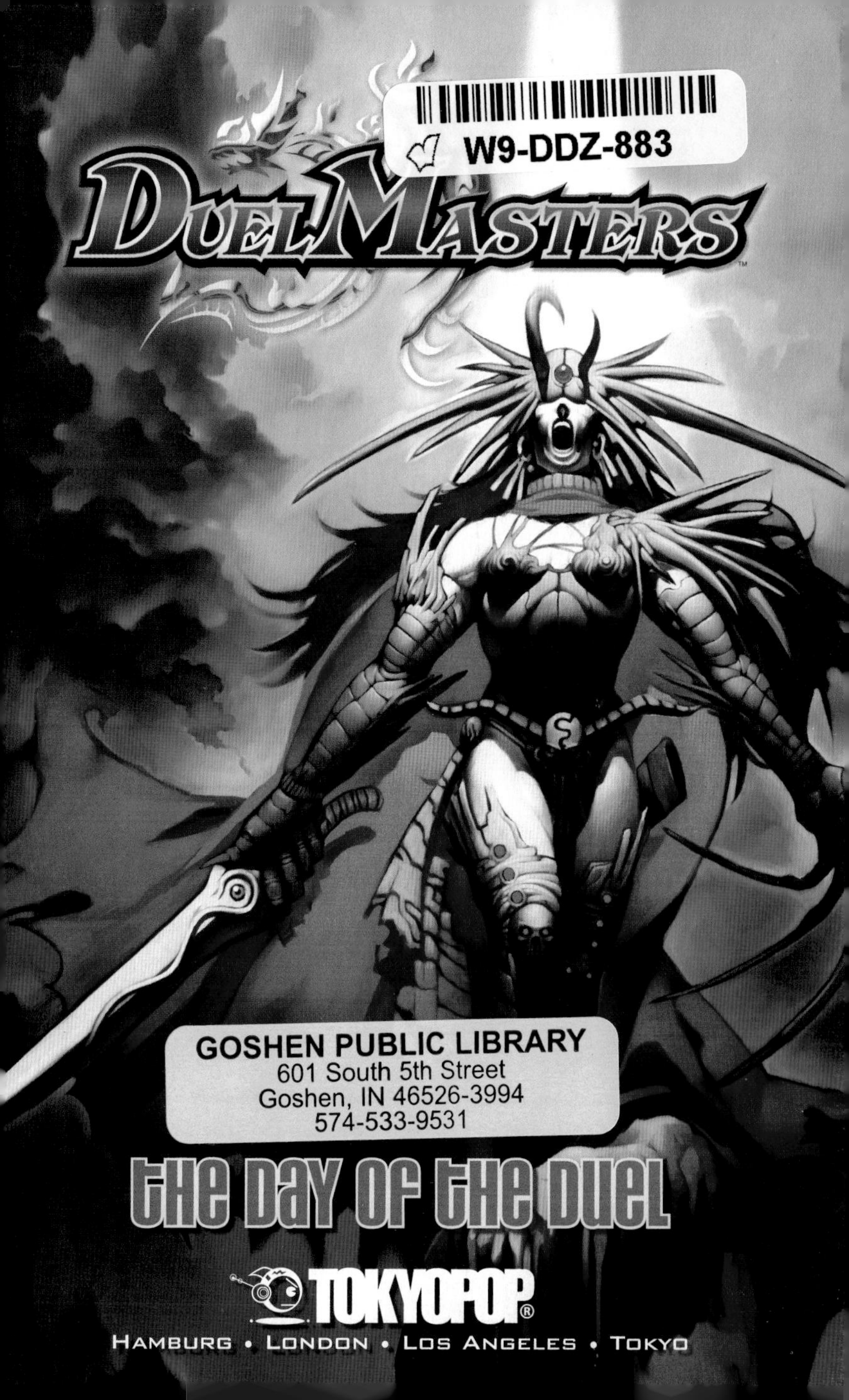
DUEL MASTERS™
THE DAY OF THE DUEL
TOKYOPOP®
HAMBURG • LONDON • LOS ANGELES • TOKYO

Editor - Erin Stein
Contributing Editor - Amy Court Kaemon
Graphic Designer and Letterer - Tomás Montalvo-Lagos
Cover Designer - Raymond Makowski
Graphic Artist - Monalisa de J. Asis

Digital Imaging Manager - Chris Buford
Pre-Press Manager - Antonio DePietro
Production Managers - Jennifer Miller and Mutsumi Miyazaki
Senior Designer - Anna Kernbaum
Art Director - Matt Alford
Senior Editor - Elizabeth Hurchalla
Managing Editor - Jill Freshney
Editor in Chief - Mike Kiley
VP of Production - Ron Klamert
President & C.O.O. - John Parker
Publisher & C.E.O. - Stuart Levy

E-mail: info@tokyopop.com
Come visit us online at www.TOKYOPOP.com

A **TOKYOPOP** Cine-Manga® Book
TOKYOPOP Inc.
5900 Wilshire Blvd., Suite 2000
Los Angeles, CA 90036

Duel Masters Volume 4: The Day of the Duel

ISBN: 1-59532-674-X

First TOKYOPOP® printing: February 2005

10 9 8 7 6 5 4 3 2 1

Printed in China

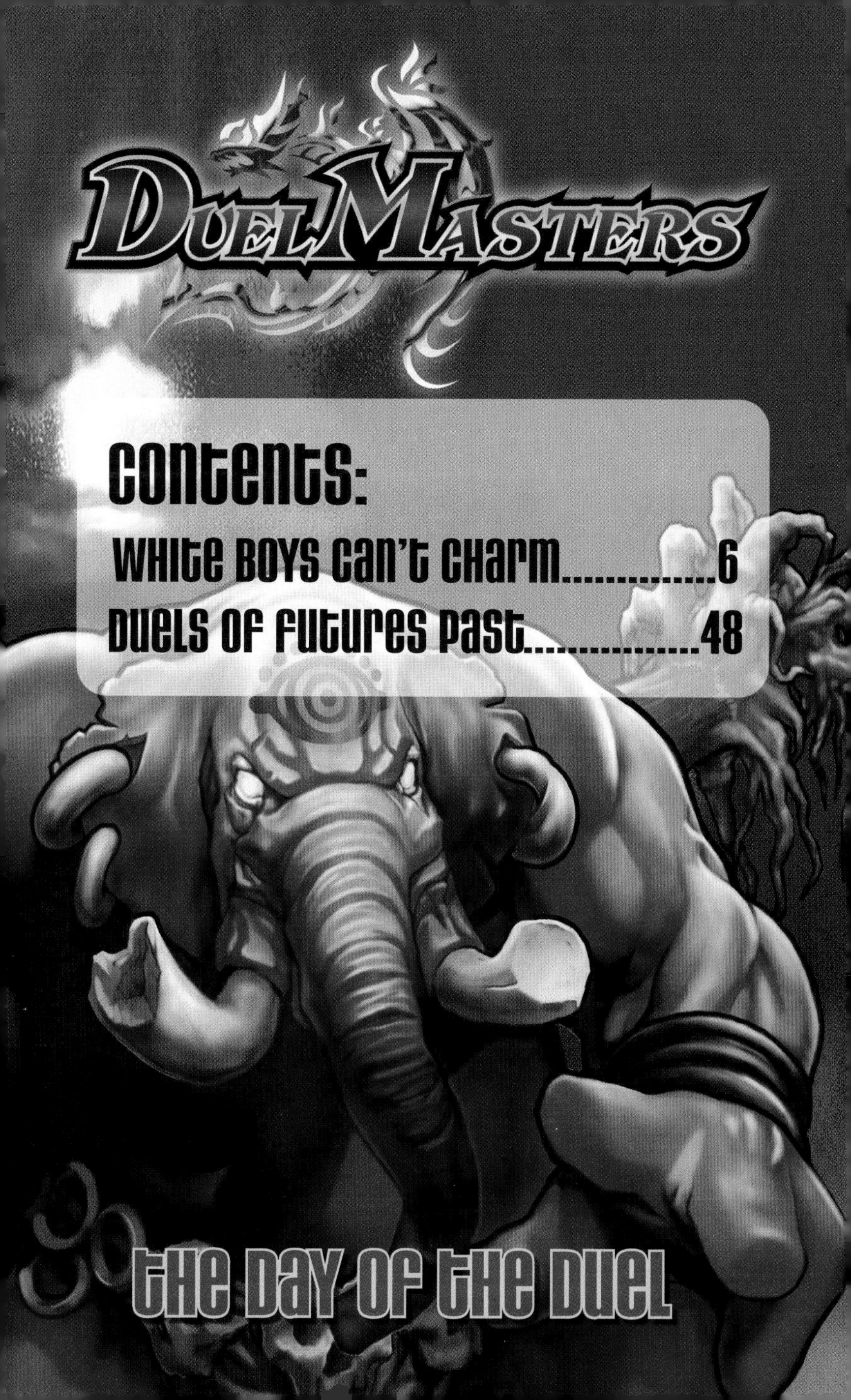
DUEL MASTERS

CONTENTS:

THE DAY OF THE DUEL

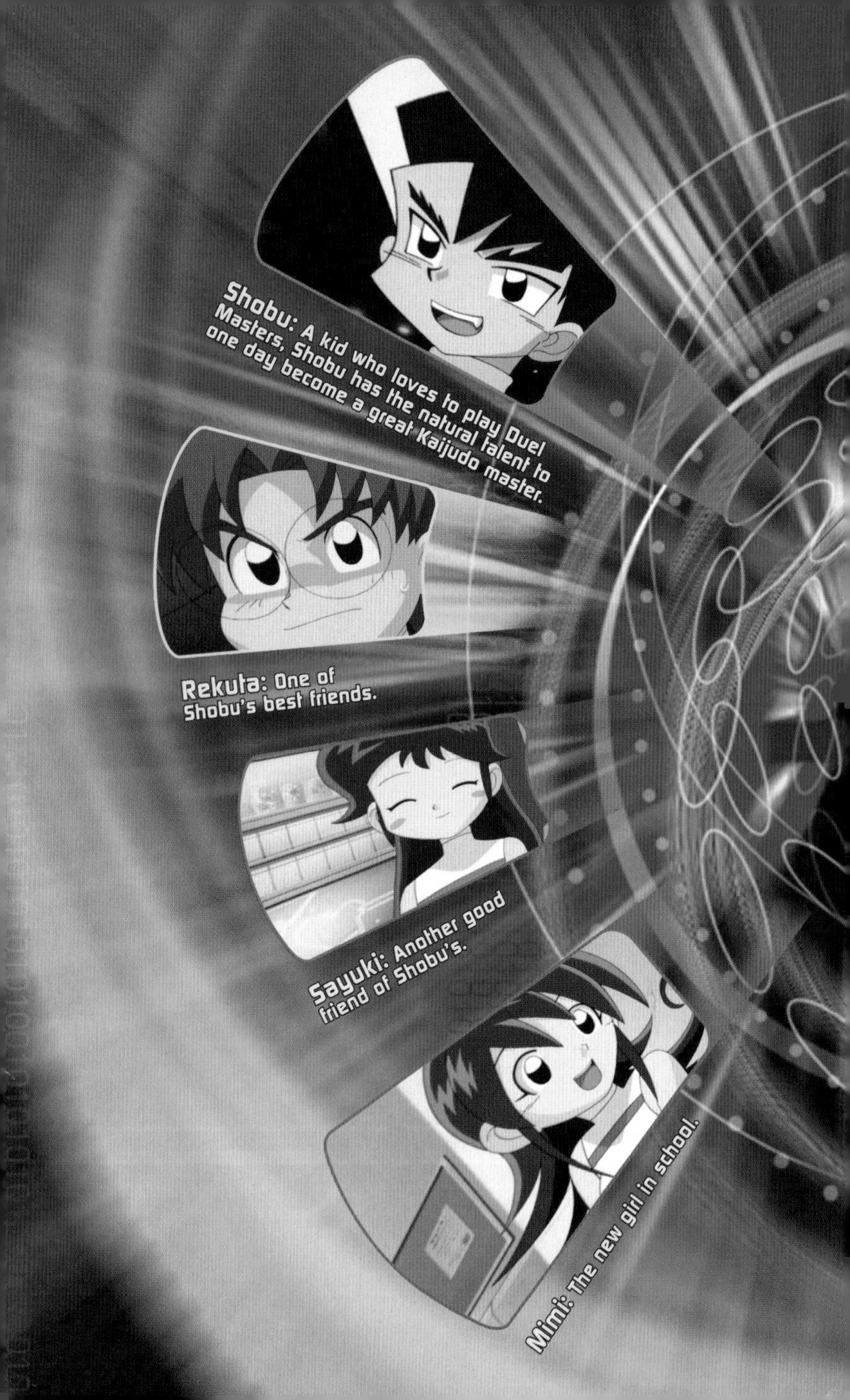
Shobu: A kid who loves to play Duel Masters, Shobu has the natural talent to one day become a great Kaijudo master.
Rekuta: One of Shobu's best friends.
Sayuki: Another good friend of Shobu's.
Mimi: The new girl in school.

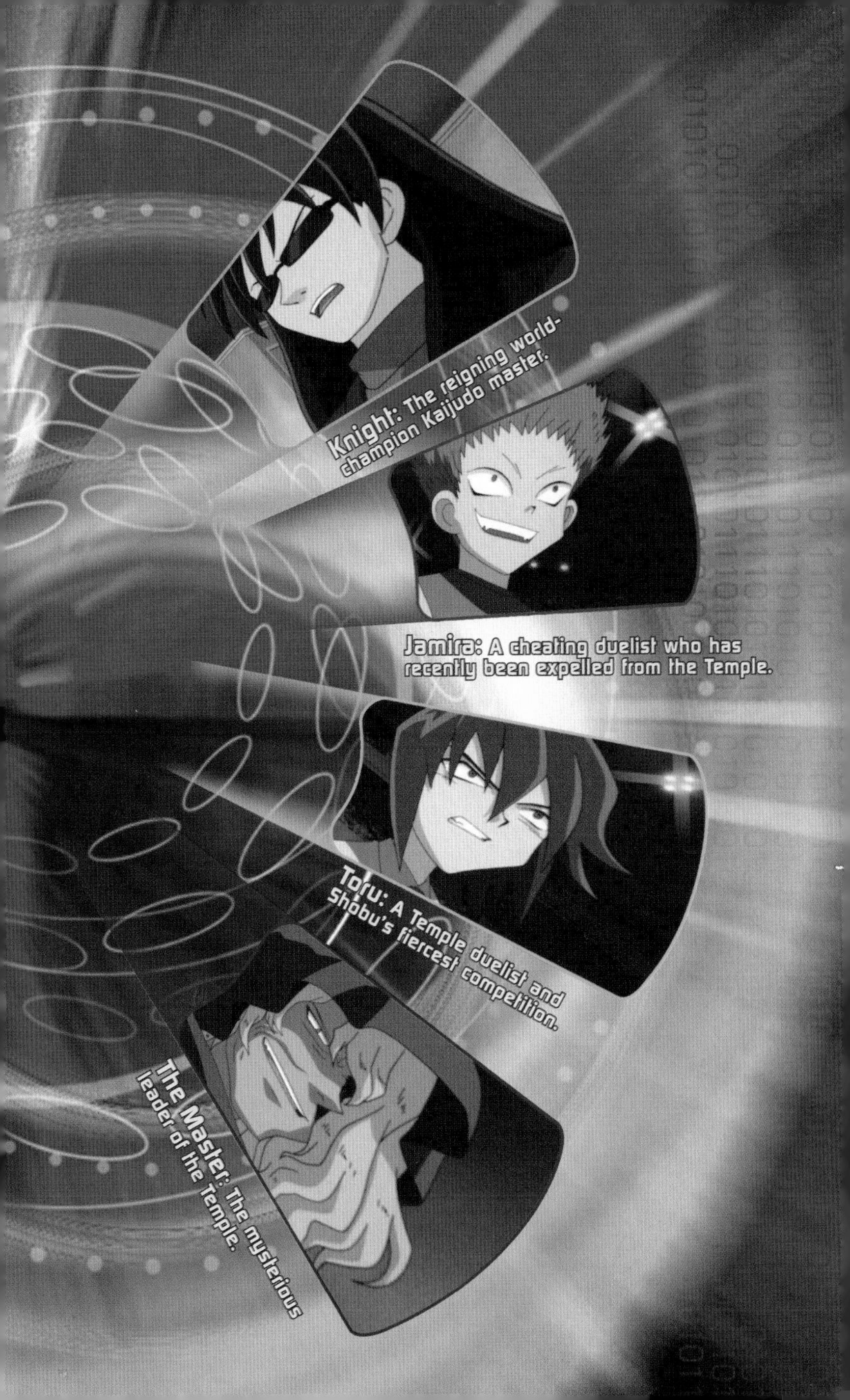
Knight: The reigning world-champion Kaijudo master.
Jamira: A cheating duelist who has recently been expelled from the Temple.
Toru: A Temple duelist and Shobu's fiercest competition.
The Master: The mysterious leader of the Temple.

WHITE BOYS CAN'T CHARM

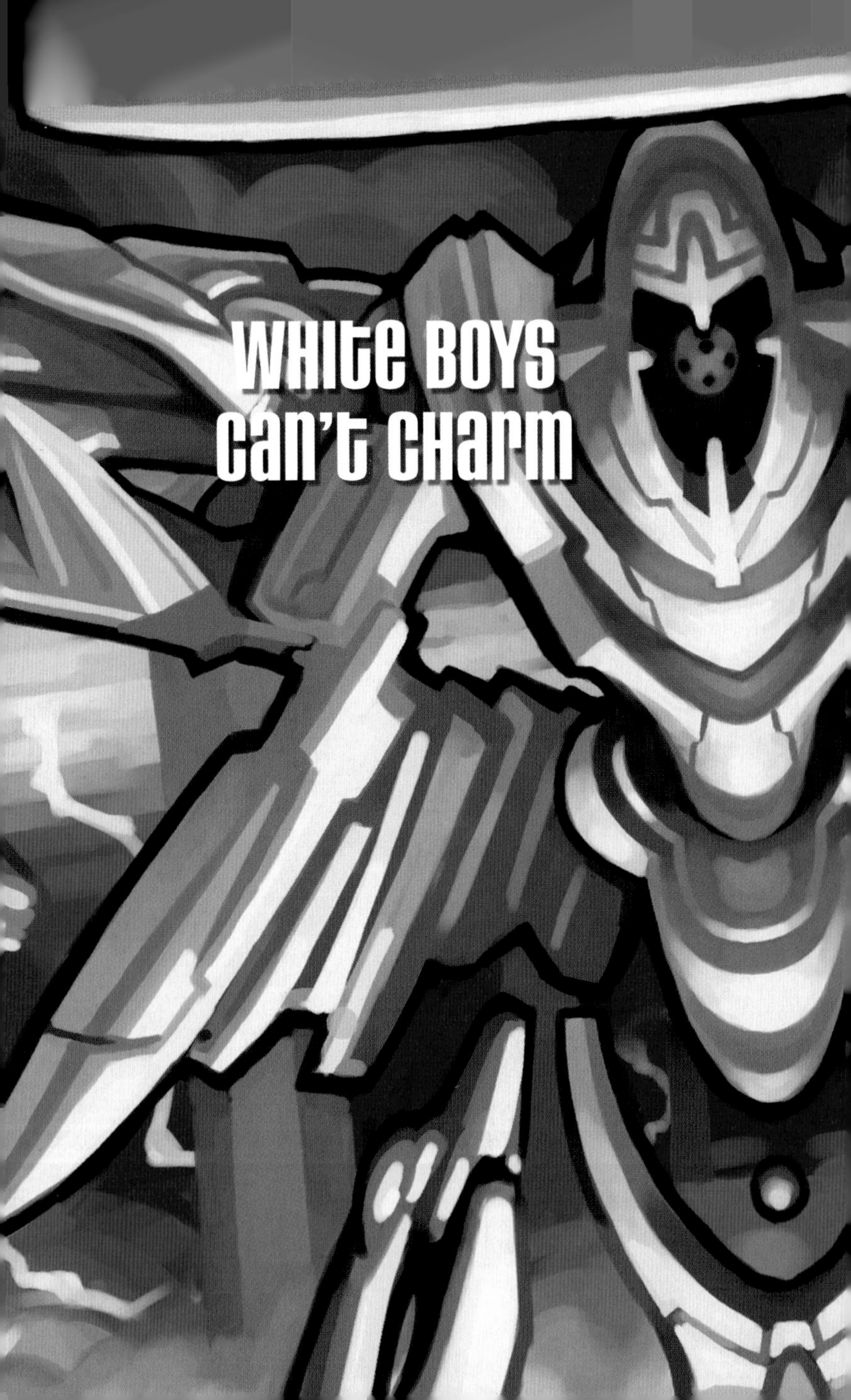

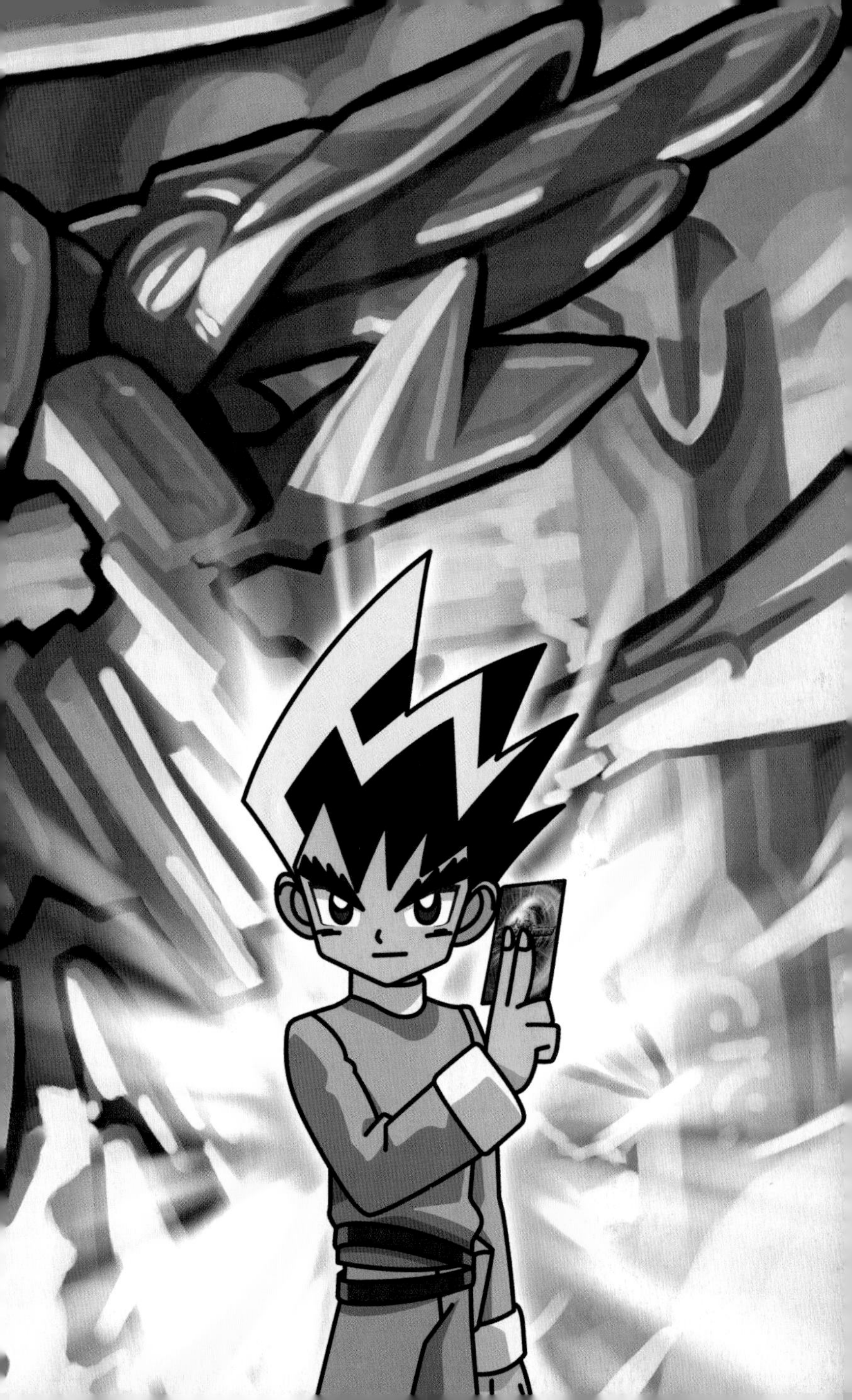

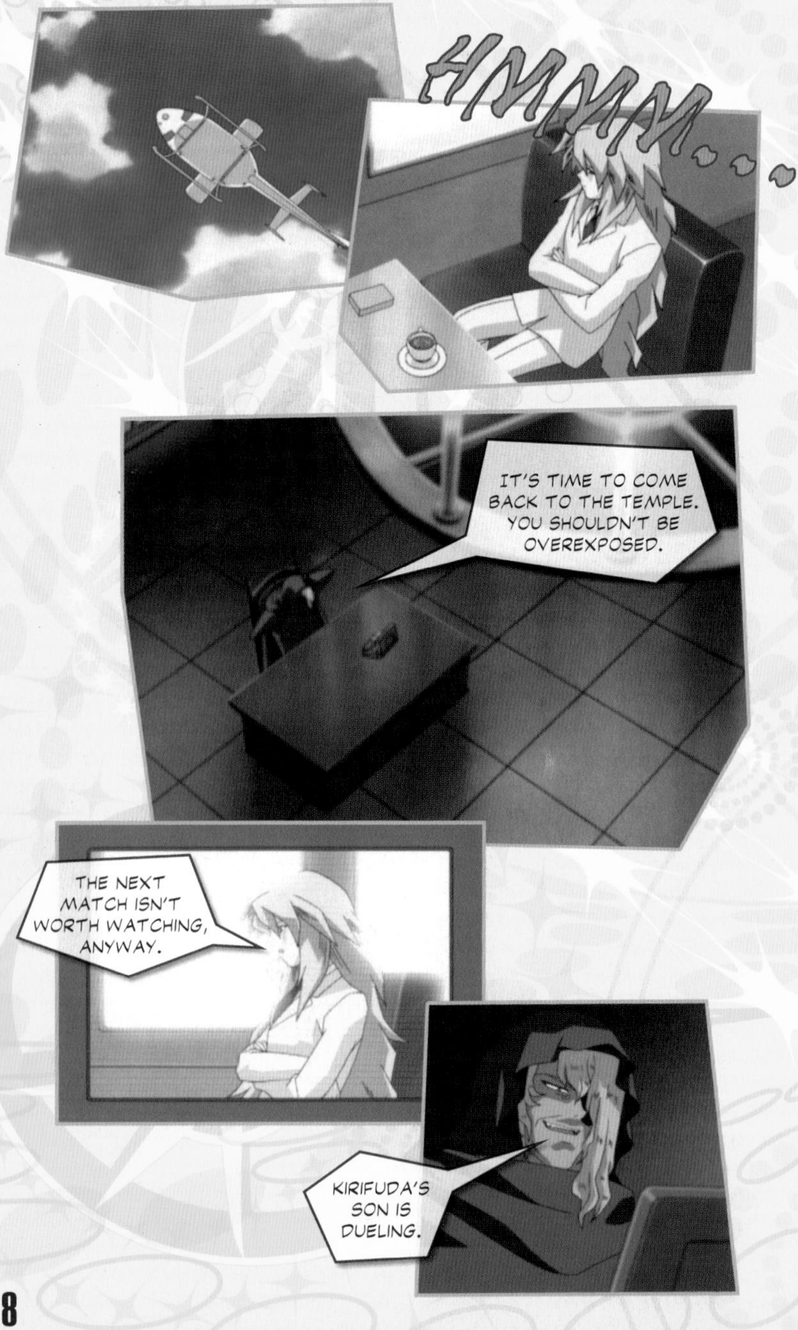
HMMM....
IT'S TIME TO COME BACK TO THE TEMPLE. YOU SHOULDN'T BE OVEREXPOSED.
THE NEXT MATCH ISN'T WORTH WATCHING, ANYWAY.
KIRIFUDA'S SON IS DUELING.

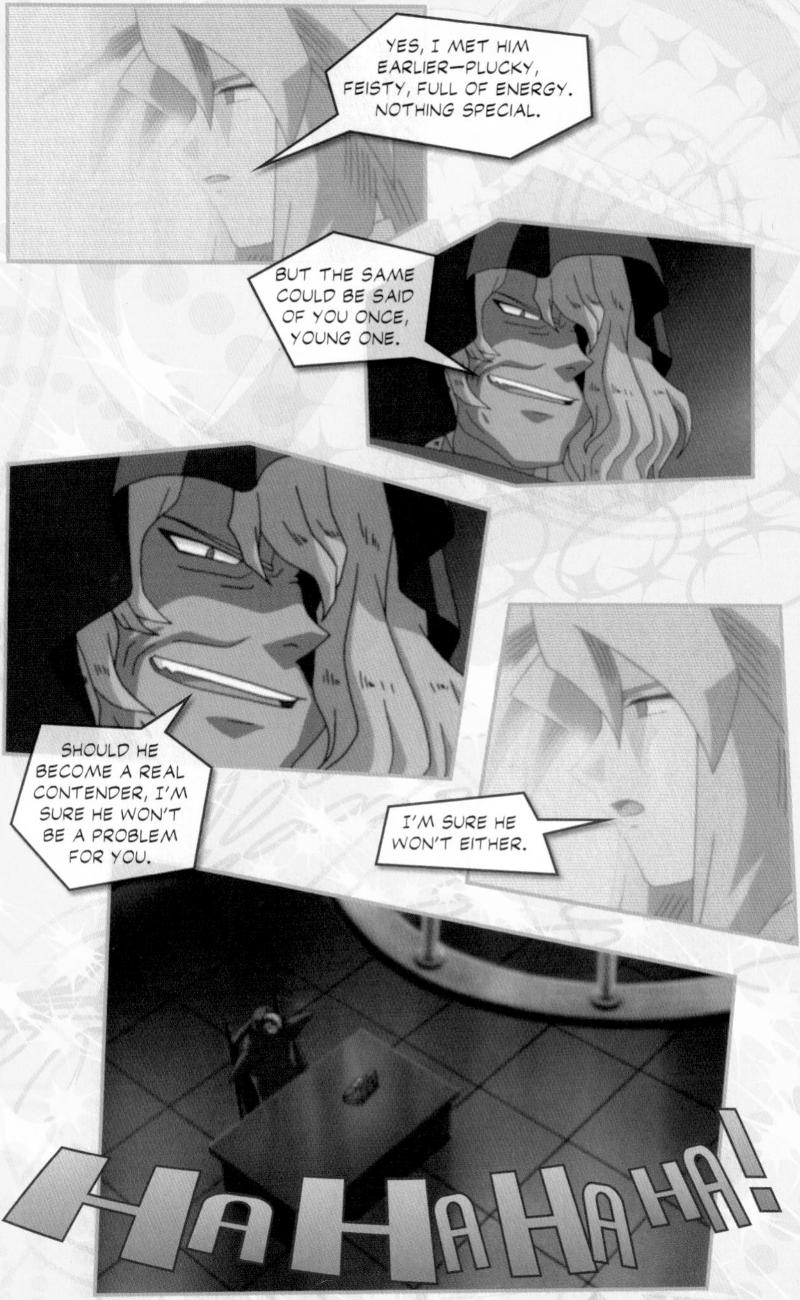
YES, I MET HIM EARLIER—PLUCKY, FEISTY, FULL OF ENERGY. NOTHING SPECIAL.
BUT THE SAME COULD BE SAID OF YOU ONCE, YOUNG ONE.
SHOULD HE BECOME A REAL CONTENDER, I'M SURE HE WON'T BE A PROBLEM FOR YOU.
I'M SURE HE WON'T EITHER.
HAHAHAHAHA!

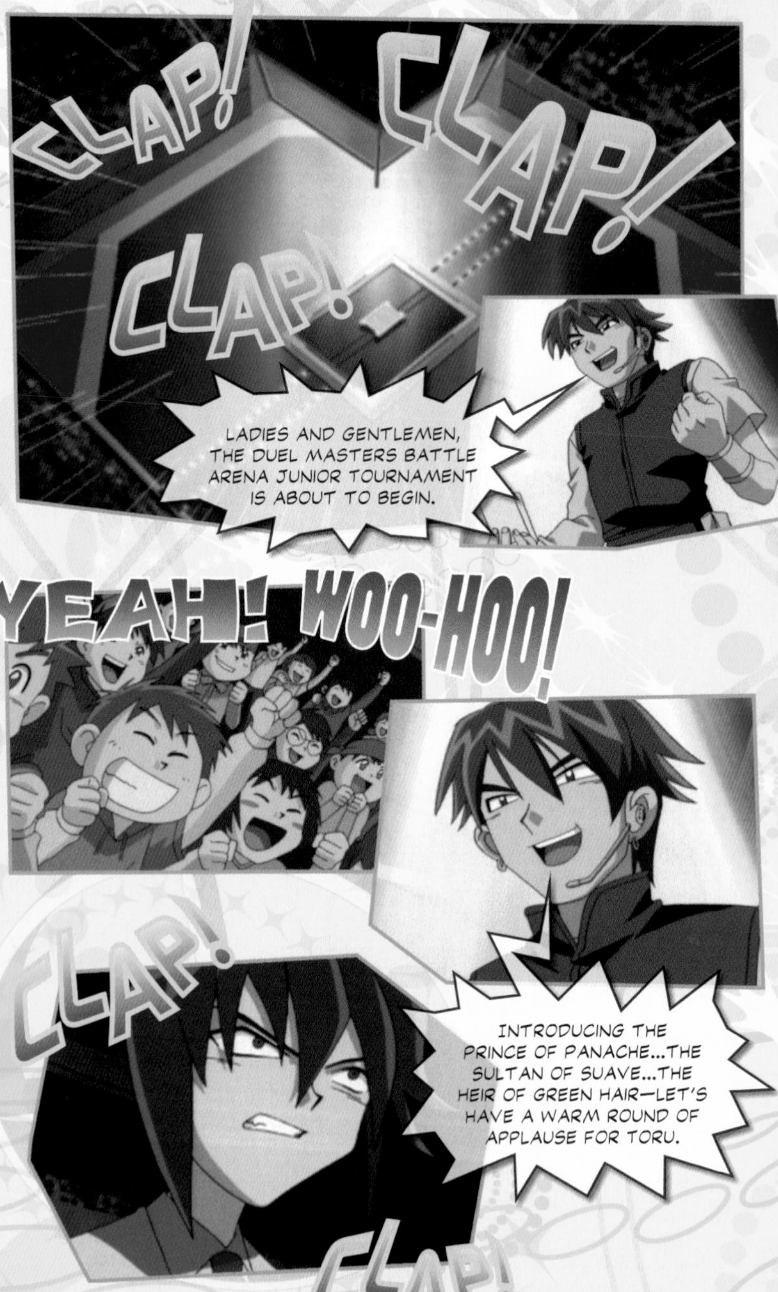
CLAP! CLAP!
CLAP!
LADIES AND GENTLEMEN, THE DUEL MASTERS BATTLE ARENA JUNIOR TOURNAMENT IS ABOUT TO BEGIN.
YEAH! WOO-HOO!
CLAP!
INTRODUCING THE PRINCE OF PANACHE...THE SULTAN OF SUAVE...THE HEIR OF GREEN HAIR—LET'S HAVE A WARM ROUND OF APPLAUSE FOR TORU.
CLAP!

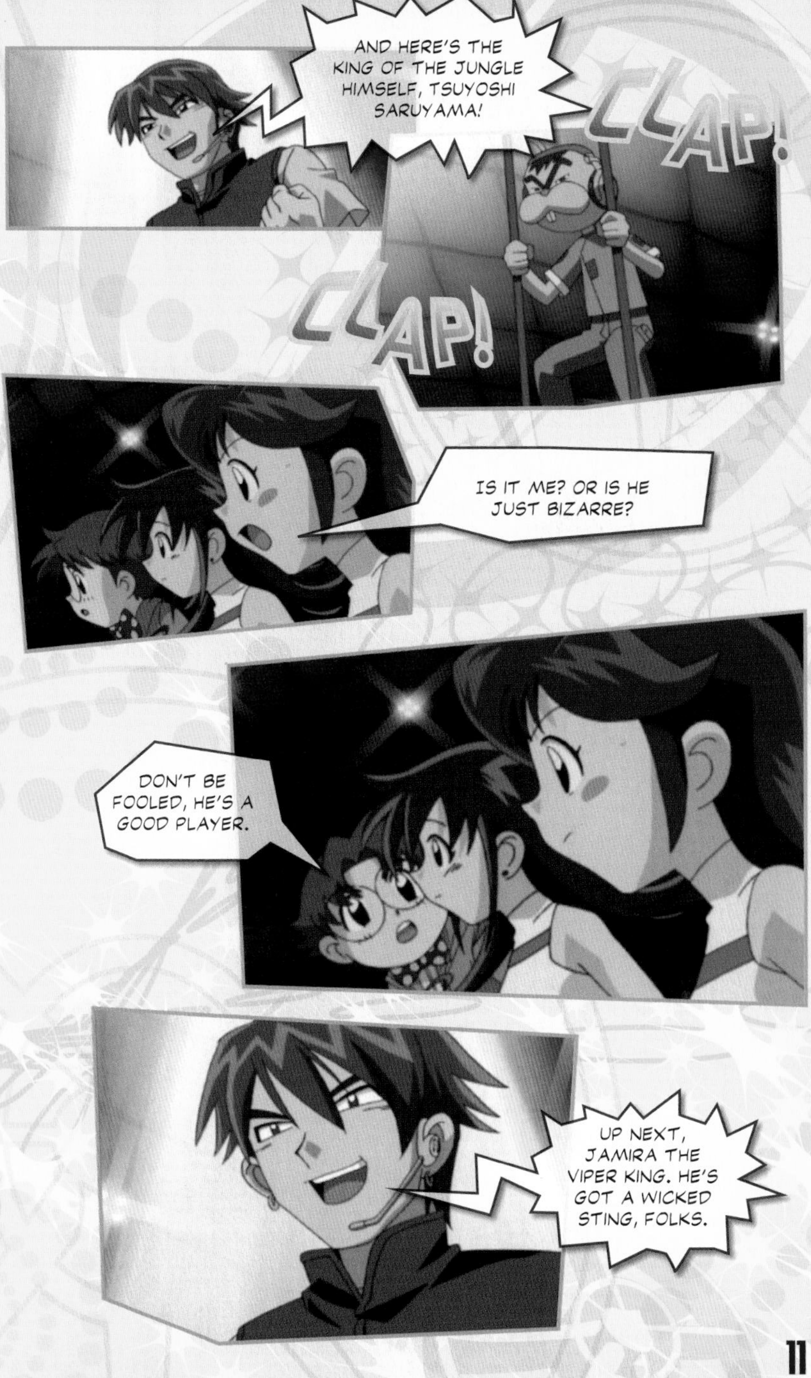
AND HERE'S THE KING OF THE JUNGLE HIMSELF, TSUYOSHI SARUYAMA!
CLAP!
CLAP!
IS IT ME? OR IS HE JUST BIZARRE?
DON'T BE FOOLED, HE'S A GOOD PLAYER.
UP NEXT, JAMIRA THE VIPER KING. HE'S GOT A WICKED STING, FOLKS.

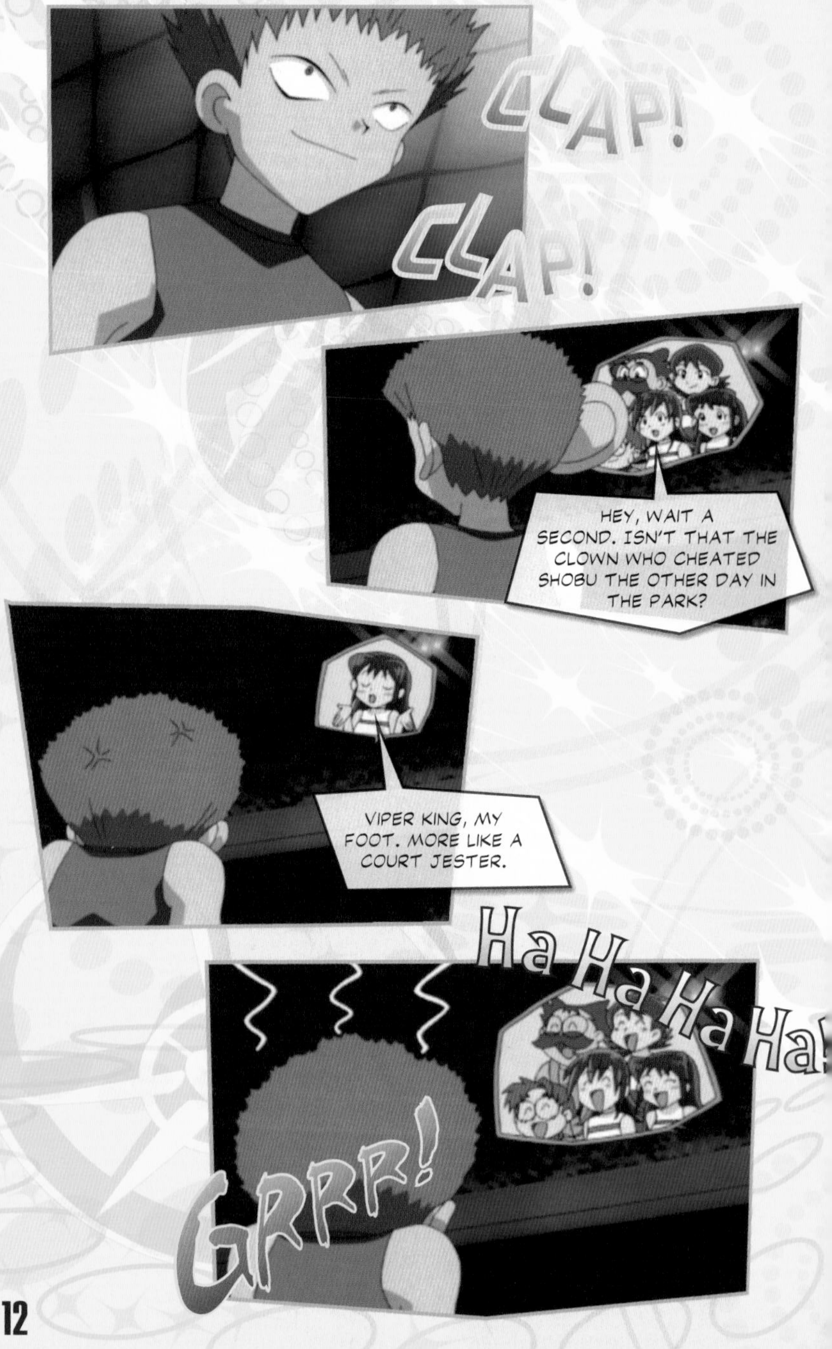
CLAP!
CLAP!
HEY, WAIT A SECOND. ISN'T THAT THE CLOWN WHO CHEATED SHOBU THE OTHER DAY IN THE PARK?
VIPER KING, MY FOOT. MORE LIKE A COURT JESTER.
Ha Ha Ha Ha!
GRRR!

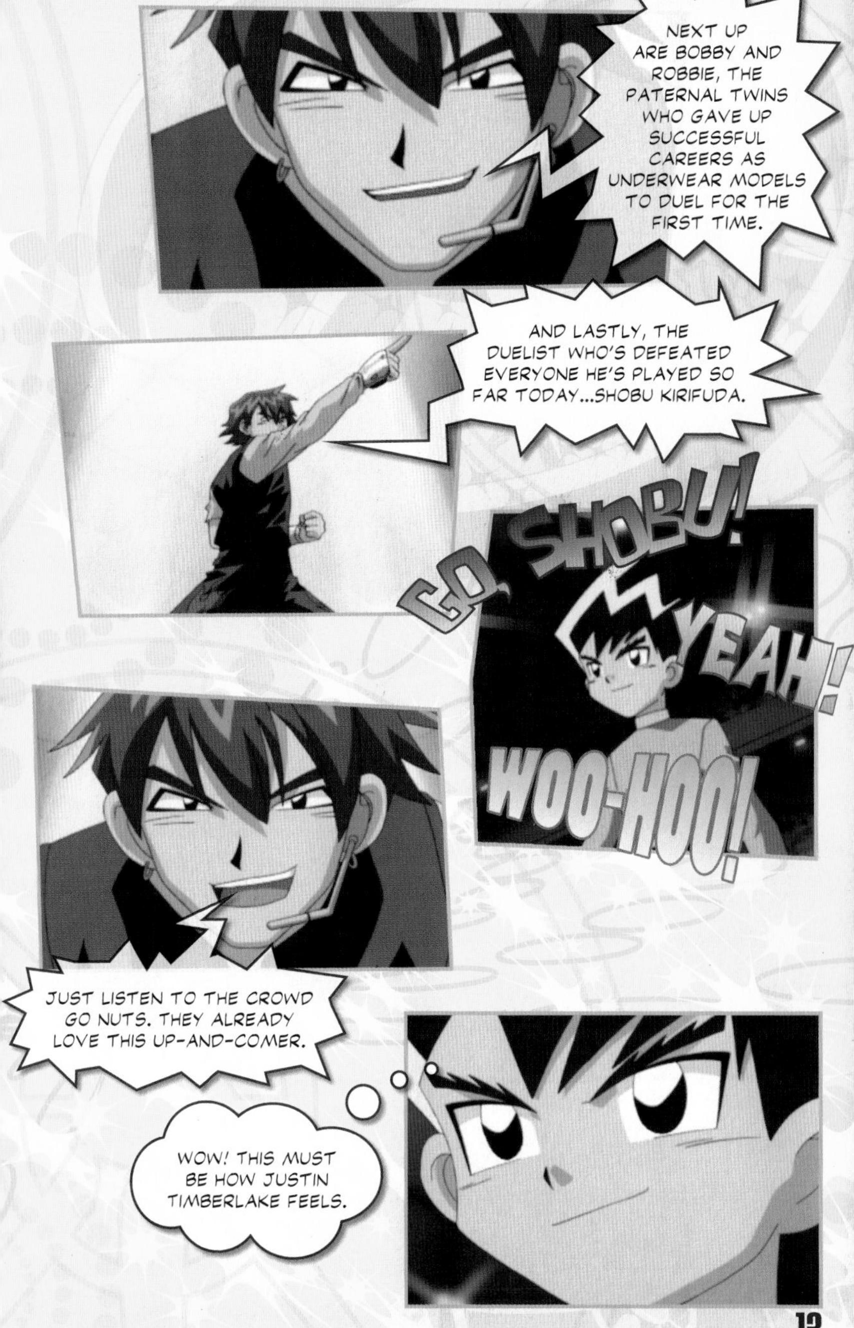
NEXT UP ARE BOBBY AND ROBBIE, THE PATERNAL TWINS WHO GAVE UP SUCCESSFUL CAREERS AS UNDERWEAR MODELS TO DUEL FOR THE FIRST TIME.
AND LASTLY, THE DUELIST WHO'S DEFEATED EVERYONE HE'S PLAYED SO FAR TODAY...SHOBU KIRIFUDA.
JUST LISTEN TO THE CROWD GO NUTS. THEY ALREADY LOVE THIS UP-AND-COMER.
GO, SHOBU!
YEAH!
WOO-HOO!
WOW! THIS MUST BE HOW JUSTIN TIMBERLAKE FEELS.

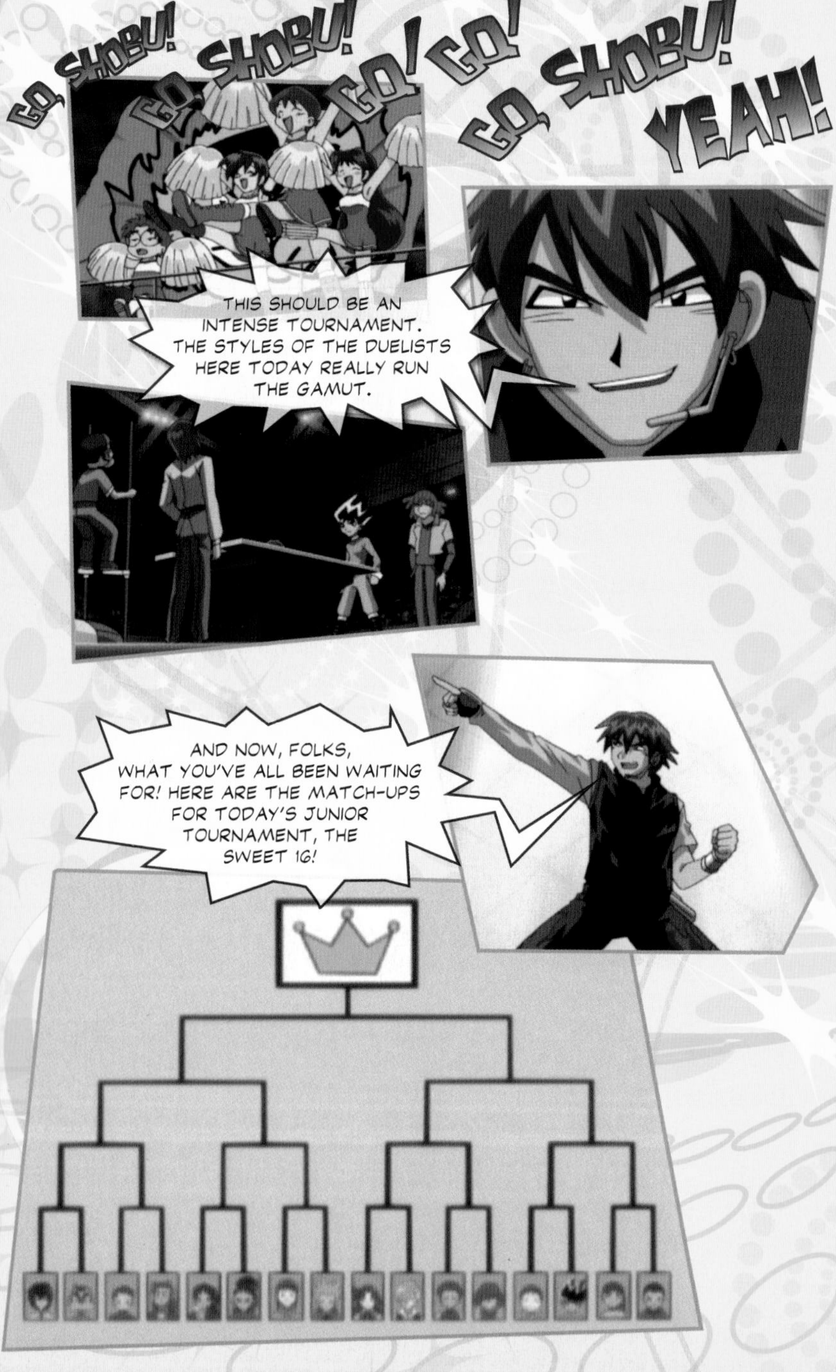
GO, SHOBU!
GO, SHOBU!
GO! GO!
GO, SHOBU!
YEAH!
THIS SHOULD BE AN INTENSE TOURNAMENT. THE STYLES OF THE DUELISTS HERE TODAY REALLY RUN THE GAMUT.
AND NOW, FOLKS, WHAT YOU'VE ALL BEEN WAITING FOR! HERE ARE THE MATCH-UPS FOR TODAY'S JUNIOR TOURNAMENT, THE SWEET 16!

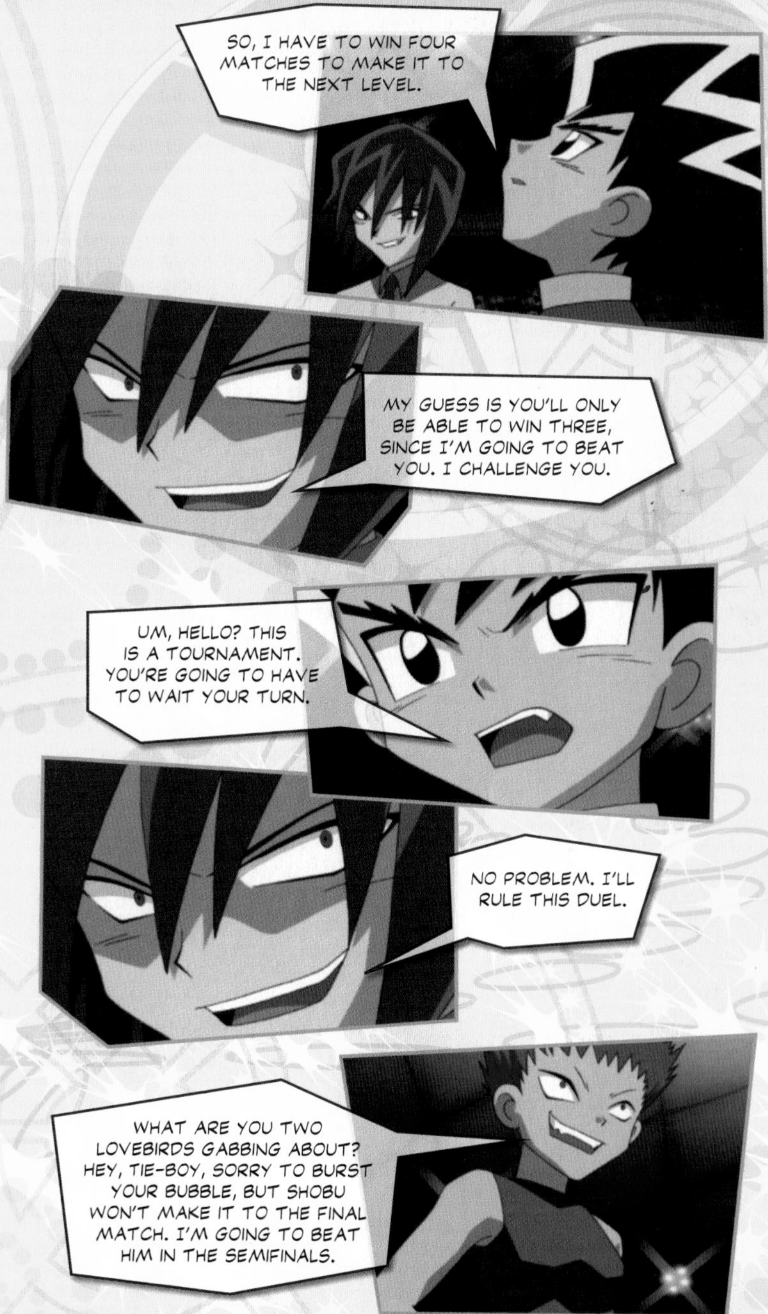
SO, I HAVE TO WIN FOUR MATCHES TO MAKE IT TO THE NEXT LEVEL.
MY GUESS IS YOU'LL ONLY BE ABLE TO WIN THREE, SINCE I'M GOING TO BEAT YOU. I CHALLENGE YOU.
UM, HELLO? THIS IS A TOURNAMENT. YOU'RE GOING TO HAVE TO WAIT YOUR TURN.
NO PROBLEM. I'LL RULE THIS DUEL.
WHAT ARE YOU TWO LOVEBIRDS GABBING ABOUT? HEY, TIE-BOY, SORRY TO BURST YOUR BUBBLE, BUT SHOBU WON'T MAKE IT TO THE FINAL MATCH. I'M GOING TO BEAT HIM IN THE SEMIFINALS.

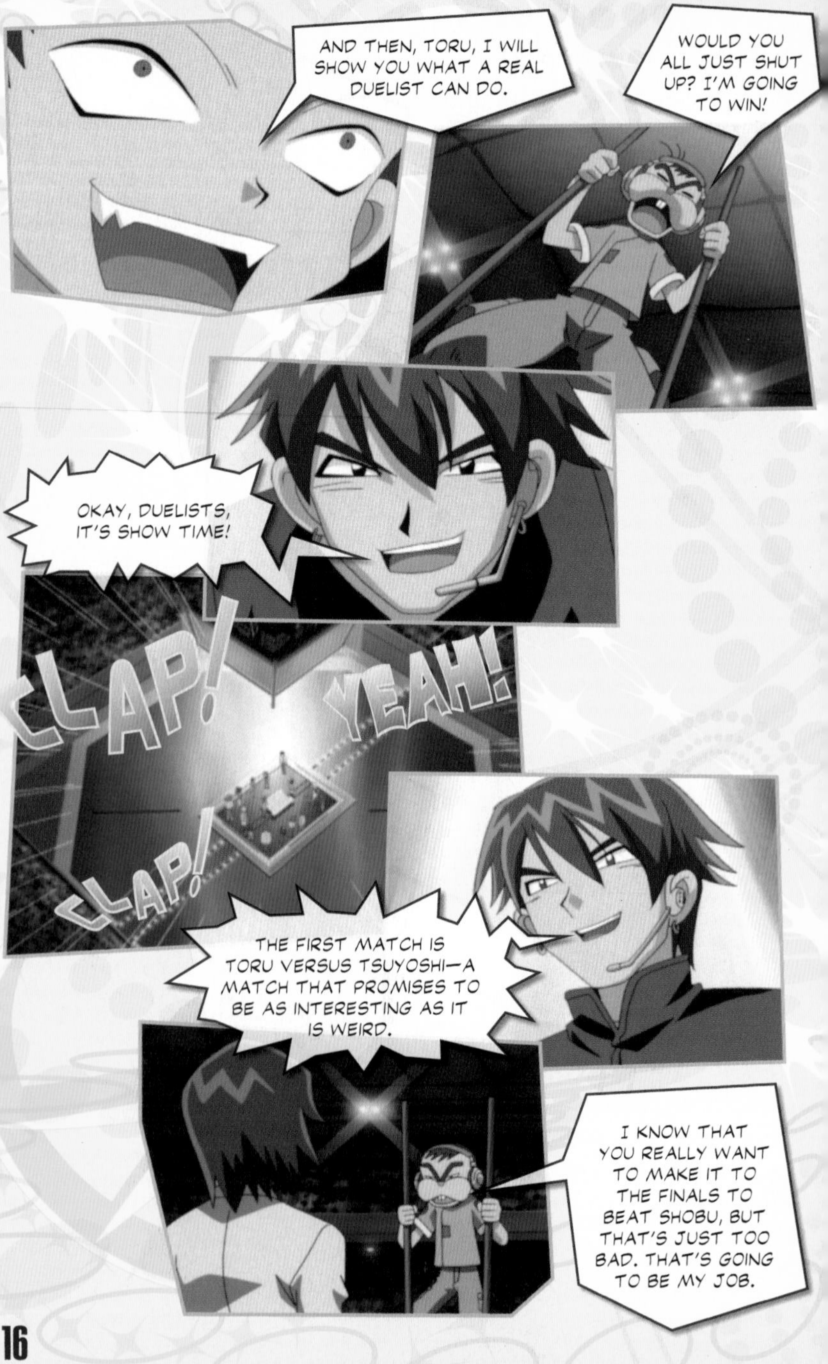
AND THEN, TORU, I WILL SHOW YOU WHAT A REAL DUELIST CAN DO.
WOULD YOU ALL JUST SHUT UP? I'M GOING TO WIN!
OKAY, DUELISTS, IT'S SHOW TIME!
CLAP!
YEAH!
CLAP!
THE FIRST MATCH IS TORU VERSUS TSUYOSHI—A MATCH THAT PROMISES TO BE AS INTERESTING AS IT IS WEIRD.
I KNOW THAT YOU REALLY WANT TO MAKE IT TO THE FINALS TO BEAT SHOBU, BUT THAT'S JUST TOO BAD. THAT'S GOING TO BE MY JOB.

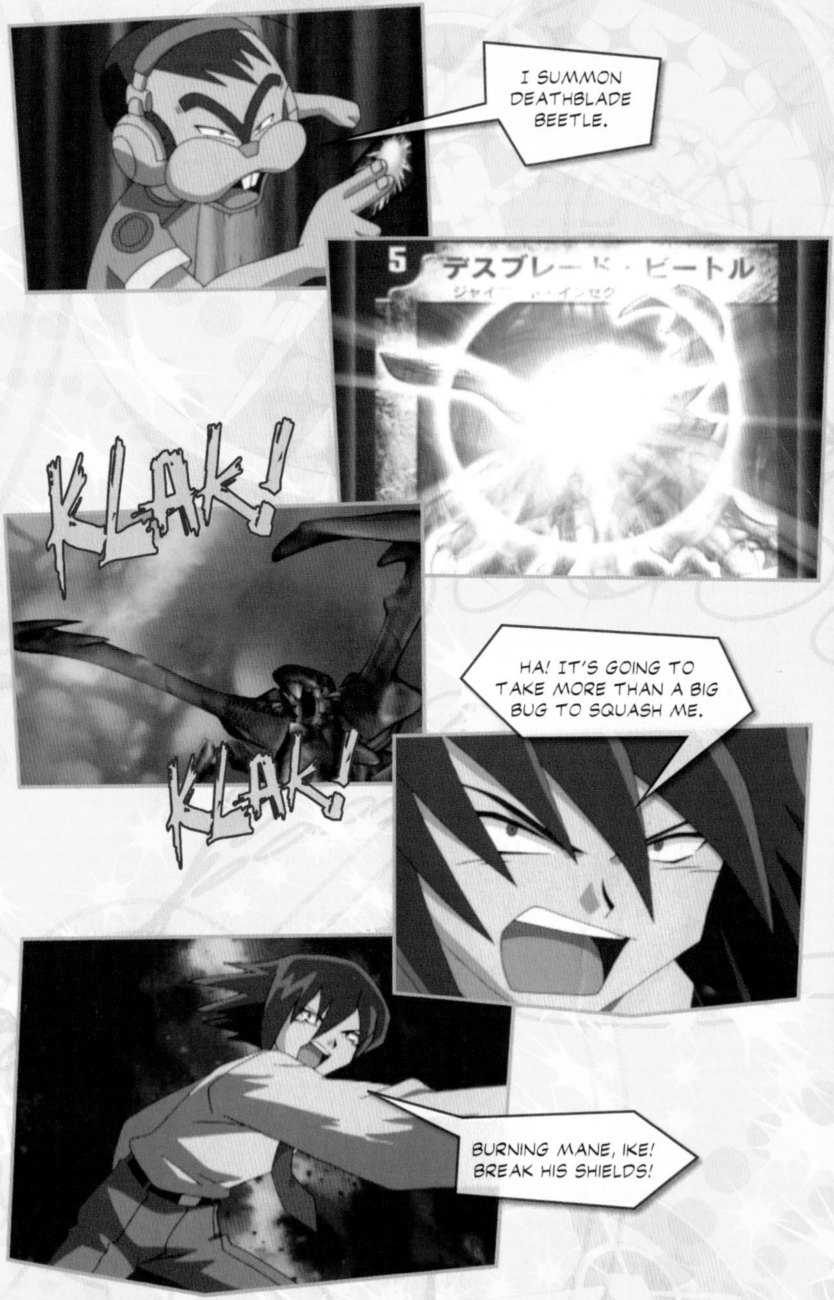
I SUMMON DEATHBLADE BEETLE.
KLAK!
KLAK!
HA! IT'S GOING TO TAKE MORE THAN A BIG BUG TO SQUASH ME.
BURNING MANE, IKE! BREAK HIS SHIELDS!

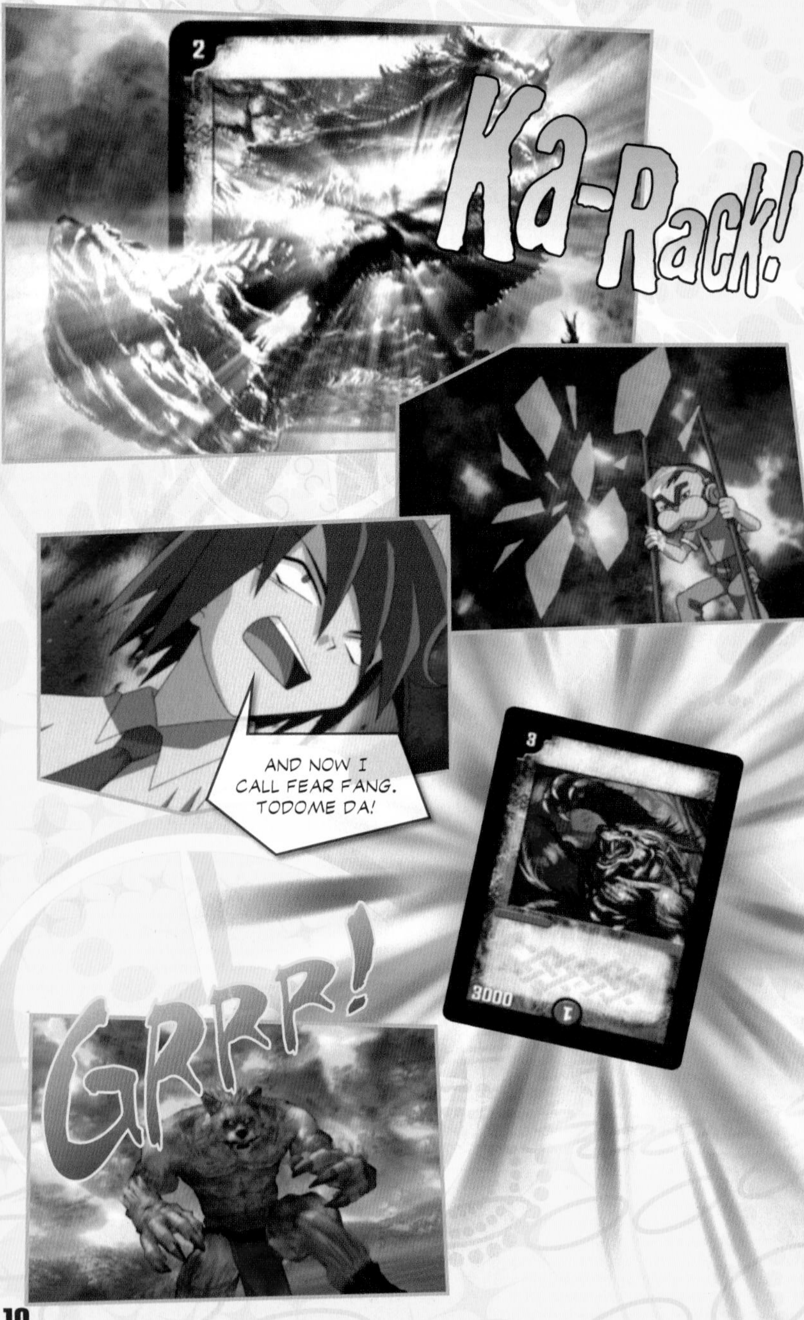
Ka-Rack!
AND NOW I CALL FEAR FANG. TODOME DA!
GRRR!

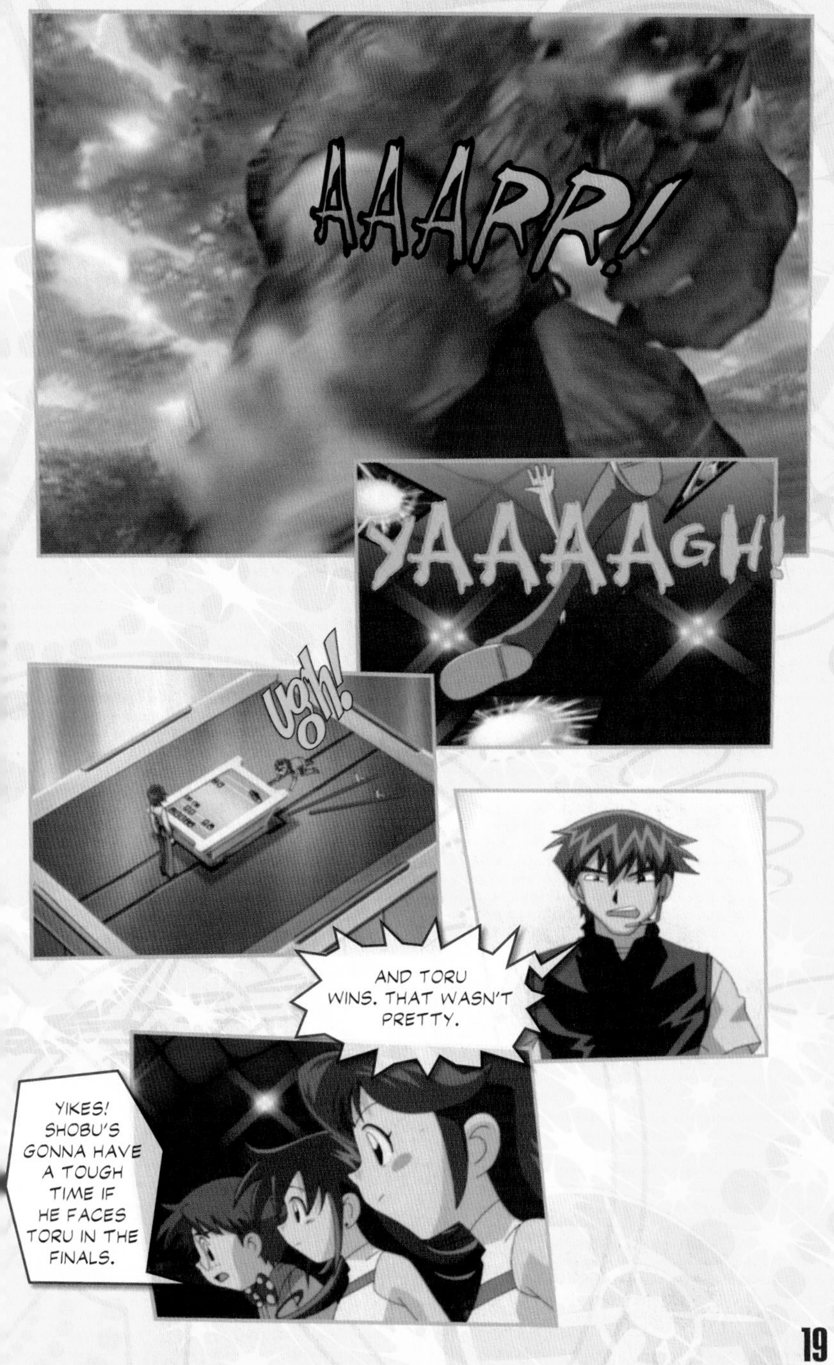
AAARR!
YAAAAAGH!
ugh!
AND TORU WINS. THAT WASN'T PRETTY.
YIKES! SHOBU'S GONNA HAVE A TOUGH TIME IF HE FACES TORU IN THE FINALS.

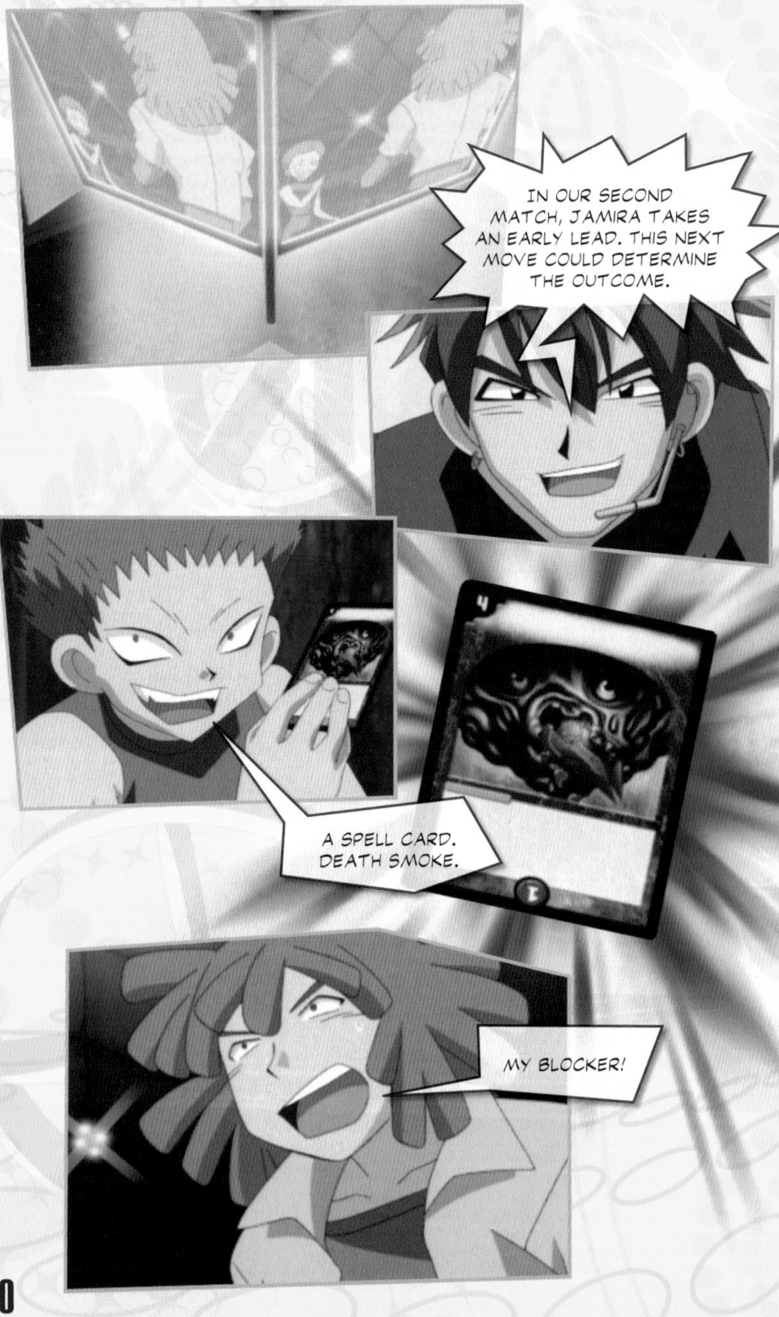
IN OUR SECOND MATCH, JAMIRA TAKES AN EARLY LEAD. THIS NEXT MOVE COULD DETERMINE THE OUTCOME.
A SPELL CARD. DEATH SMOKE.
MY BLOCKER!

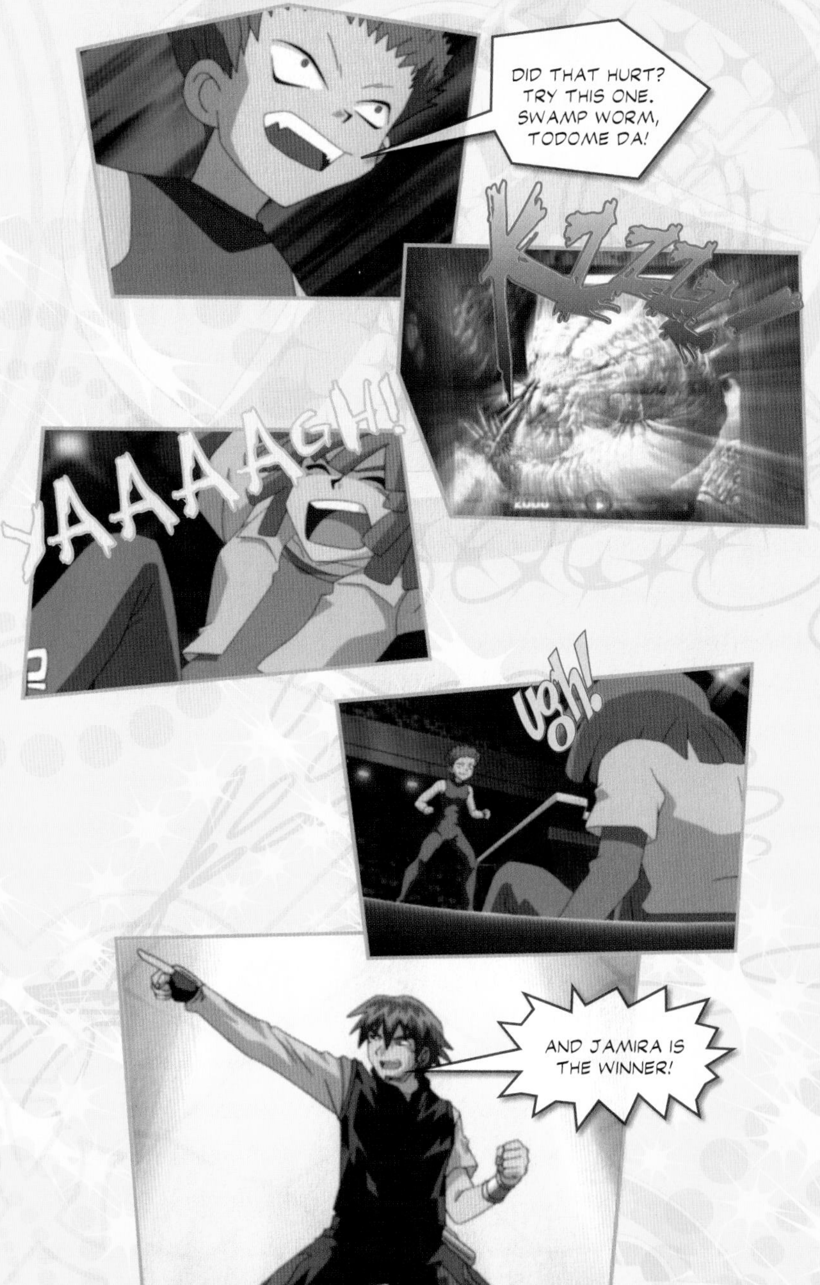
DID THAT HURT? TRY THIS ONE. SWAMP WORM, TODOME DA!
KZZZ!
YAAAAAGH!
Ugh!
AND JAMIRA IS THE WINNER!

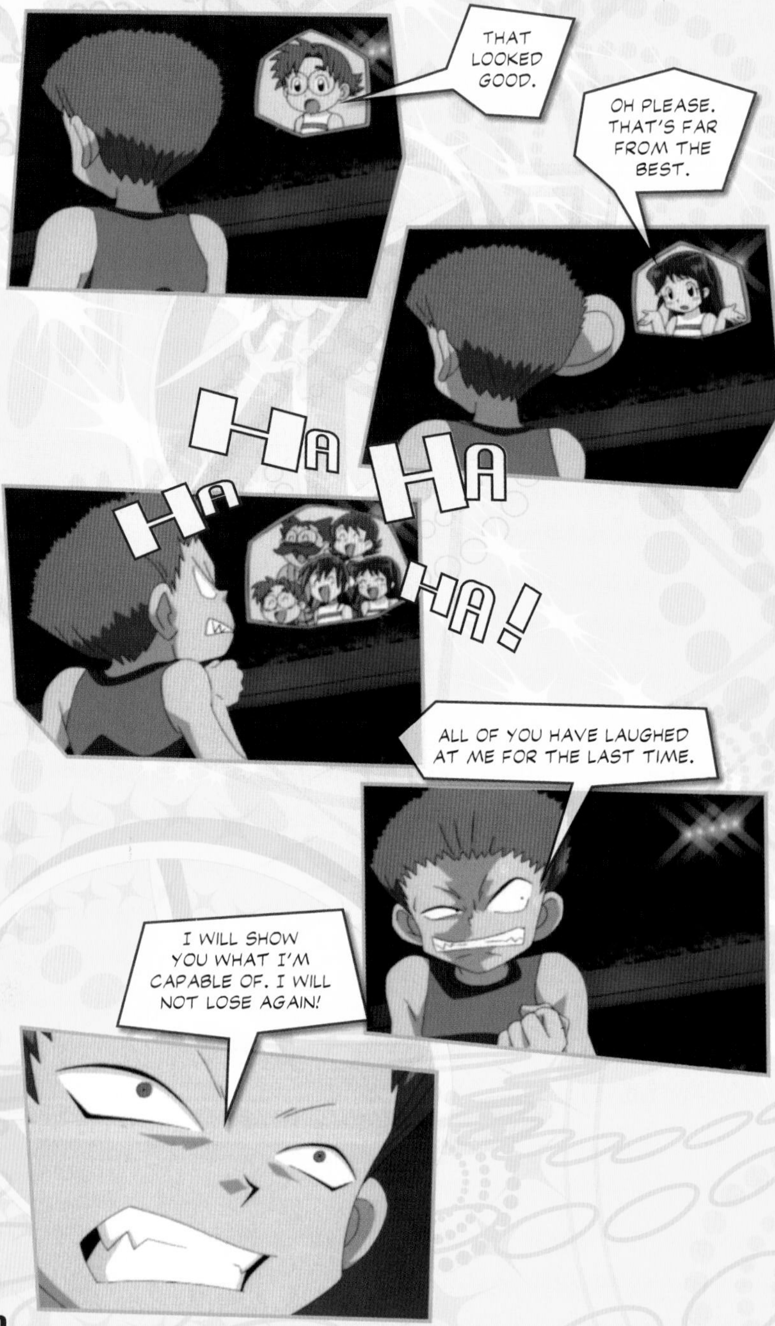
THAT LOOKED GOOD.
OH PLEASE. THAT'S FAR FROM THE BEST.
HA HA HA HA!
ALL OF YOU HAVE LAUGHED AT ME FOR THE LAST TIME.
I WILL SHOW YOU WHAT I'M CAPABLE OF. I WILL NOT LOSE AGAIN!

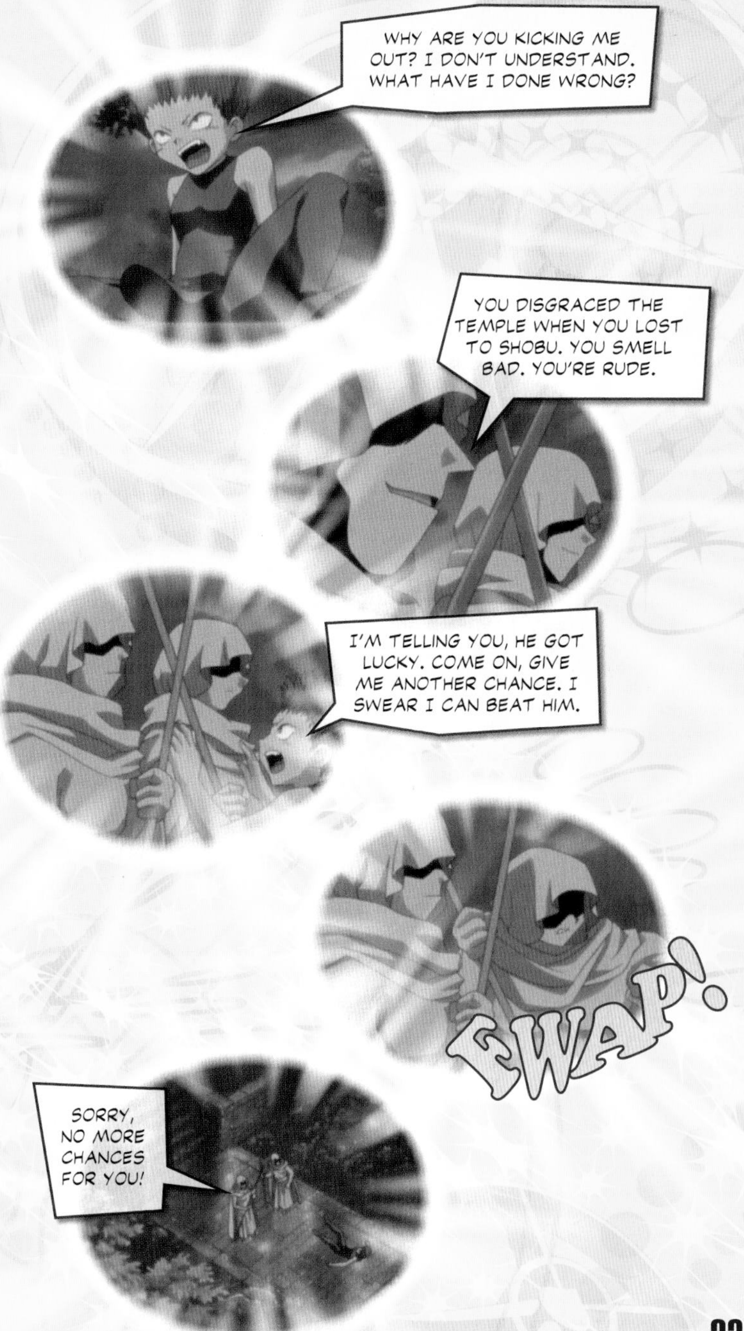
WHY ARE YOU KICKING ME OUT? I DON'T UNDERSTAND. WHAT HAVE I DONE WRONG?
YOU DISGRACED THE TEMPLE WHEN YOU LOST TO SHOBU. YOU SMELL BAD. YOU'RE RUDE.
I'M TELLING YOU, HE GOT LUCKY. COME ON, GIVE ME ANOTHER CHANCE. I SWEAR I CAN BEAT HIM.
FWAP!
SORRY, NO MORE CHANCES FOR YOU!

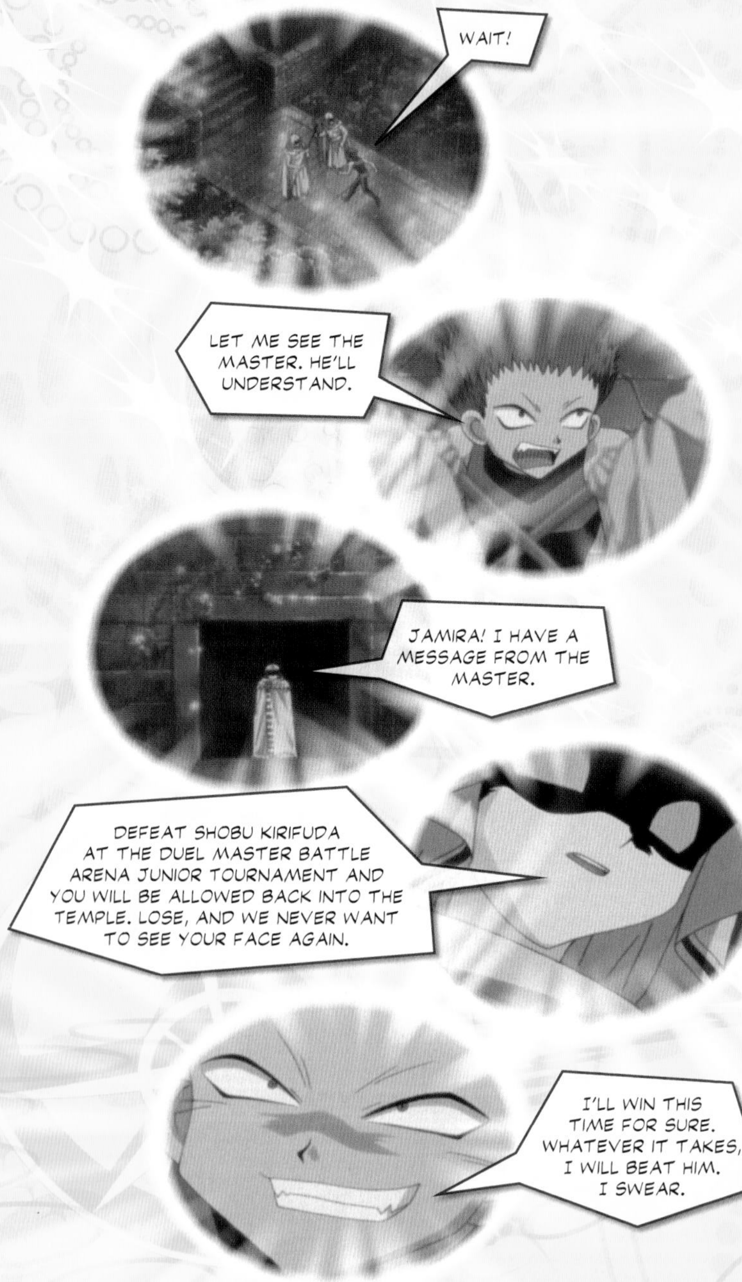
WAIT!
LET ME SEE THE MASTER. HE'LL UNDERSTAND.
JAMIRA! I HAVE A MESSAGE FROM THE MASTER.
DEFEAT SHOBU KIRIFUDA AT THE DUEL MASTER BATTLE ARENA JUNIOR TOURNAMENT AND YOU WILL BE ALLOWED BACK INTO THE TEMPLE. LOSE, AND WE NEVER WANT TO SEE YOUR FACE AGAIN.
I'LL WIN THIS TIME FOR SURE. WHATEVER IT TAKES, I WILL BEAT HIM. I SWEAR.

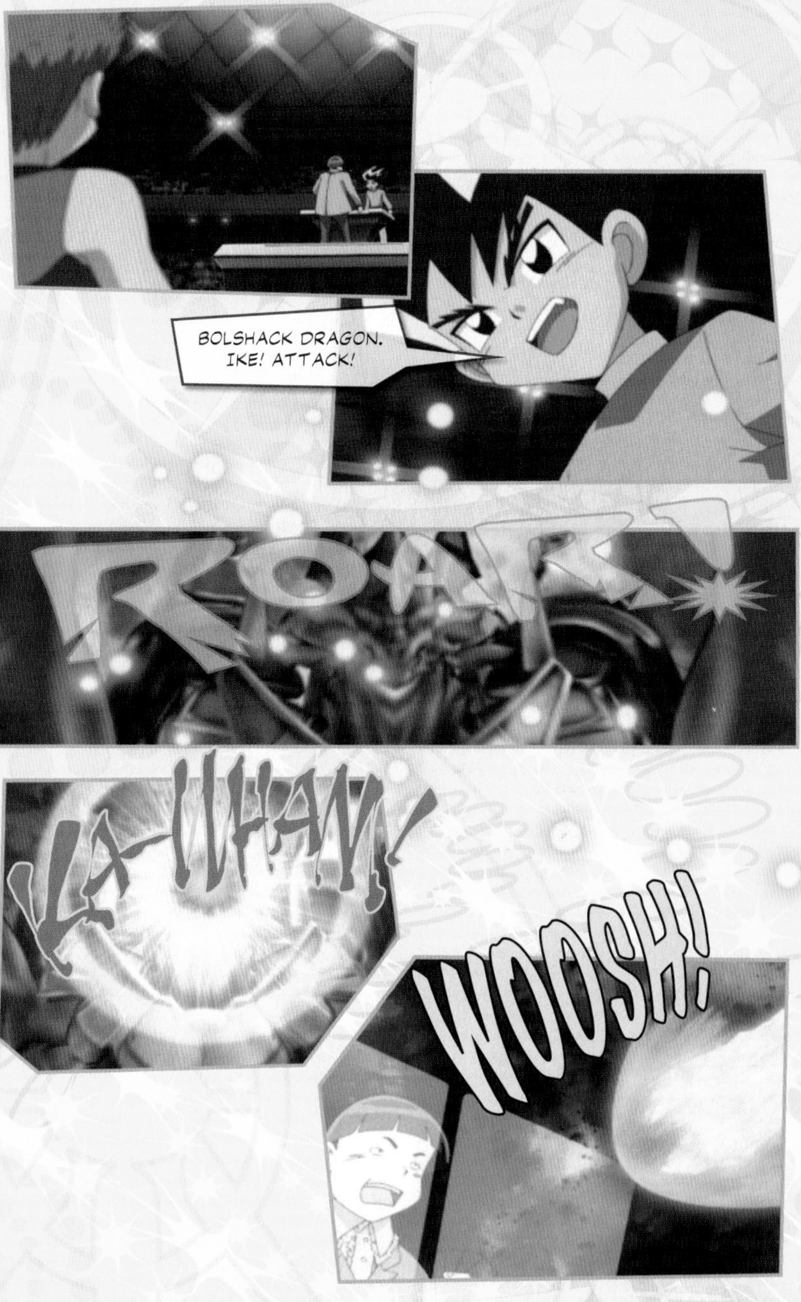
BOLSHACK DRAGON.
IKE! ATTACK!
ROAR!
KA-WHAM!
WOOSH!

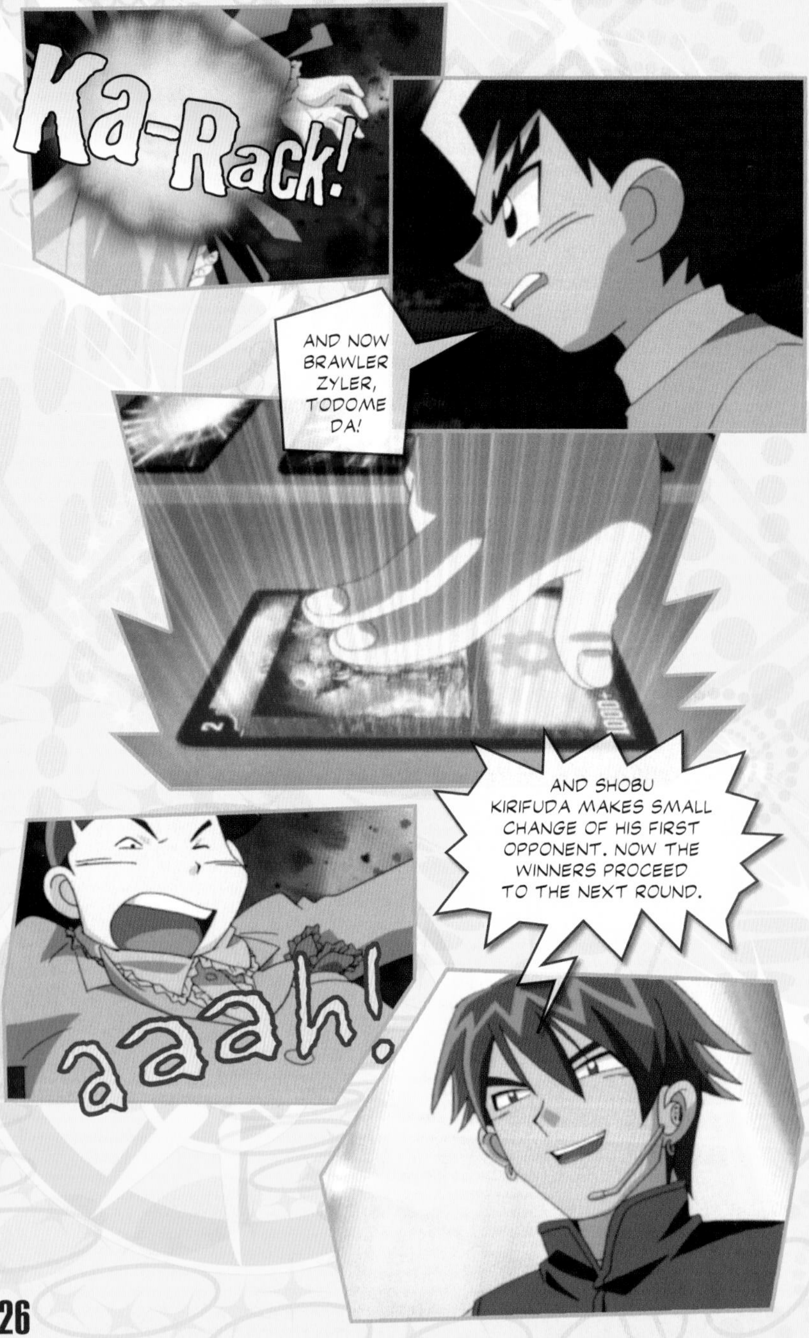
Ka-Rack!
AND NOW BRAWLER ZYLER, TODOME DA!
aaah!
AND SHOBU KIRIFUDA MAKES SMALL CHANGE OF HIS FIRST OPPONENT. NOW THE WINNERS PROCEED TO THE NEXT ROUND.

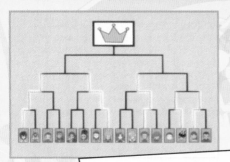

BOLSHACK DRAGON, SHOW 'EM WHAT YOU GOT! TODOME DA!

OUR MAN SHOBU, HE'S SO HOT. OUR MAN SHOBU, SHOW 'EM WHAT YOU GOT. OWN THE ZONE!

KIRIFUDA ADVANCES.

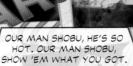

WE'VE GOT SOME VERY STRONG DUELISTS HEADING INTO THE SEMIFINALS. THE FIRST MATCH WILL BE JAMIRA AND SHOBU KIRIFUDA.

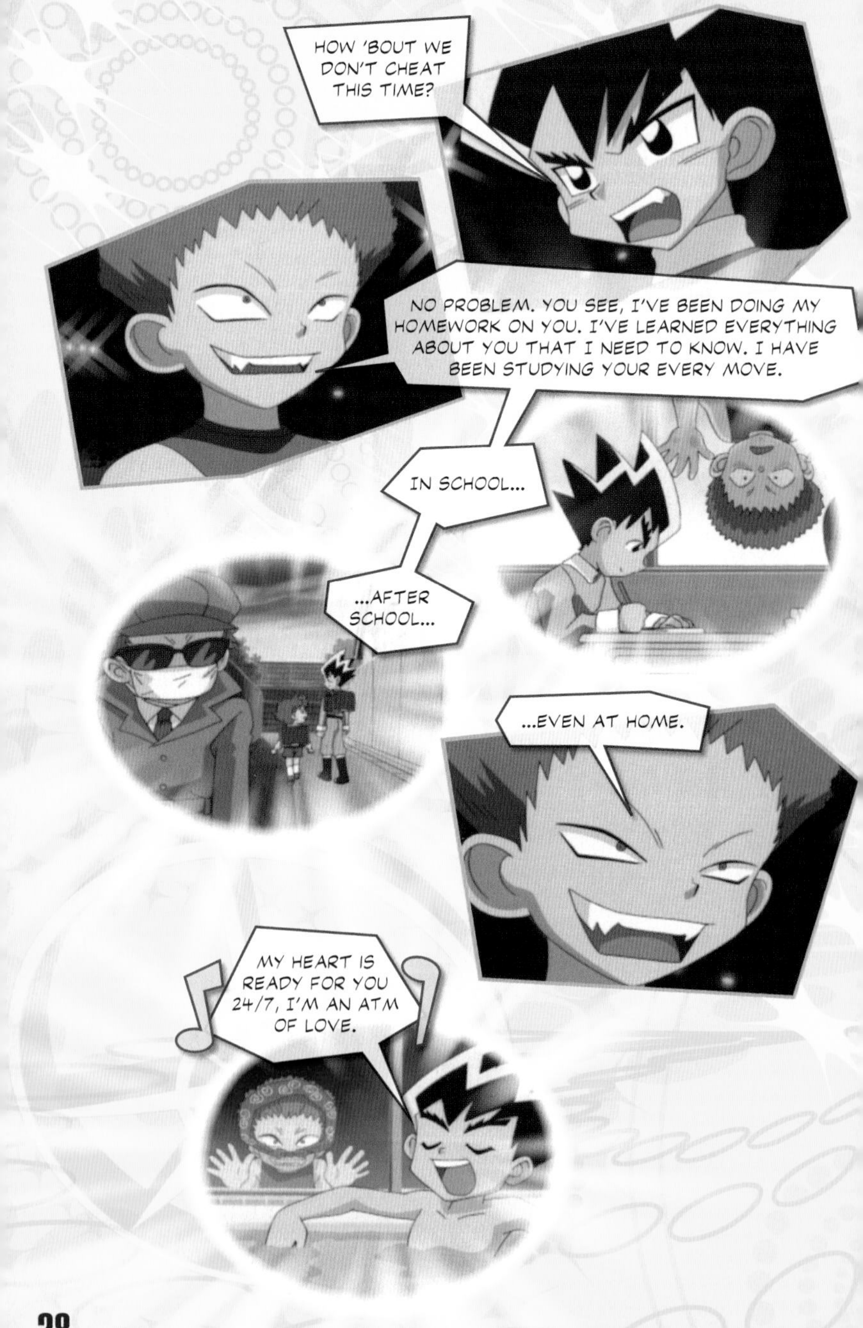
HOW 'BOUT WE DON'T CHEAT THIS TIME?
NO PROBLEM. YOU SEE, I'VE BEEN DOING MY HOMEWORK ON YOU. I'VE LEARNED EVERYTHING ABOUT YOU THAT I NEED TO KNOW. I HAVE BEEN STUDYING YOUR EVERY MOVE.
IN SCHOOL...
...AFTER SCHOOL...
...EVEN AT HOME.
MY HEART IS READY FOR YOU 24/7, I'M AN ATM OF LOVE.

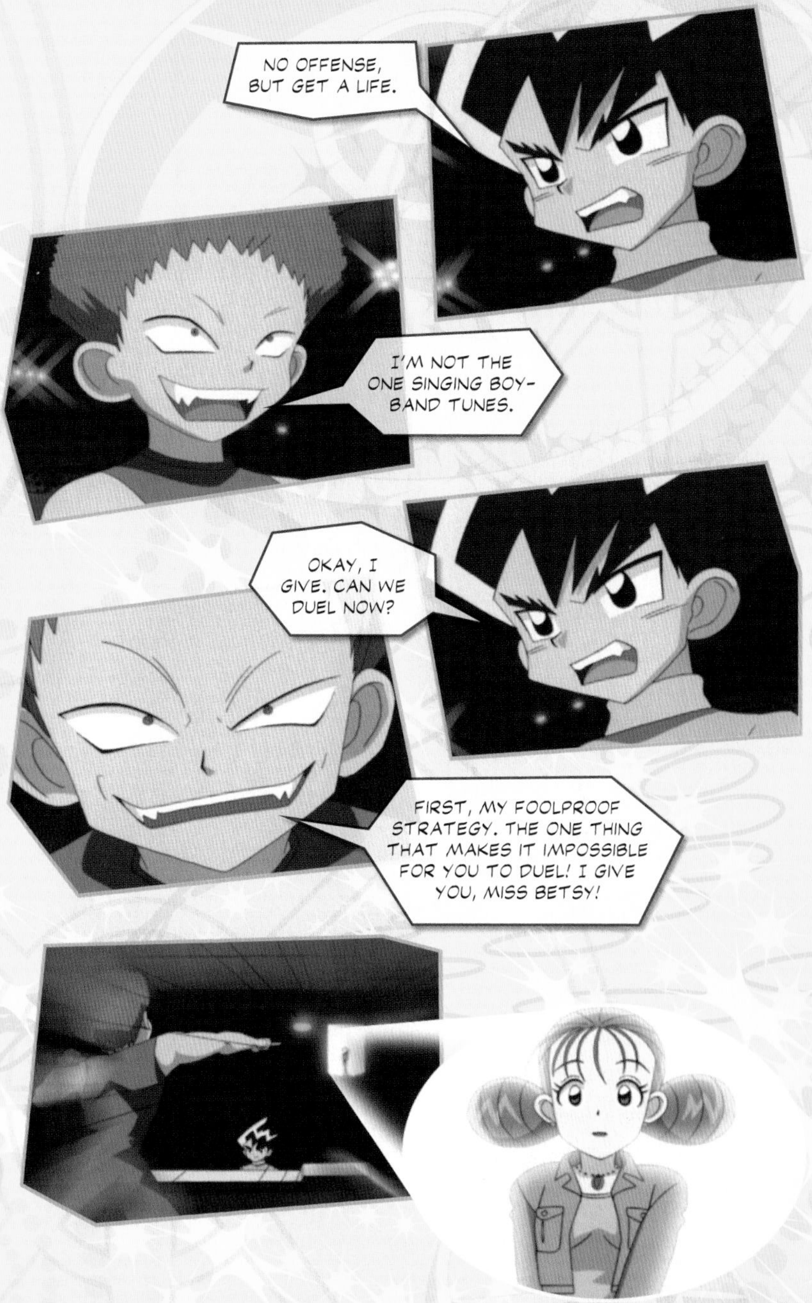

NO OFFENSE, BUT GET A LIFE.
I'M NOT THE ONE SINGING BOY-BAND TUNES.
OKAY, I GIVE. CAN WE DUEL NOW?
FIRST, MY FOOLPROOF STRATEGY. THE ONE THING THAT MAKES IT IMPOSSIBLE FOR YOU TO DUEL! I GIVE YOU, MISS BETSY!

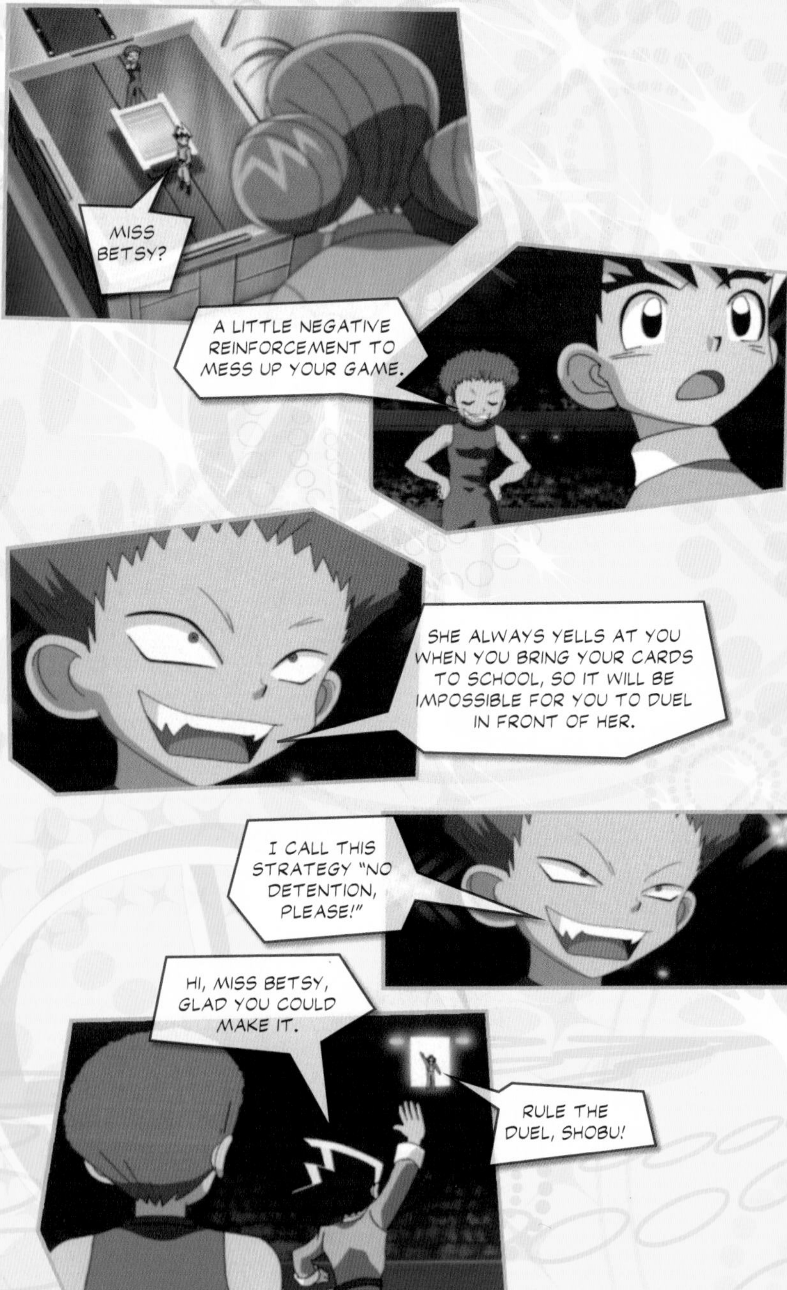

MISS BETSY?
A LITTLE NEGATIVE REINFORCEMENT TO MESS UP YOUR GAME.
SHE ALWAYS YELLS AT YOU WHEN YOU BRING YOUR CARDS TO SCHOOL, SO IT WILL BE IMPOSSIBLE FOR YOU TO DUEL IN FRONT OF HER.
I CALL THIS STRATEGY "NO DETENTION, PLEASE!"
HI, MISS BETSY, GLAD YOU COULD MAKE IT.
RULE THE DUEL, SHOBU!

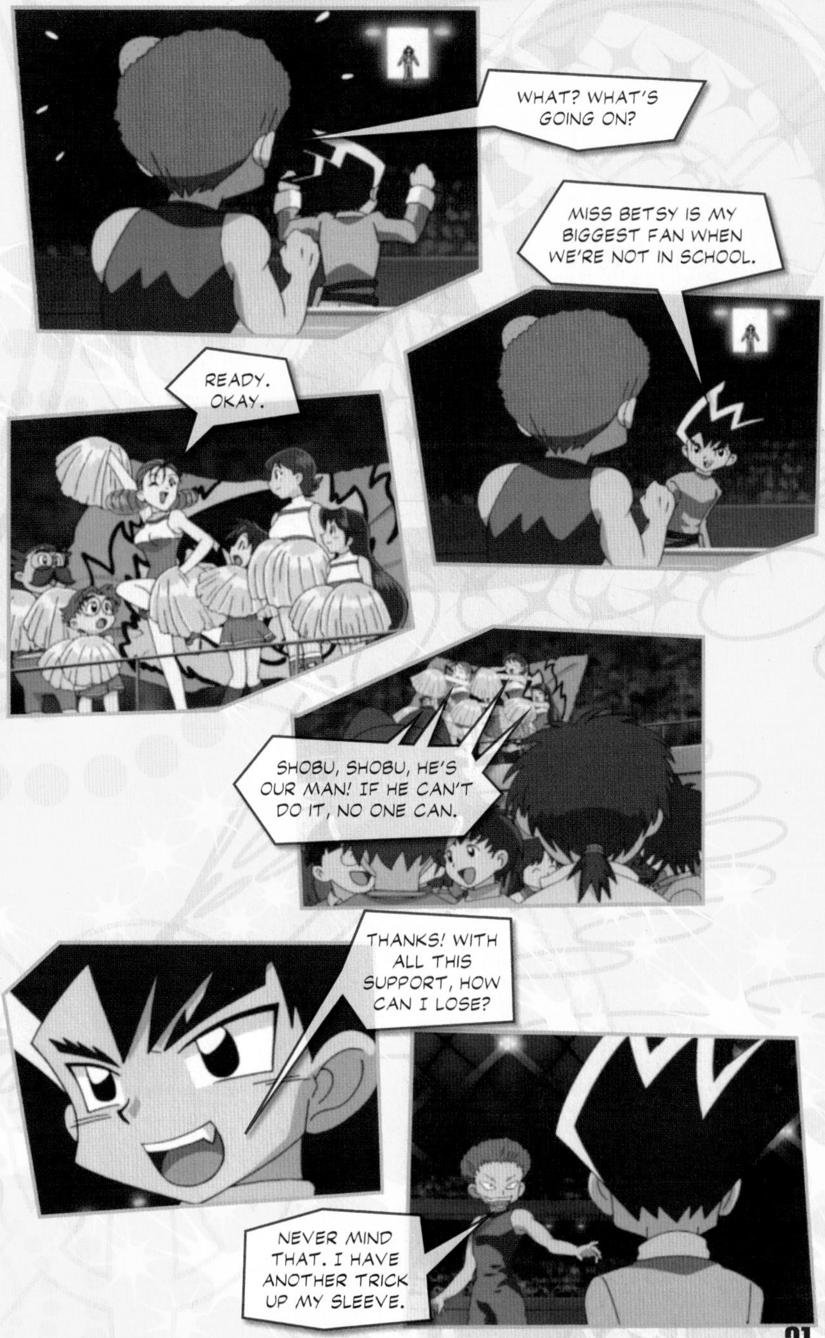
WHAT? WHAT'S GOING ON?
MISS BETSY IS MY BIGGEST FAN WHEN WE'RE NOT IN SCHOOL.
READY. OKAY.
SHOBU, SHOBU, HE'S OUR MAN! IF HE CAN'T DO IT, NO ONE CAN.
THANKS! WITH ALL THIS SUPPORT, HOW CAN I LOSE?
NEVER MIND THAT. I HAVE ANOTHER TRICK UP MY SLEEVE.

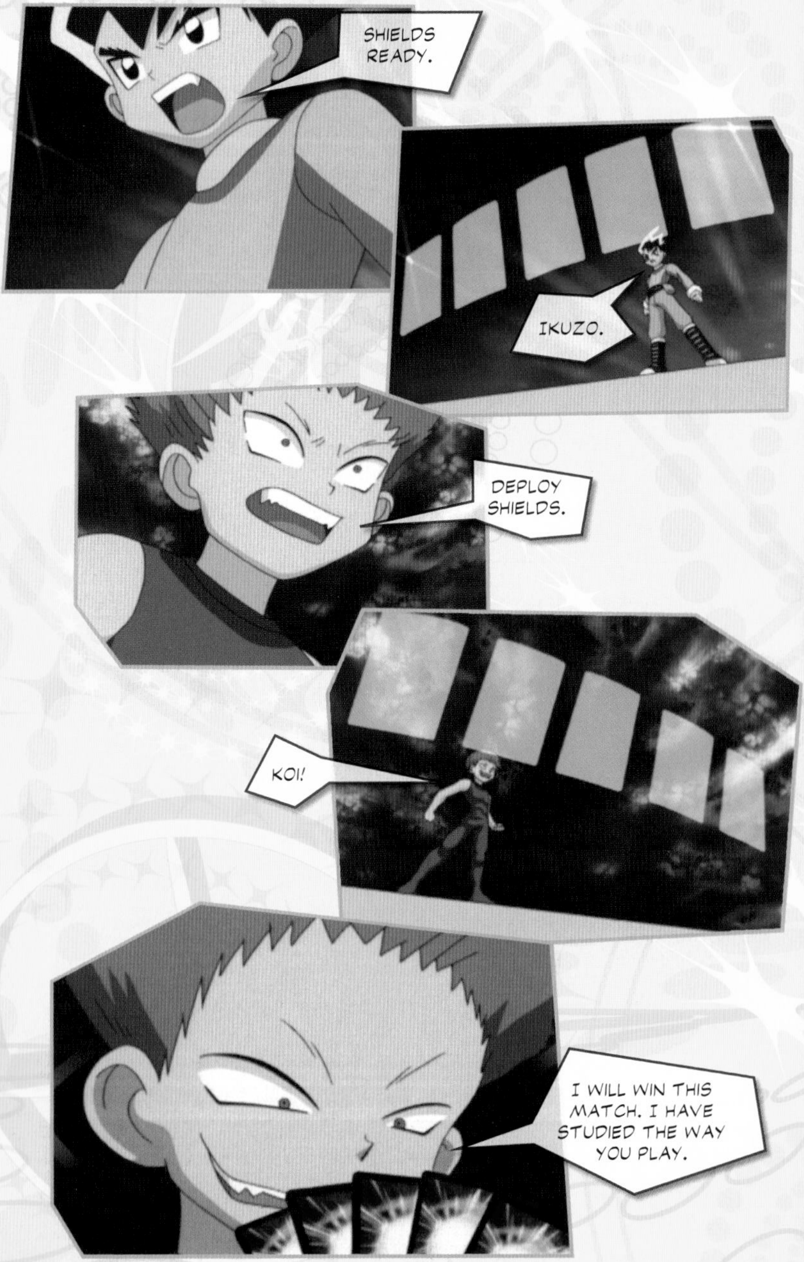
SHIELDS READY.
IKUZO.
DEPLOY SHIELDS.
KOI!
I WILL WIN THIS MATCH. I HAVE STUDIED THE WAY YOU PLAY.

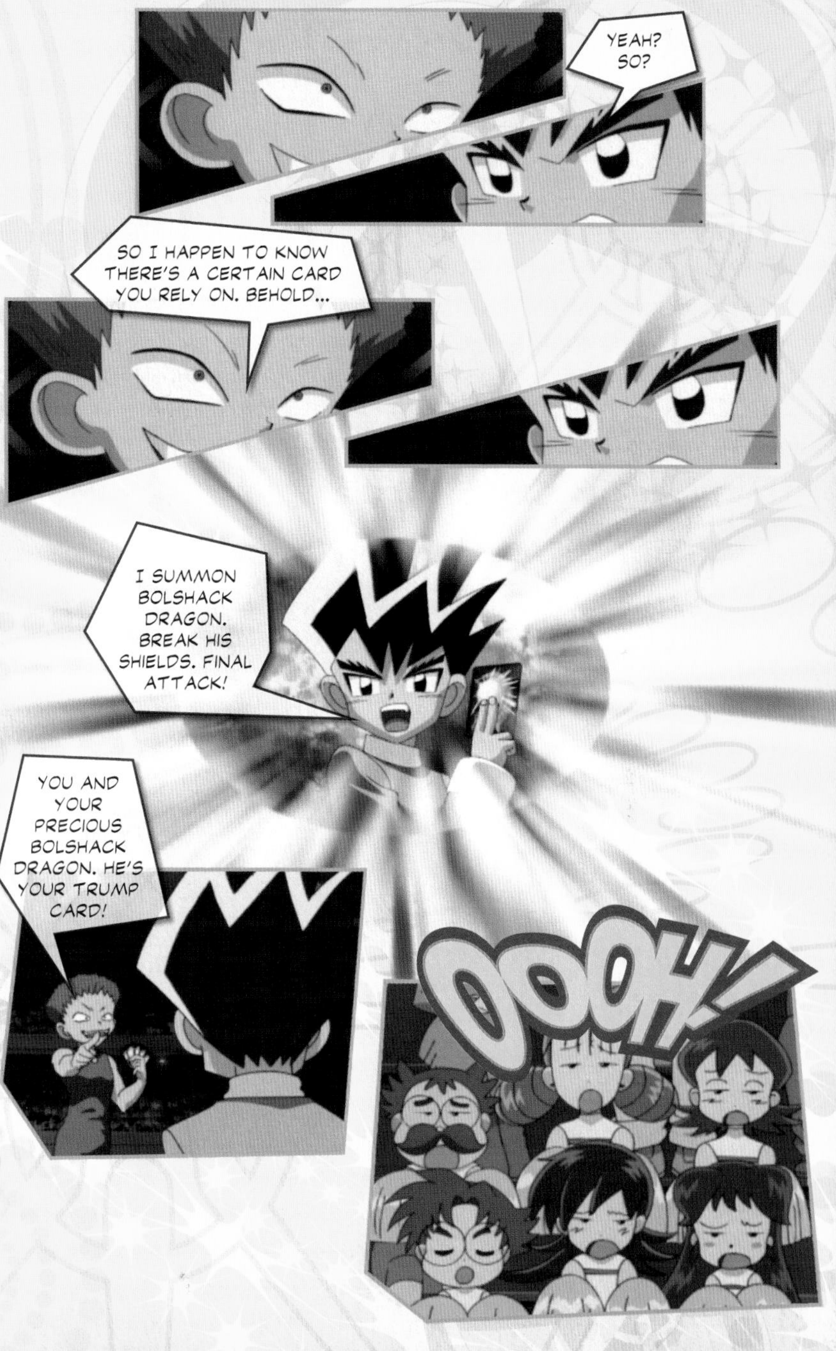
YEAH? SO?
SO I HAPPEN TO KNOW THERE'S A CERTAIN CARD YOU RELY ON. BEHOLD...
I SUMMON BOLSHACK DRAGON. BREAK HIS SHIELDS. FINAL ATTACK!
YOU AND YOUR PRECIOUS BOLSHACK DRAGON. HE'S YOUR TRUMP CARD!
OOOH!

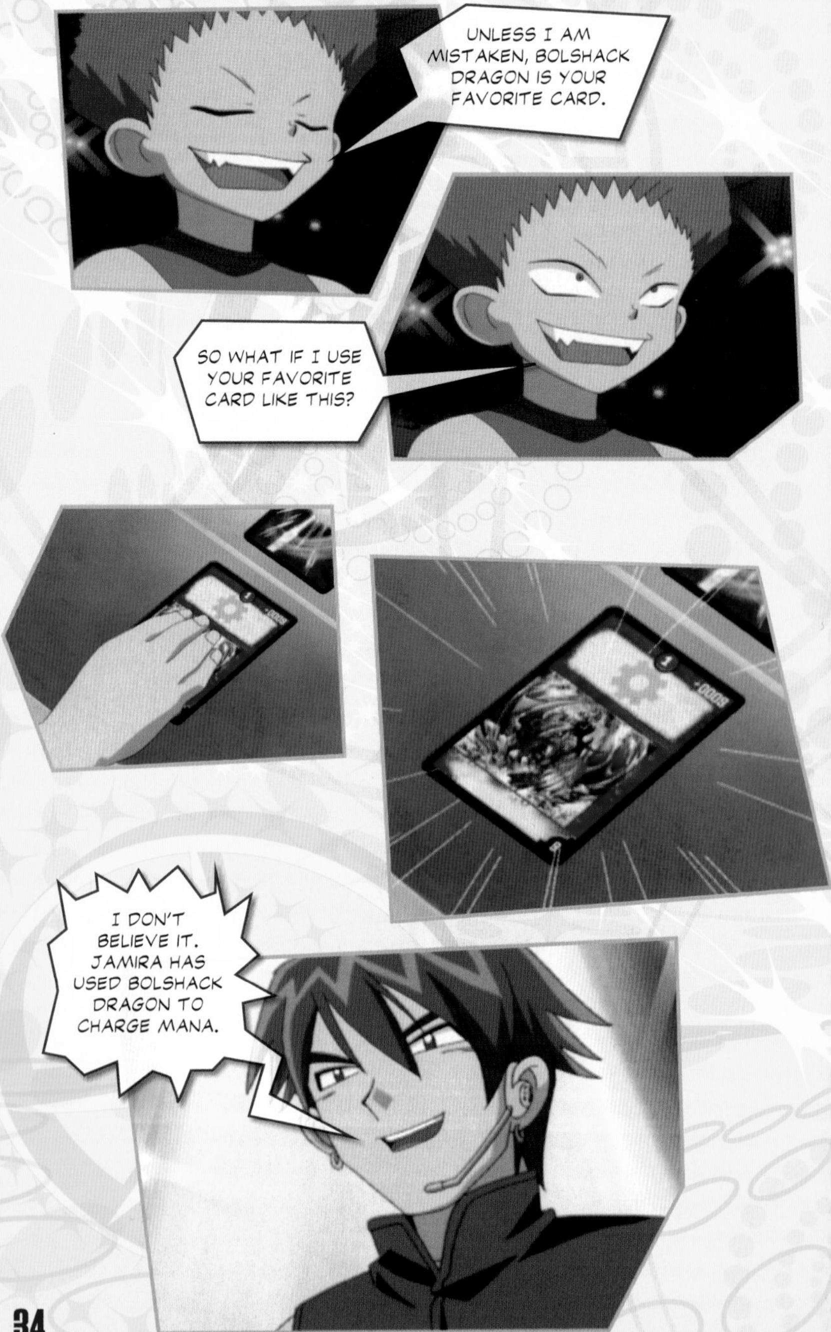
UNLESS I AM MISTAKEN, BOLSHACK DRAGON IS YOUR FAVORITE CARD.
SO WHAT IF I USE YOUR FAVORITE CARD LIKE THIS?
I DON'T BELIEVE IT. JAMIRA HAS USED BOLSHACK DRAGON TO CHARGE MANA.

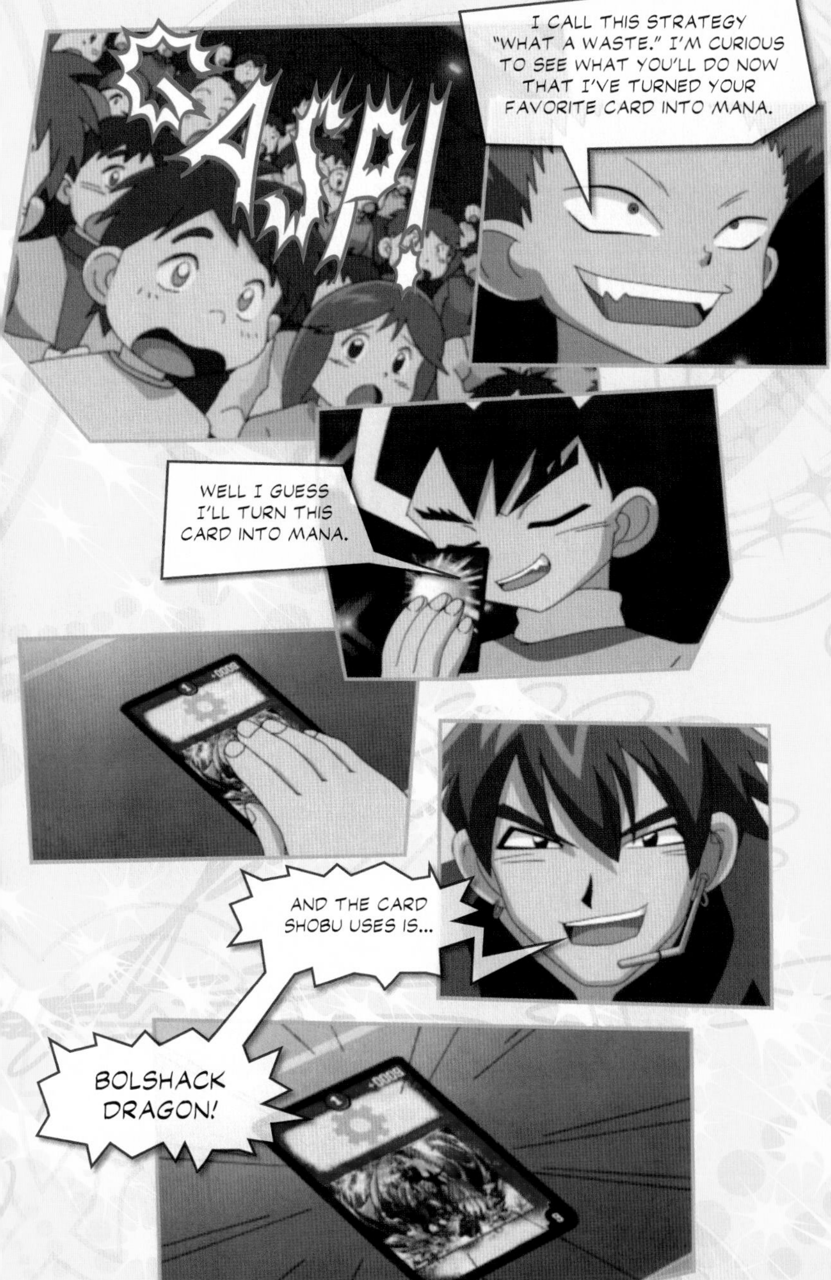

GASP!
I CALL THIS STRATEGY "WHAT A WASTE." I'M CURIOUS TO SEE WHAT YOU'LL DO NOW THAT I'VE TURNED YOUR FAVORITE CARD INTO MANA.
WELL I GUESS I'LL TURN THIS CARD INTO MANA.
AND THE CARD SHOBU USES IS...
BOLSHACK DRAGON!

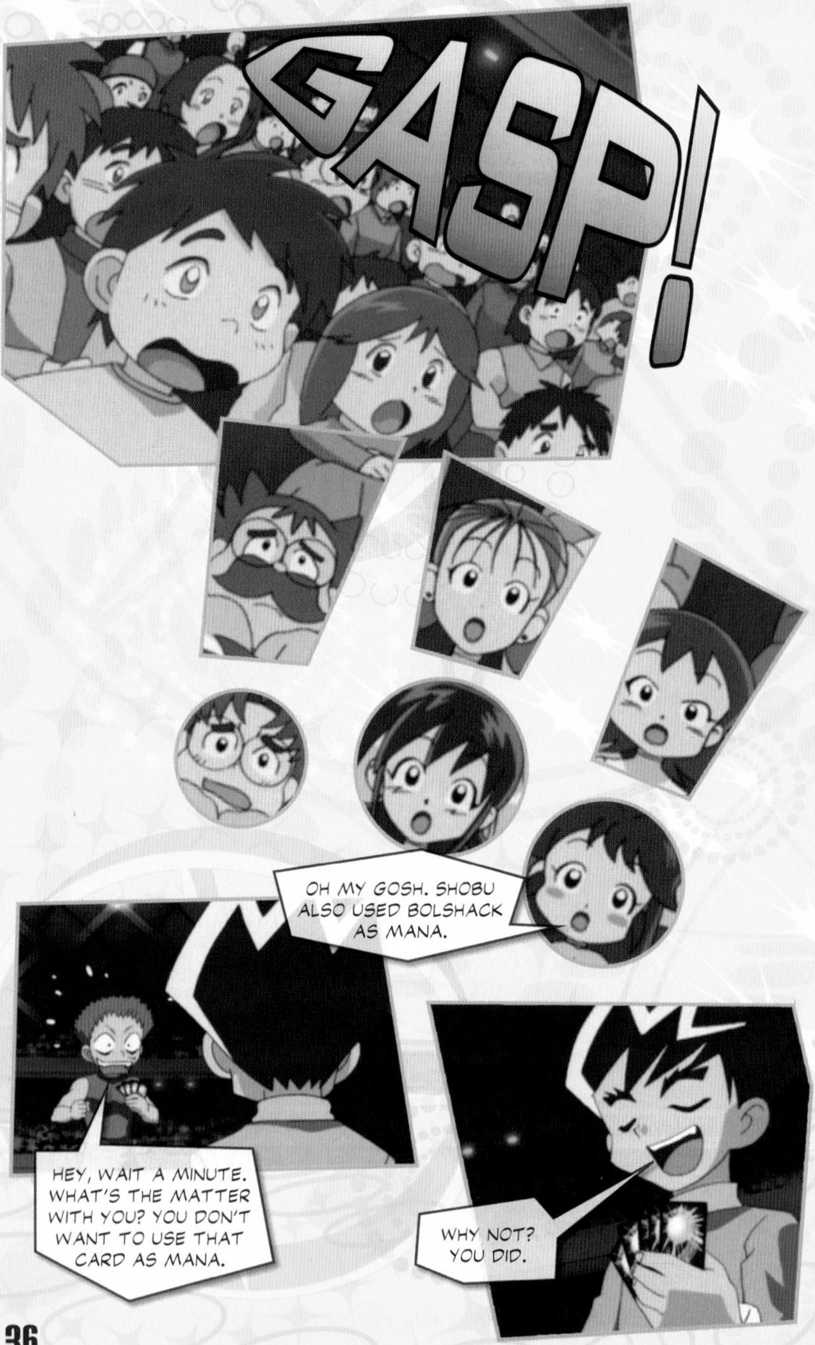
GASP!
OH MY GOSH. SHOBU ALSO USED BOLSHACK AS MANA.
HEY, WAIT A MINUTE. WHAT'S THE MATTER WITH YOU? YOU DON'T WANT TO USE THAT CARD AS MANA.
WHY NOT? YOU DID.

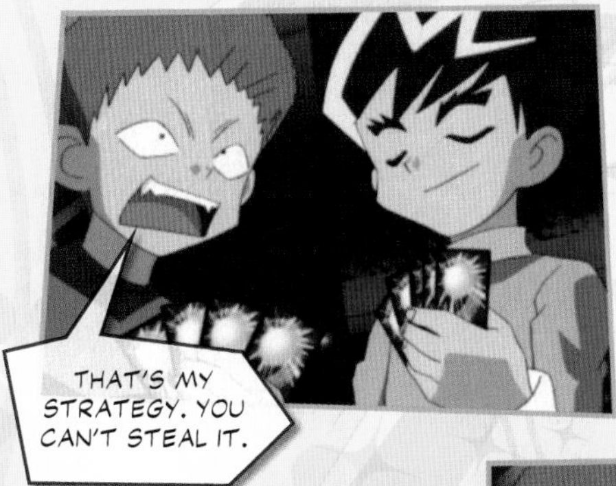
THAT'S MY STRATEGY. YOU CAN'T STEAL IT.

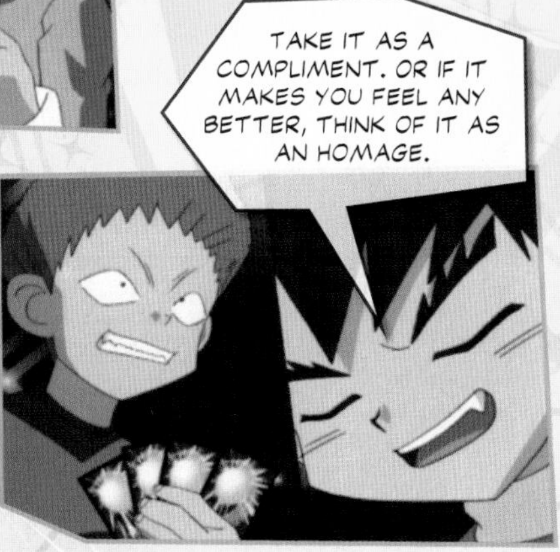
TAKE IT AS A COMPLIMENT. OR IF IT MAKES YOU FEEL ANY BETTER, THINK OF IT AS AN HOMAGE.

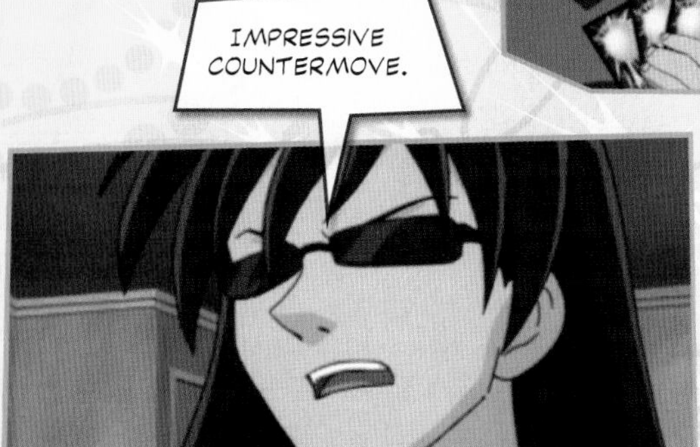
IMPRESSIVE COUNTERMOVE.

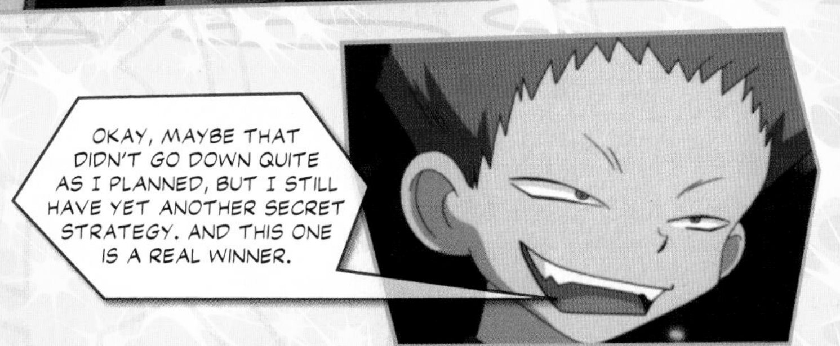
OKAY, MAYBE THAT DIDN'T GO DOWN QUITE AS I PLANNED, BUT I STILL HAVE YET ANOTHER SECRET STRATEGY. AND THIS ONE IS A REAL WINNER.

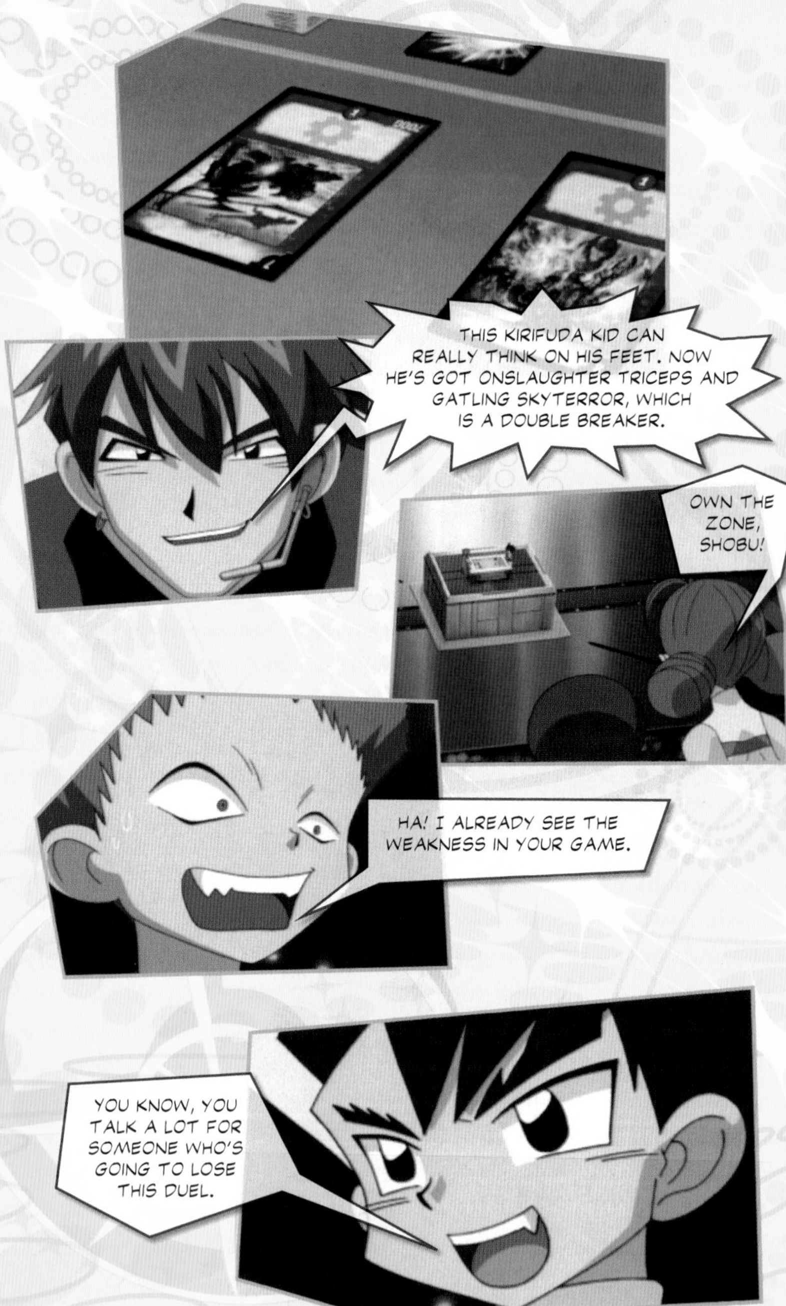
THIS KIRIFUDA KID CAN REALLY THINK ON HIS FEET. NOW HE'S GOT ONSLAUGHTER TRICEPS AND GATLING SKYTERROR, WHICH IS A DOUBLE BREAKER.
OWN THE ZONE, SHOBU!
HA! I ALREADY SEE THE WEAKNESS IN YOUR GAME.
YOU KNOW, YOU TALK A LOT FOR SOMEONE WHO'S GOING TO LOSE THIS DUEL.

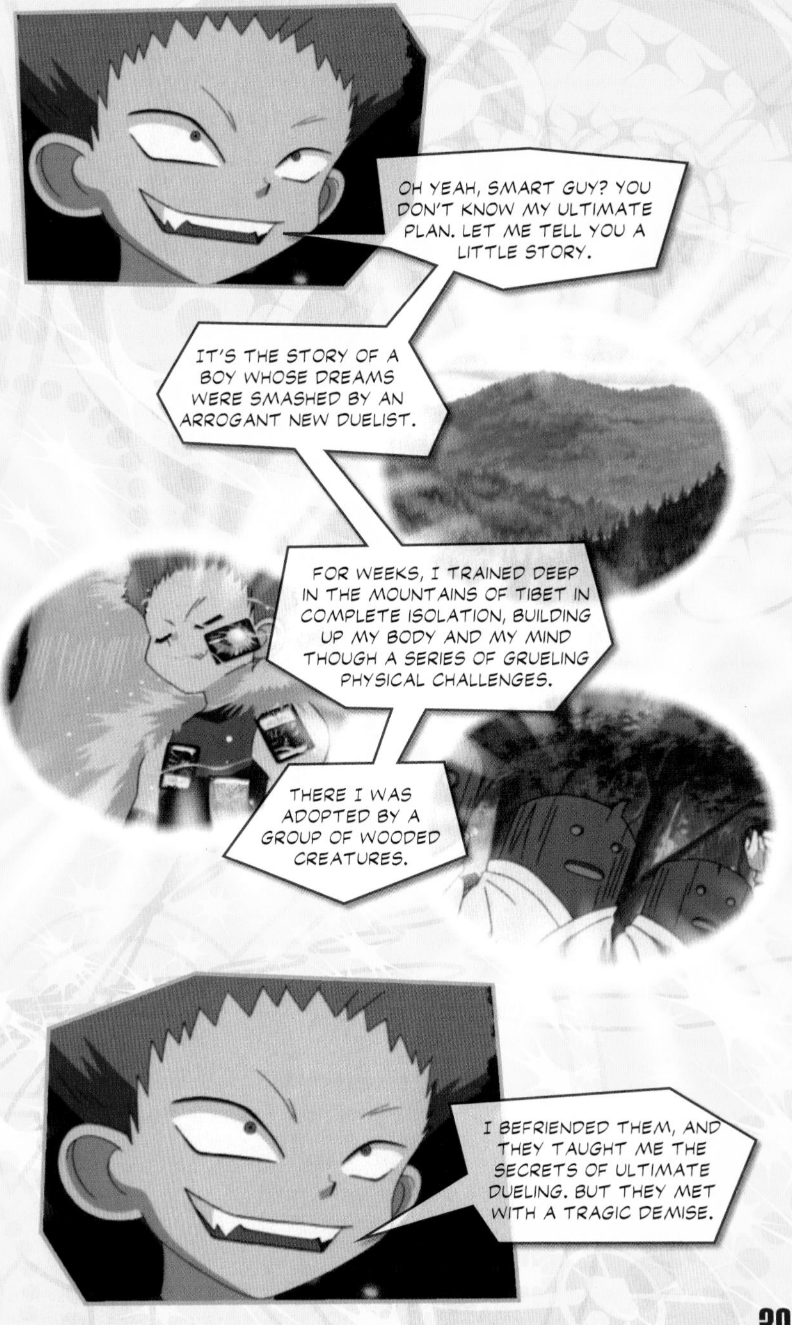

OH YEAH, SMART GUY? YOU DON'T KNOW MY ULTIMATE PLAN. LET ME TELL YOU A LITTLE STORY.
IT'S THE STORY OF A BOY WHOSE DREAMS WERE SMASHED BY AN ARROGANT NEW DUELIST.
FOR WEEKS, I TRAINED DEEP IN THE MOUNTAINS OF TIBET IN COMPLETE ISOLATION, BUILDING UP MY BODY AND MY MIND THOUGH A SERIES OF GRUELING PHYSICAL CHALLENGES.
THERE I WAS ADOPTED BY A GROUP OF WOODED CREATURES.
I BEFRIENDED THEM, AND THEY TAUGHT ME THE SECRETS OF ULTIMATE DUELING. BUT THEY MET WITH A TRAGIC DEMISE.

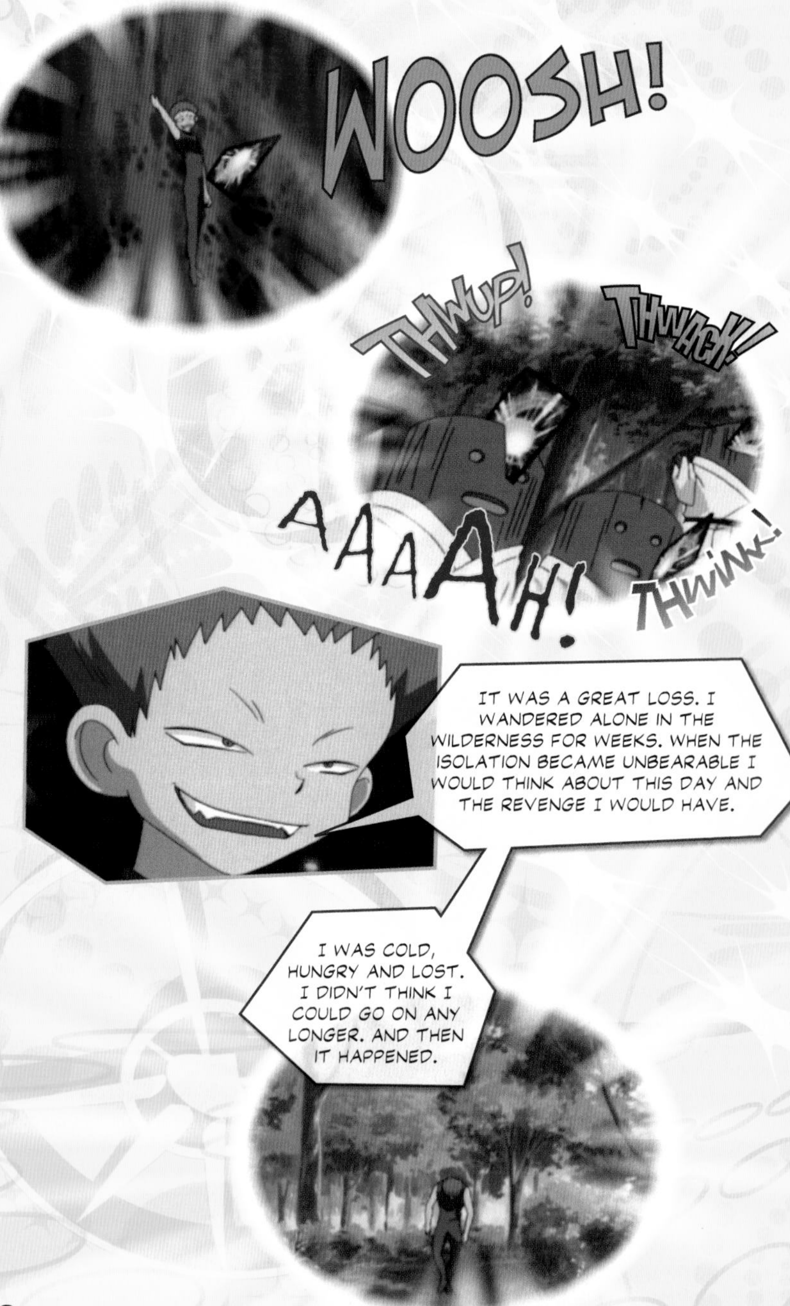
WOOSH!
THWUP!
THWACK!!
AAAAH!
THWINK!
IT WAS A GREAT LOSS. I WANDERED ALONE IN THE WILDERNESS FOR WEEKS. WHEN THE ISOLATION BECAME UNBEARABLE I WOULD THINK ABOUT THIS DAY AND THE REVENGE I WOULD HAVE.
I WAS COLD, HUNGRY AND LOST. I DIDN'T THINK I COULD GO ON ANY LONGER. AND THEN IT HAPPENED.

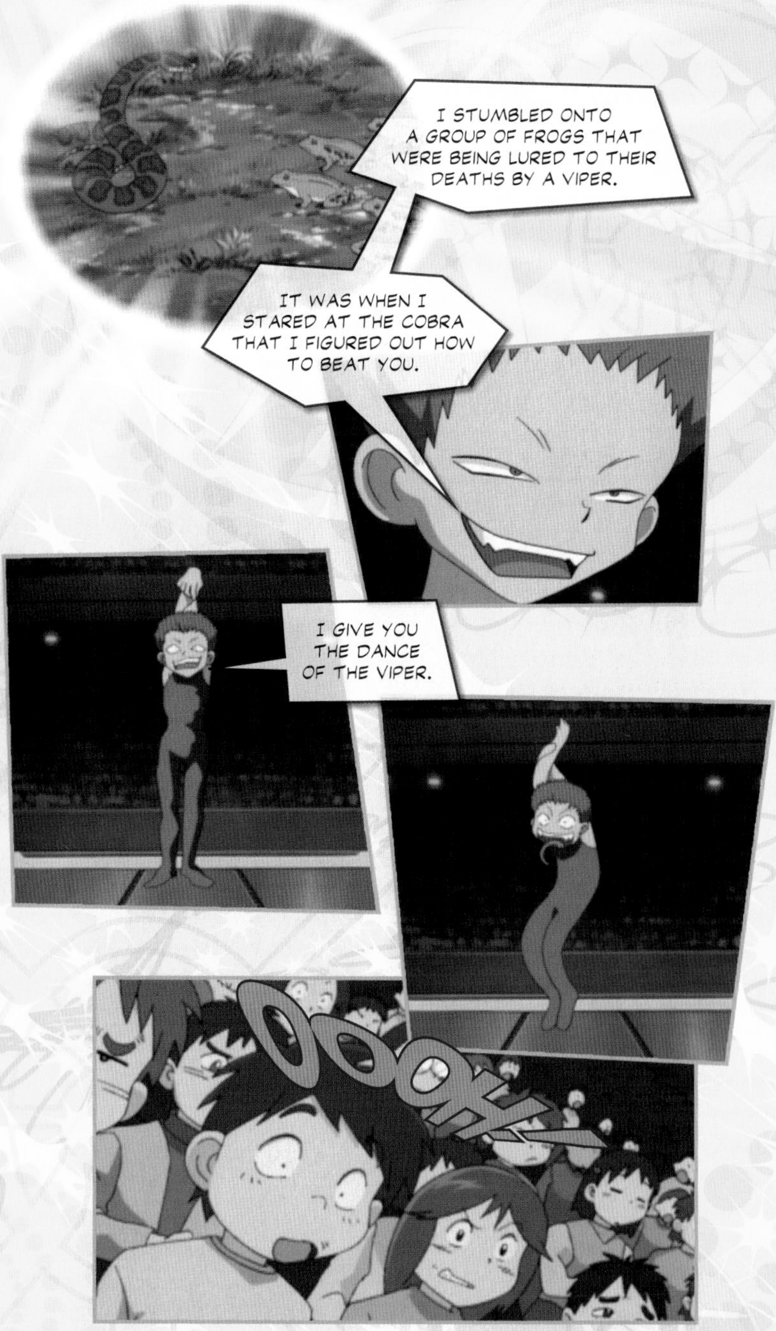
I STUMBLED ONTO A GROUP OF FROGS THAT WERE BEING LURED TO THEIR DEATHS BY A VIPER.
IT WAS WHEN I STARED AT THE COBRA THAT I FIGURED OUT HOW TO BEAT YOU.
I GIVE YOU THE DANCE OF THE VIPER.
OOOOH

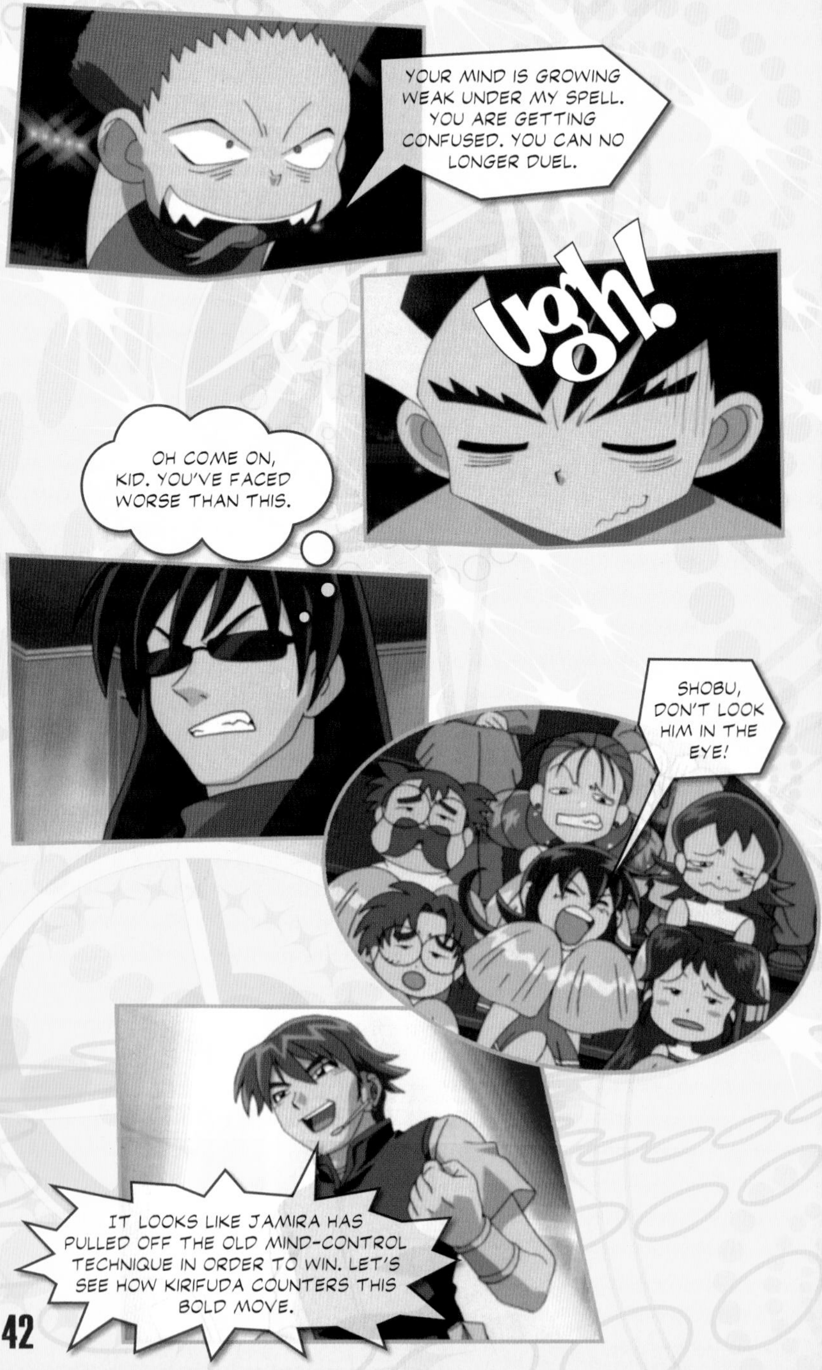
YOUR MIND IS GROWING WEAK UNDER MY SPELL. YOU ARE GETTING CONFUSED. YOU CAN NO LONGER DUEL.
UGH!
OH COME ON, KID. YOU'VE FACED WORSE THAN THIS.
SHOBU, DON'T LOOK HIM IN THE EYE!
IT LOOKS LIKE JAMIRA HAS PULLED OFF THE OLD MIND-CONTROL TECHNIQUE IN ORDER TO WIN. LET'S SEE HOW KIRIFUDA COUNTERS THIS BOLD MOVE.

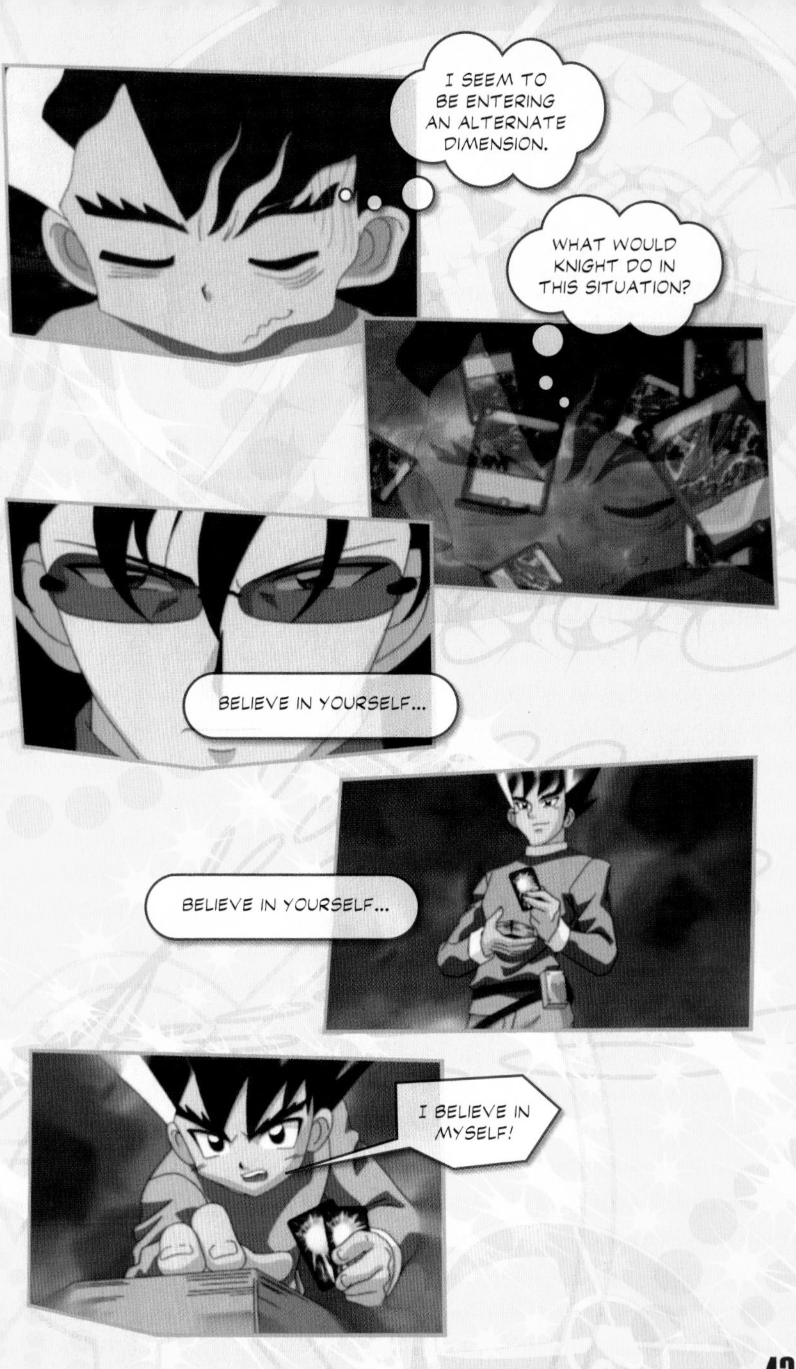
I SEEM TO BE ENTERING AN ALTERNATE DIMENSION.
WHAT WOULD KNIGHT DO IN THIS SITUATION?
BELIEVE IN YOURSELF...
BELIEVE IN YOURSELF...
I BELIEVE IN MYSELF!

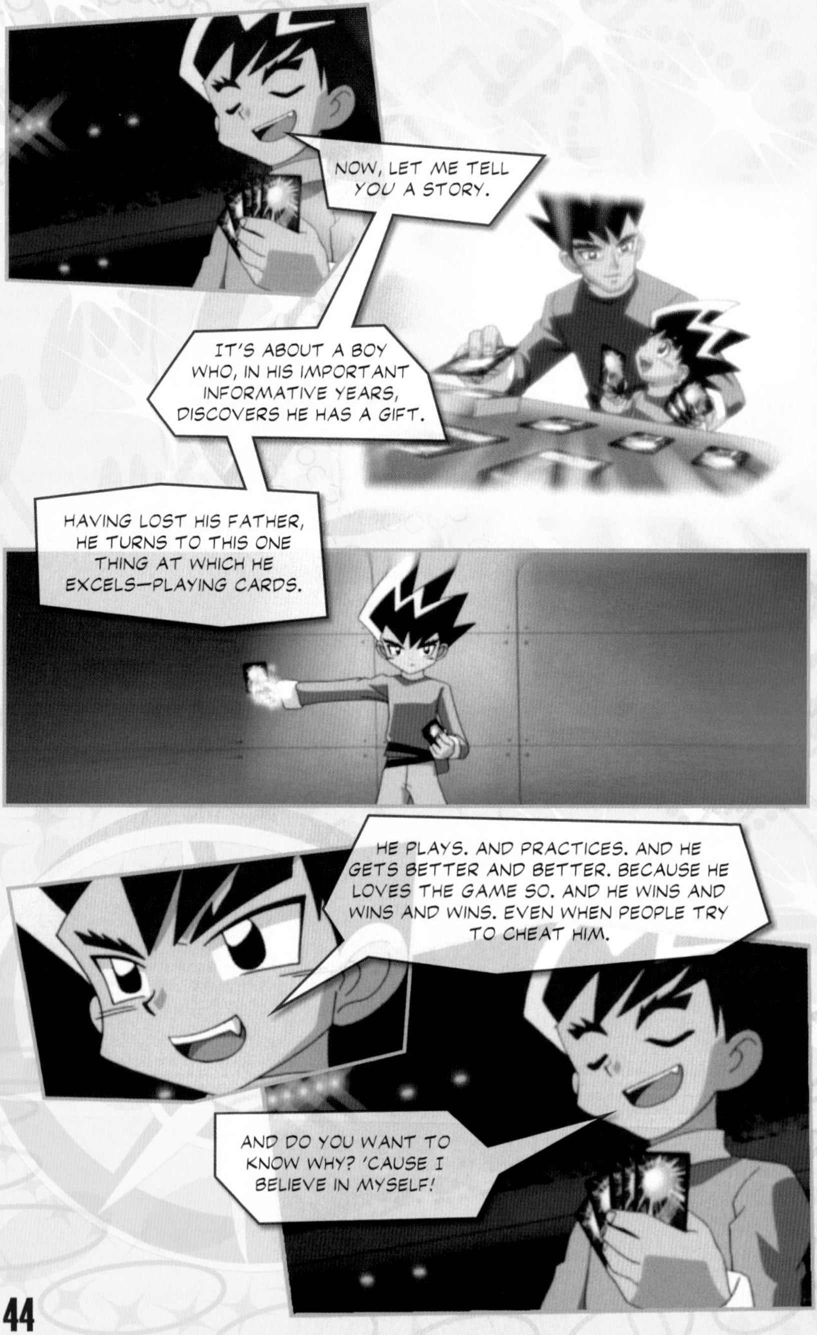
NOW, LET ME TELL YOU A STORY.
IT'S ABOUT A BOY WHO, IN HIS IMPORTANT INFORMATIVE YEARS, DISCOVERS HE HAS A GIFT.
HAVING LOST HIS FATHER, HE TURNS TO THIS ONE THING AT WHICH HE EXCELS—PLAYING CARDS.
HE PLAYS. AND PRACTICES. AND HE GETS BETTER AND BETTER. BECAUSE HE LOVES THE GAME SO. AND HE WINS AND WINS AND WINS. EVEN WHEN PEOPLE TRY TO CHEAT HIM.
AND DO YOU WANT TO KNOW WHY? 'CAUSE I BELIEVE IN MYSELF!

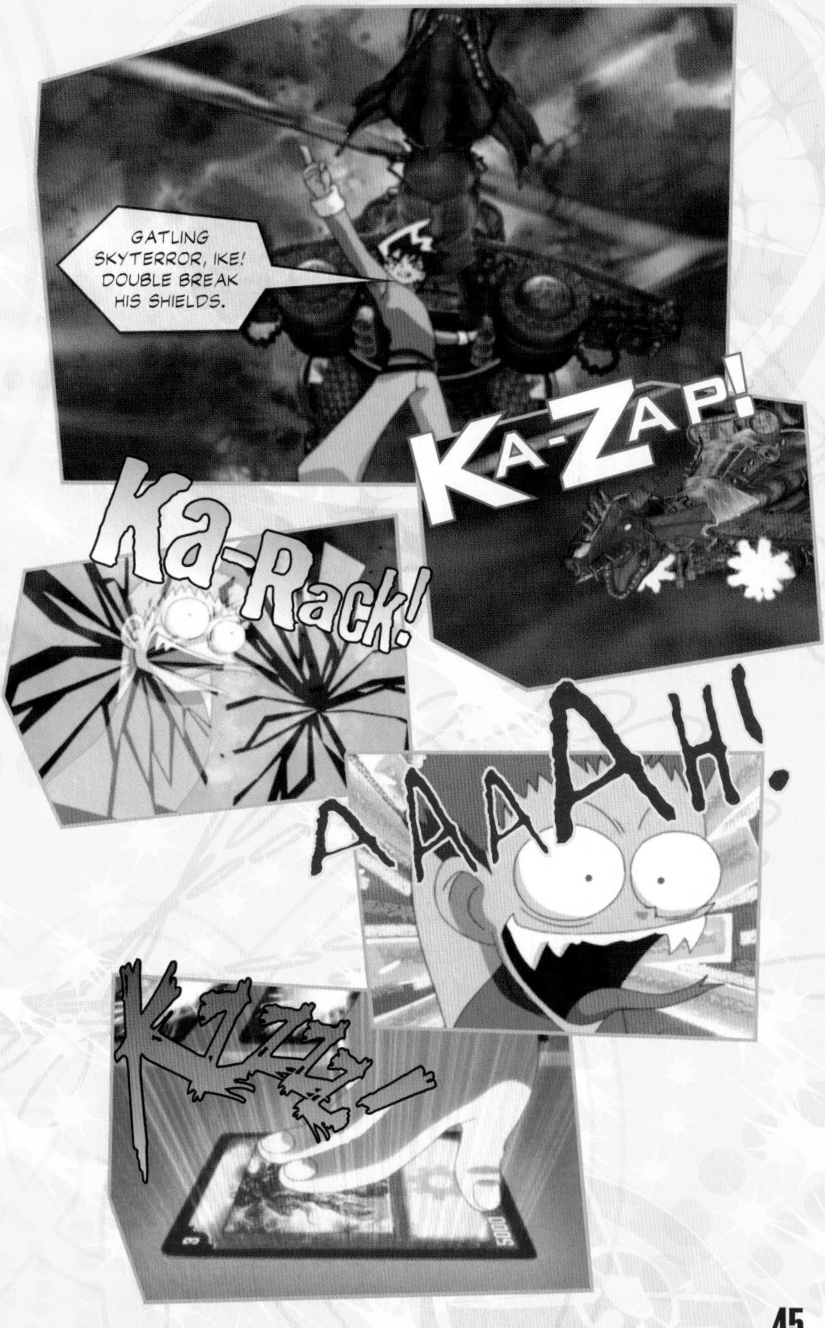
GATLING SKYTERROR, IKE! DOUBLE BREAK HIS SHIELDS.
Ka-Rack!
KA-ZAP!
AAAAH!

TRICEPS, ATTACK! TODOME DA!

AAAH!

Yaaah!

OOF!

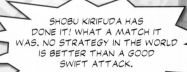

SHOBU KIRIFUDA HAS DONE IT! WHAT A MATCH IT WAS. NO STRATEGY IN THE WORLD IS BETTER THAN A GOOD SWIFT ATTACK.

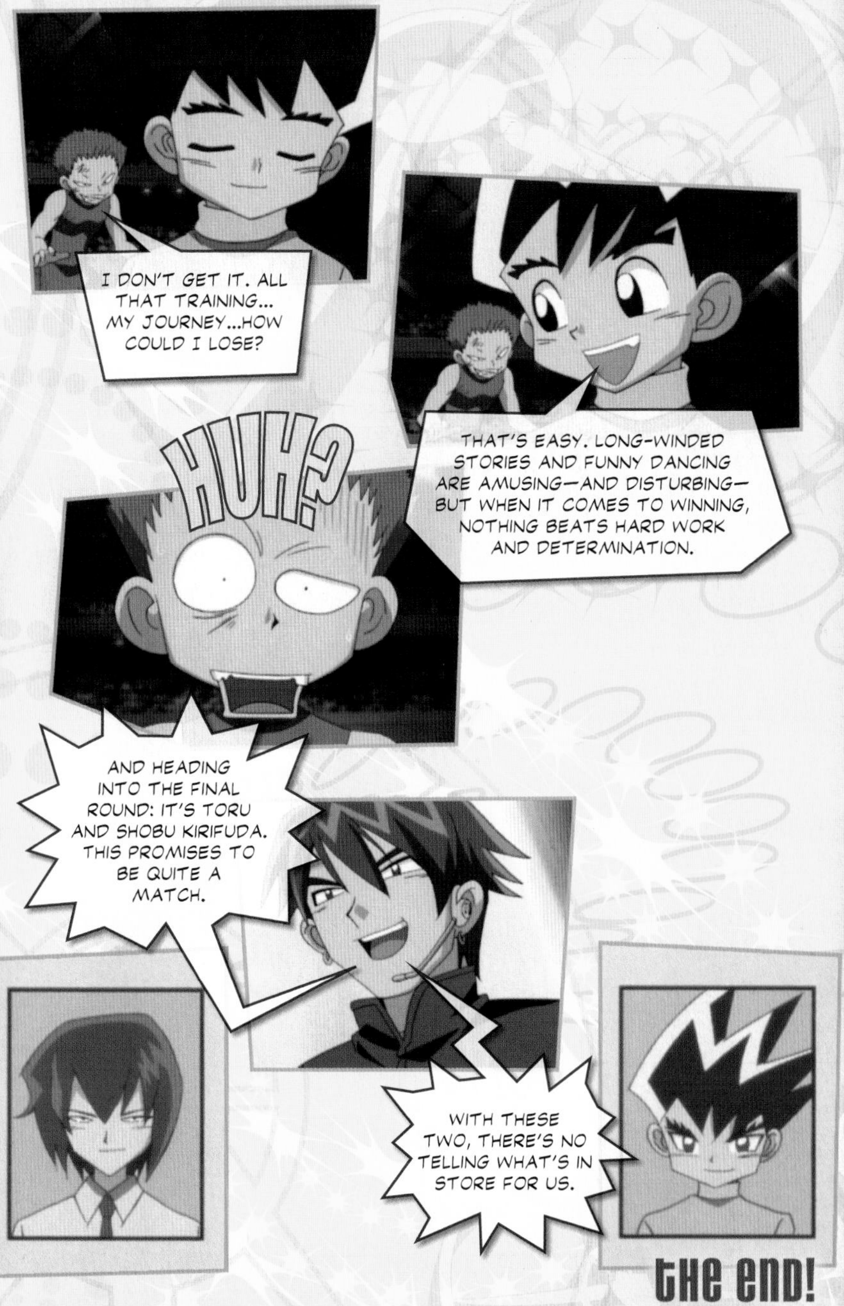
I DON'T GET IT. ALL THAT TRAINING... MY JOURNEY...HOW COULD I LOSE?
THAT'S EASY. LONG-WINDED STORIES AND FUNNY DANCING ARE AMUSING—AND DISTURBING—BUT WHEN IT COMES TO WINNING, NOTHING BEATS HARD WORK AND DETERMINATION.
HUH?
AND HEADING INTO THE FINAL ROUND: IT'S TORU AND SHOBU KIRIFUDA. THIS PROMISES TO BE QUITE A MATCH.
WITH THESE TWO, THERE'S NO TELLING WHAT'S IN STORE FOR US.
THE END!

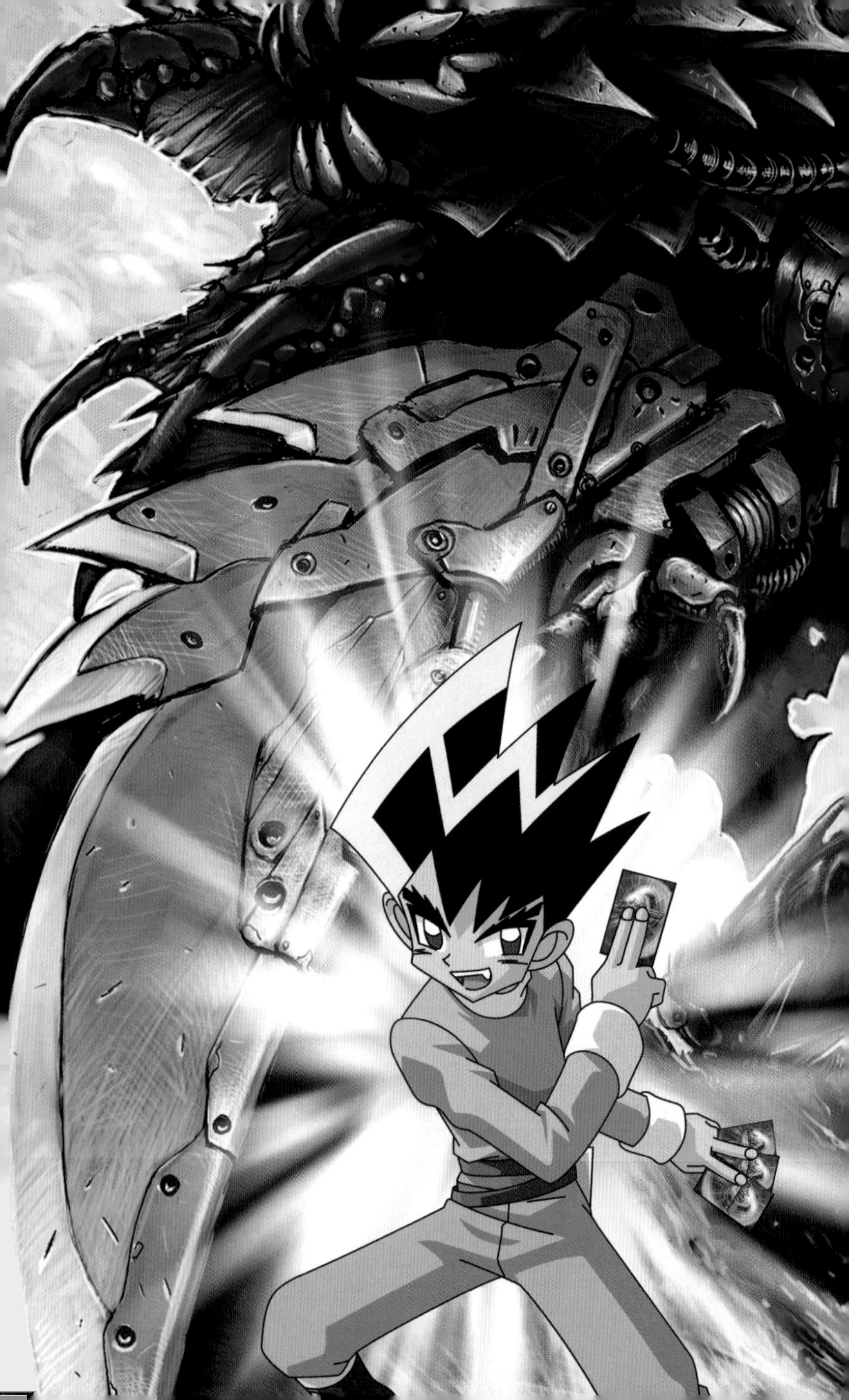

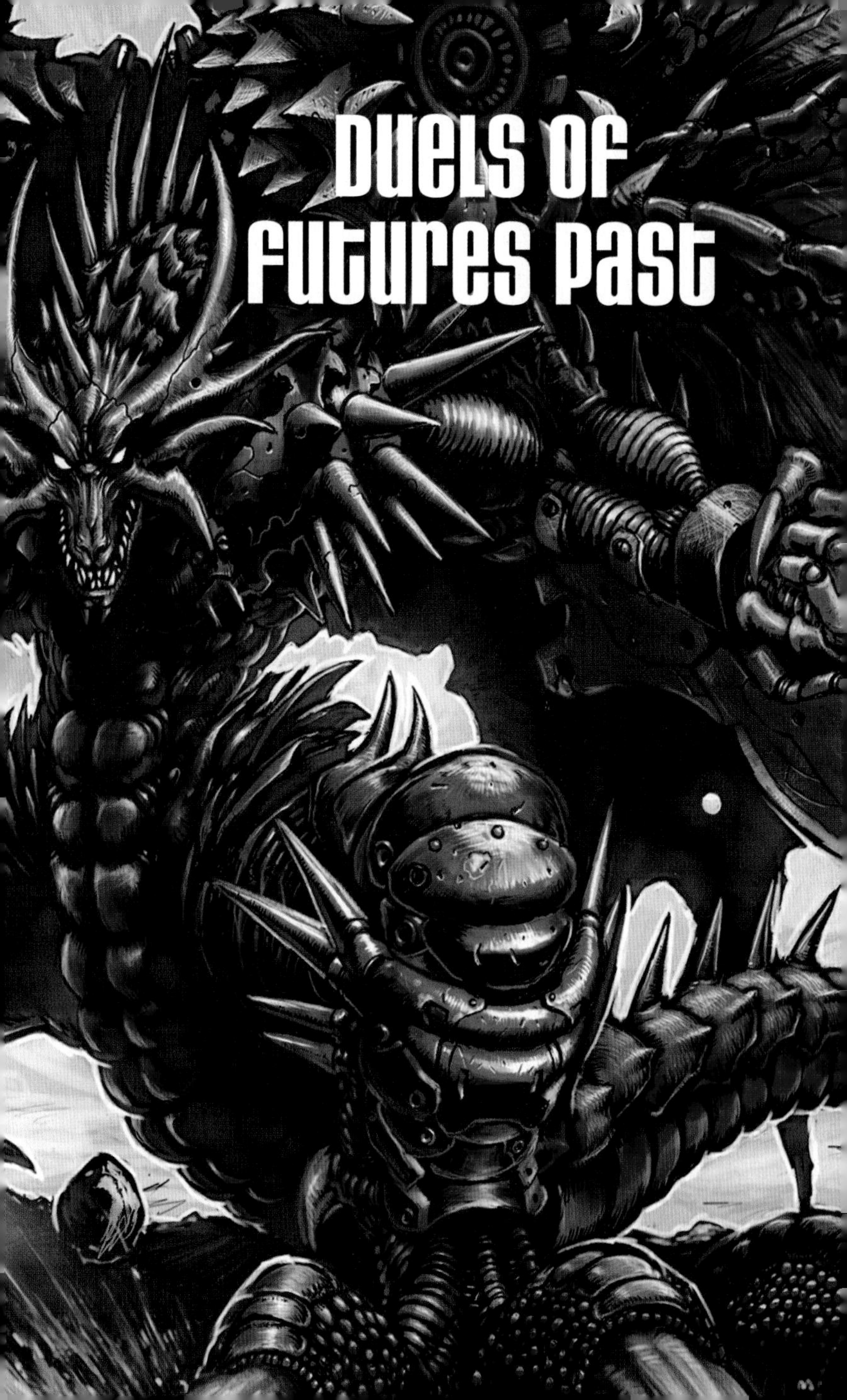
Duels of
Futures Past

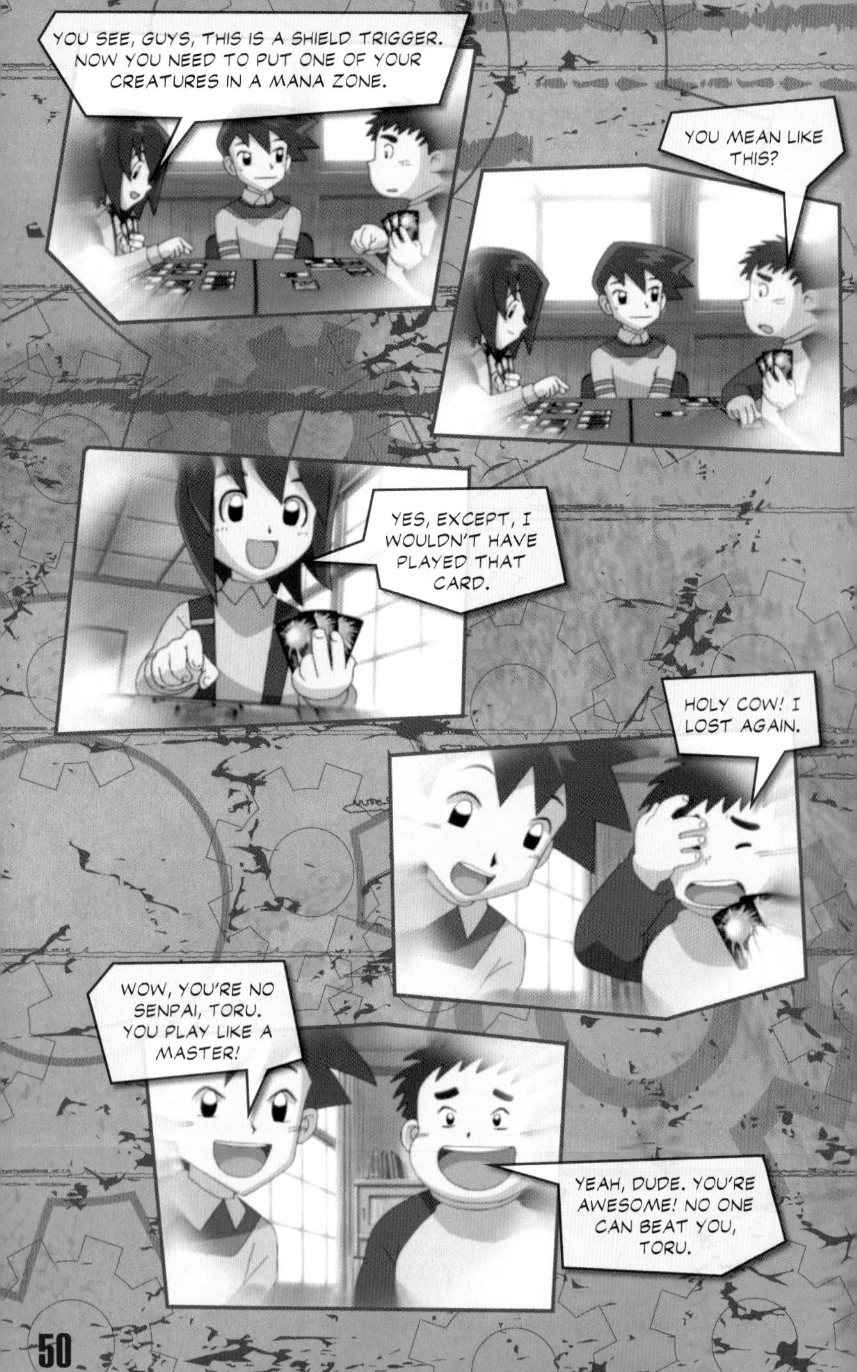
YOU SEE, GUYS, THIS IS A SHIELD TRIGGER. NOW YOU NEED TO PUT ONE OF YOUR CREATURES IN A MANA ZONE.
YOU MEAN LIKE THIS?
YES, EXCEPT, I WOULDN'T HAVE PLAYED THAT CARD.
HOLY COW! I LOST AGAIN.
WOW, YOU'RE NO SENPAI, TORU. YOU PLAY LIKE A MASTER!
YEAH, DUDE. YOU'RE AWESOME! NO ONE CAN BEAT YOU, TORU.

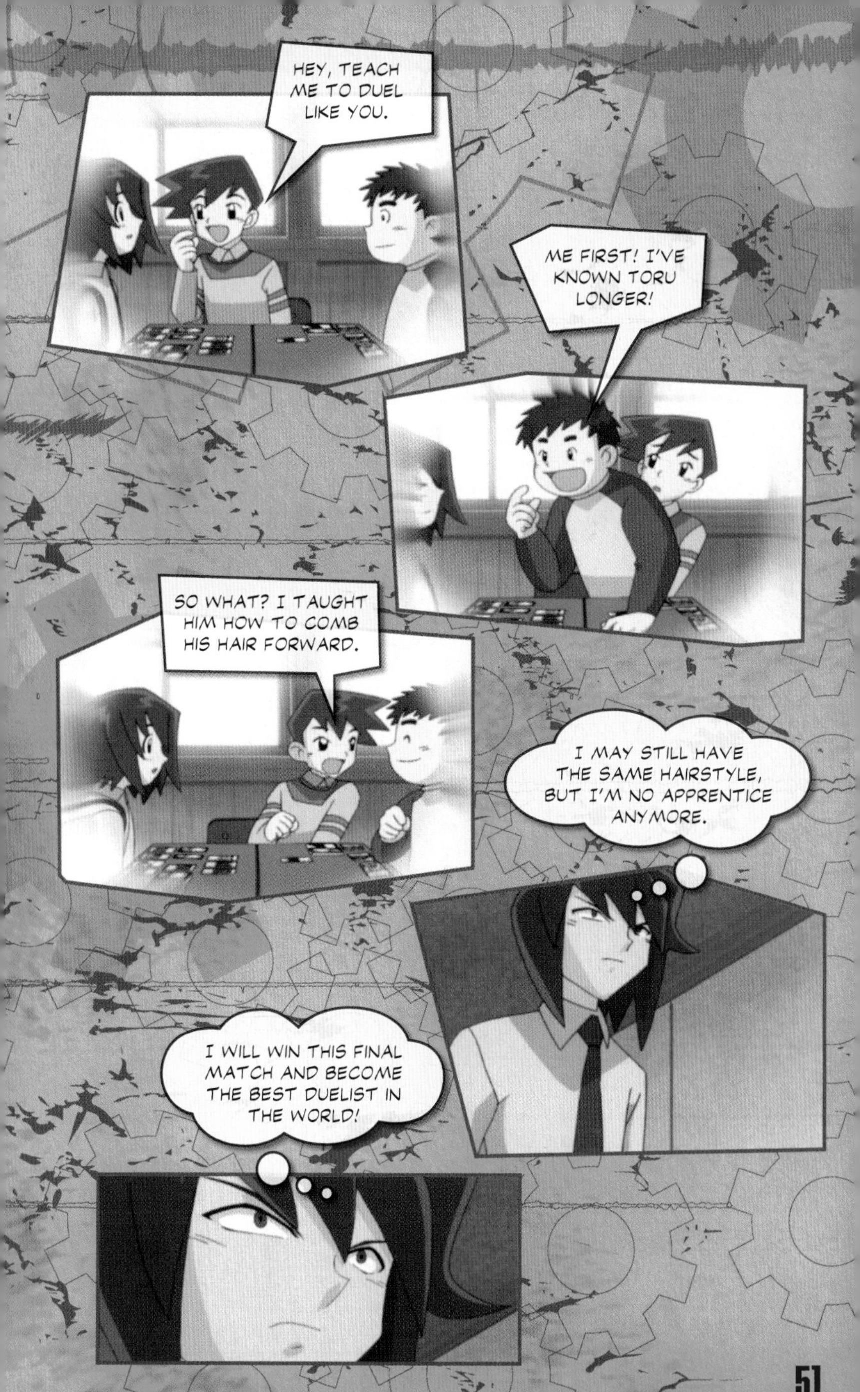
HEY, TEACH ME TO DUEL LIKE YOU.
ME FIRST! I'VE KNOWN TORU LONGER!
SO WHAT? I TAUGHT HIM HOW TO COMB HIS HAIR FORWARD.
I MAY STILL HAVE THE SAME HAIRSTYLE, BUT I'M NO APPRENTICE ANYMORE.
I WILL WIN THIS FINAL MATCH AND BECOME THE BEST DUELIST IN THE WORLD!

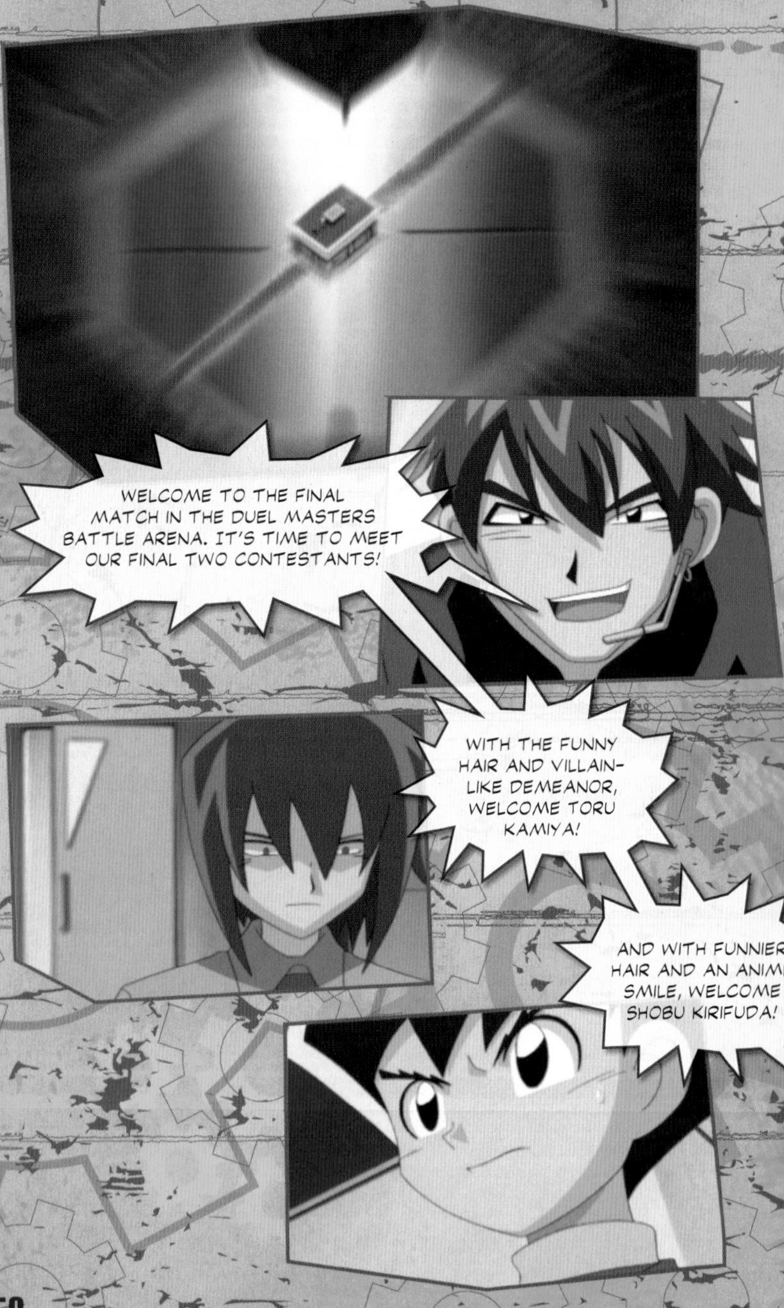
WELCOME TO THE FINAL MATCH IN THE DUEL MASTERS BATTLE ARENA. IT'S TIME TO MEET OUR FINAL TWO CONTESTANTS!
WITH THE FUNNY HAIR AND VILLAIN-LIKE DEMEANOR, WELCOME TORU KAMIYA!
AND WITH FUNNIER HAIR AND AN ANIME SMILE, WELCOME SHOBU KIRIFUDA!

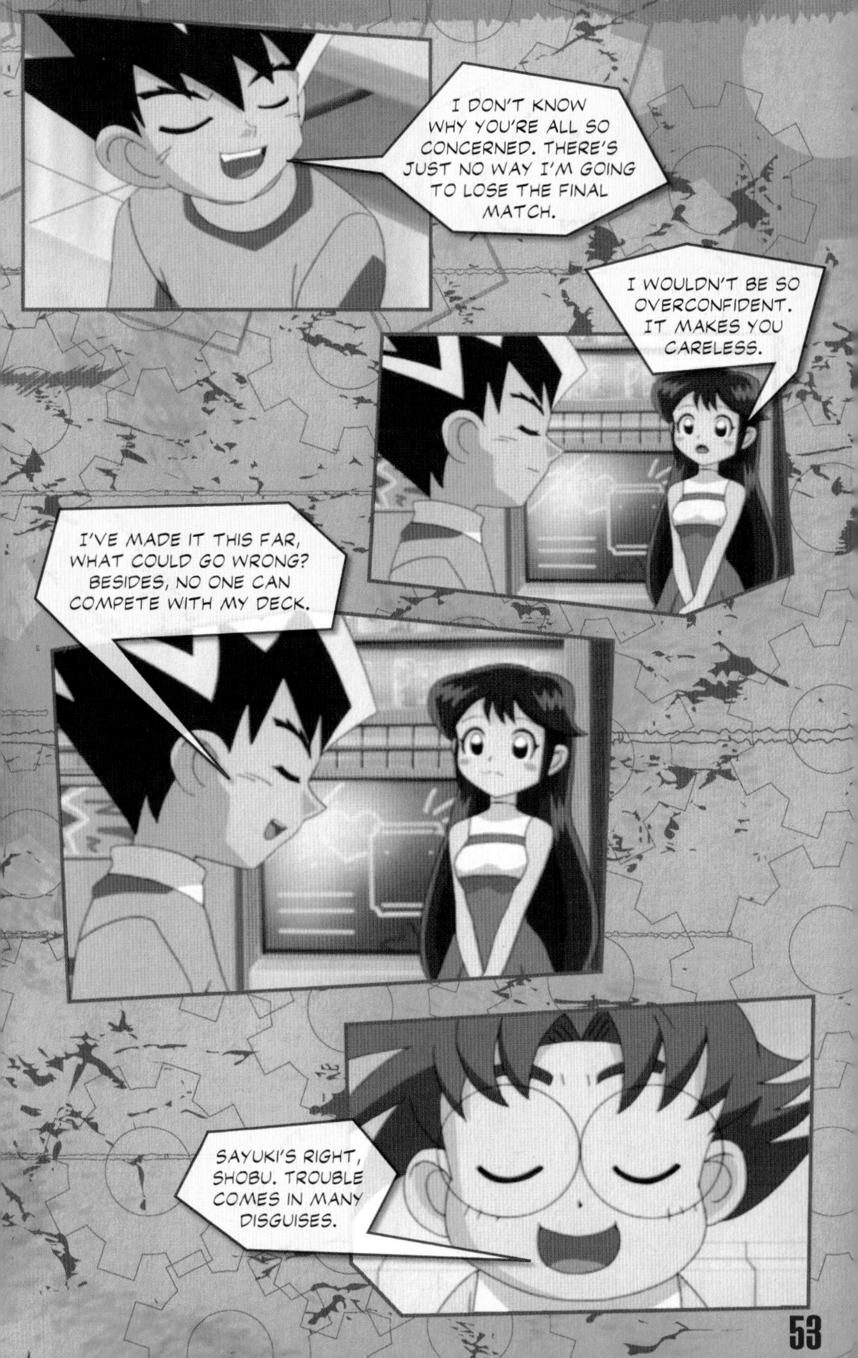
I DON'T KNOW WHY YOU'RE ALL SO CONCERNED. THERE'S JUST NO WAY I'M GOING TO LOSE THE FINAL MATCH.
I WOULDN'T BE SO OVERCONFIDENT. IT MAKES YOU CARELESS.
I'VE MADE IT THIS FAR, WHAT COULD GO WRONG? BESIDES, NO ONE CAN COMPETE WITH MY DECK.
SAYUKI'S RIGHT, SHOBU. TROUBLE COMES IN MANY DISGUISES.

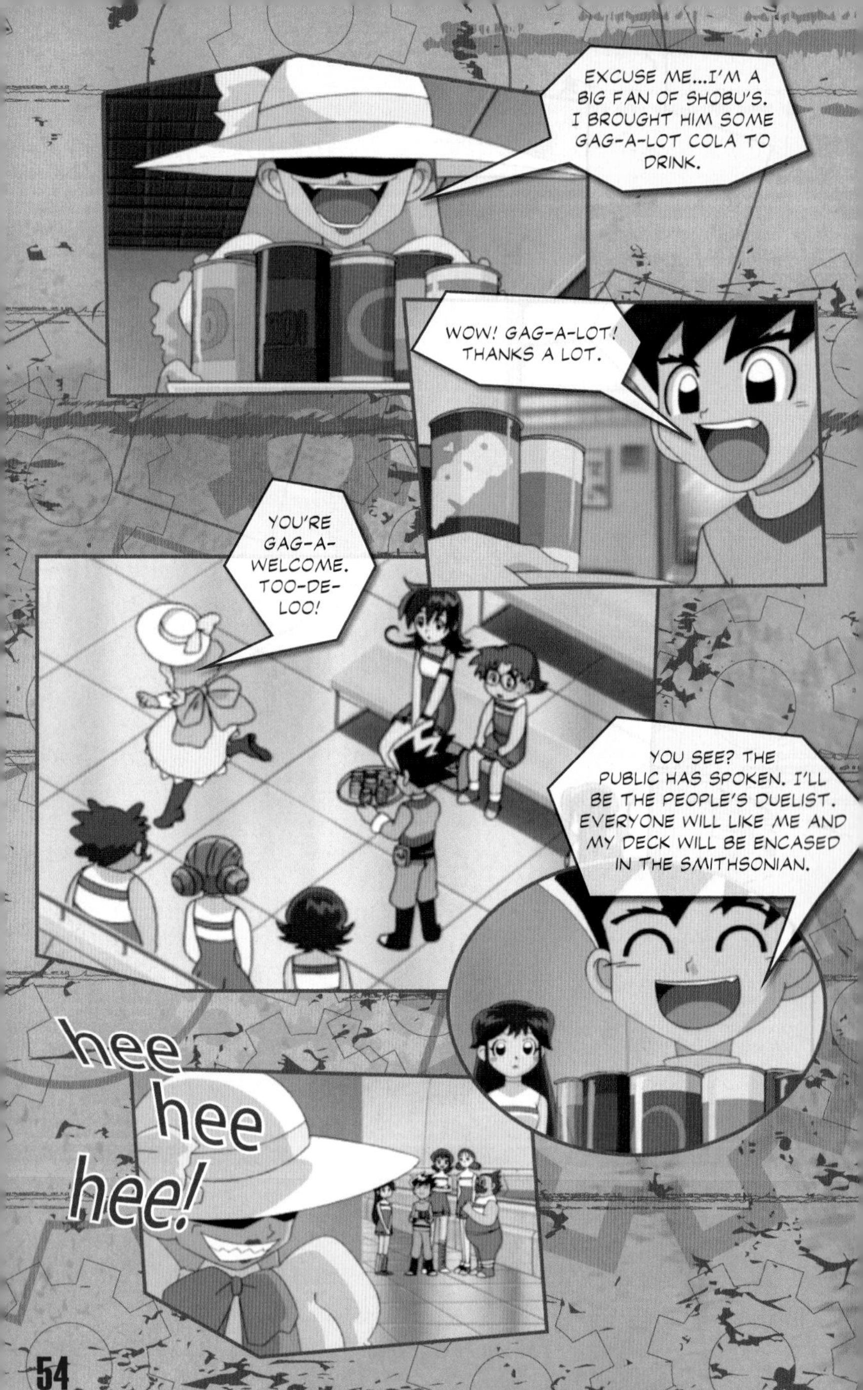
EXCUSE ME...I'M A BIG FAN OF SHOBU'S. I BROUGHT HIM SOME GAG-A-LOT COLA TO DRINK.
WOW! GAG-A-LOT! THANKS A LOT.
YOU'RE GAG-A-WELCOME. TOO-DE-LOO!
YOU SEE? THE PUBLIC HAS SPOKEN. I'LL BE THE PEOPLE'S DUELIST. EVERYONE WILL LIKE ME AND MY DECK WILL BE ENCASED IN THE SMITHSONIAN.
hee hee hee!

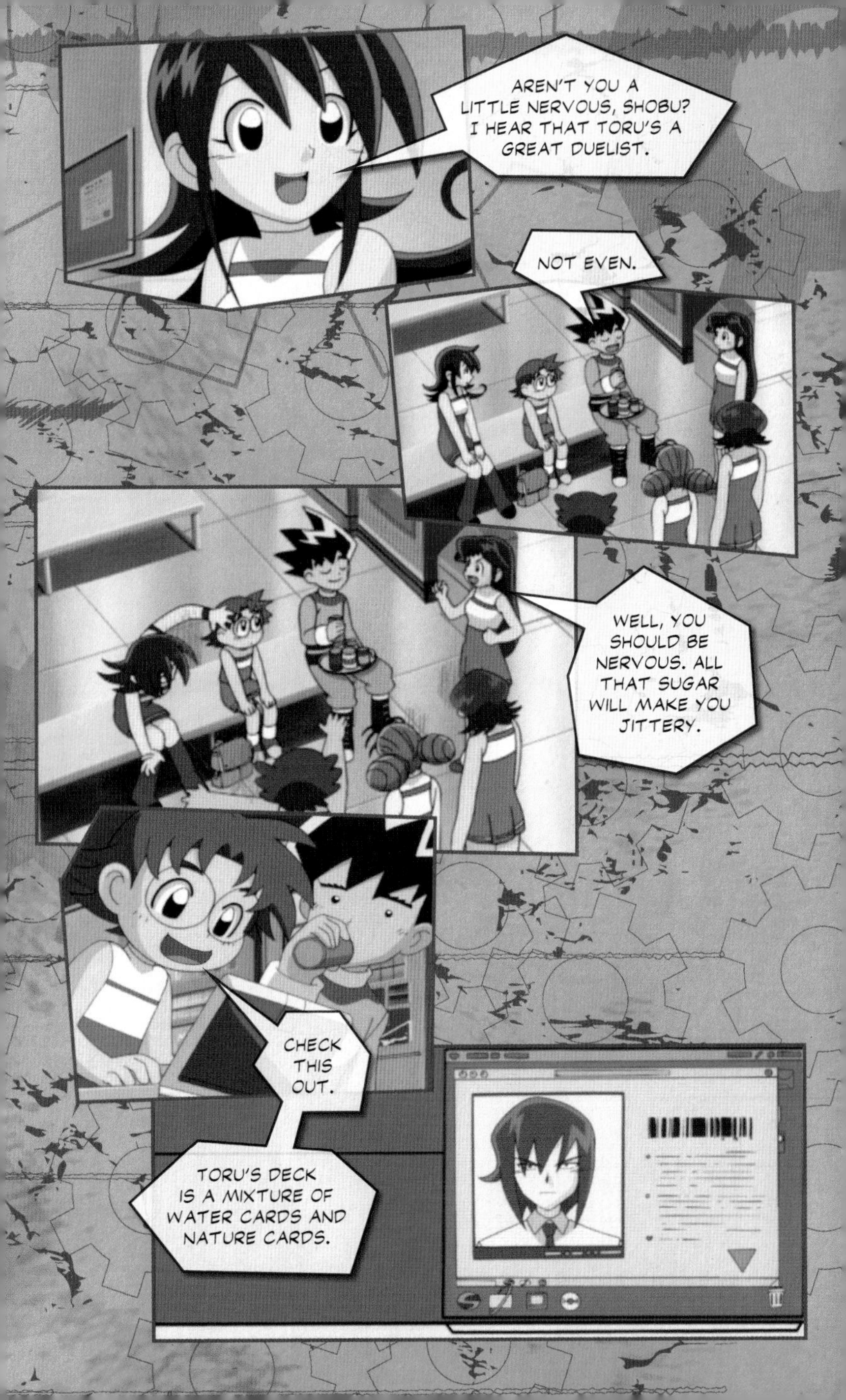
AREN'T YOU A LITTLE NERVOUS, SHOBU? I HEAR THAT TORU'S A GREAT DUELIST.
NOT EVEN.
WELL, YOU SHOULD BE NERVOUS. ALL THAT SUGAR WILL MAKE YOU JITTERY.
CHECK THIS OUT.
TORU'S DECK IS A MIXTURE OF WATER CARDS AND NATURE CARDS.

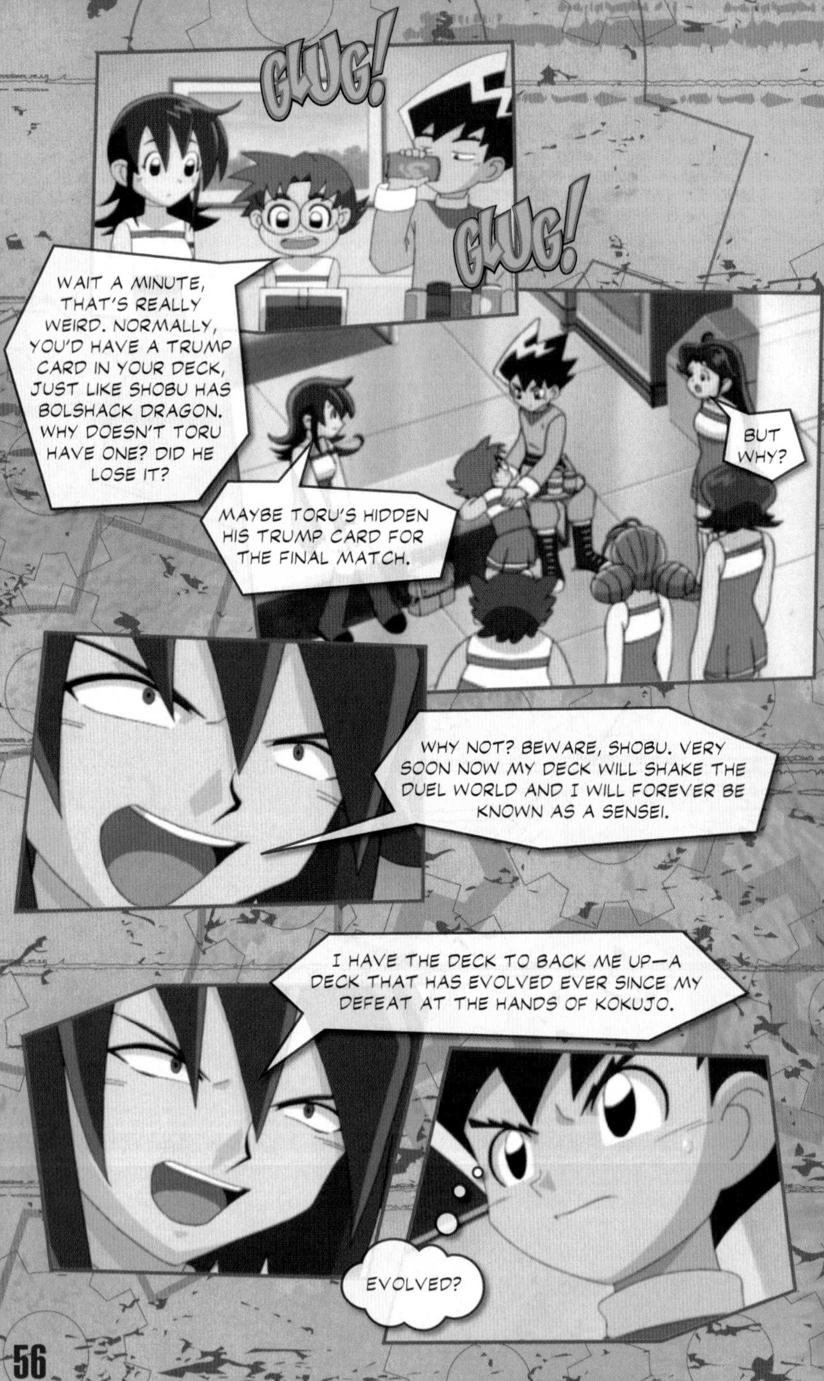
GLUG!
GLUG!
WAIT A MINUTE, THAT'S REALLY WEIRD. NORMALLY, YOU'D HAVE A TRUMP CARD IN YOUR DECK, JUST LIKE SHOBU HAS BOLSHACK DRAGON. WHY DOESN'T TORU HAVE ONE? DID HE LOSE IT?
MAYBE TORU'S HIDDEN HIS TRUMP CARD FOR THE FINAL MATCH.
BUT WHY?
WHY NOT? BEWARE, SHOBU. VERY SOON NOW MY DECK WILL SHAKE THE DUEL WORLD AND I WILL FOREVER BE KNOWN AS A SENSEI.
I HAVE THE DECK TO BACK ME UP—A DECK THAT HAS EVOLVED EVER SINCE MY DEFEAT AT THE HANDS OF KOKUJO.
EVOLVED?

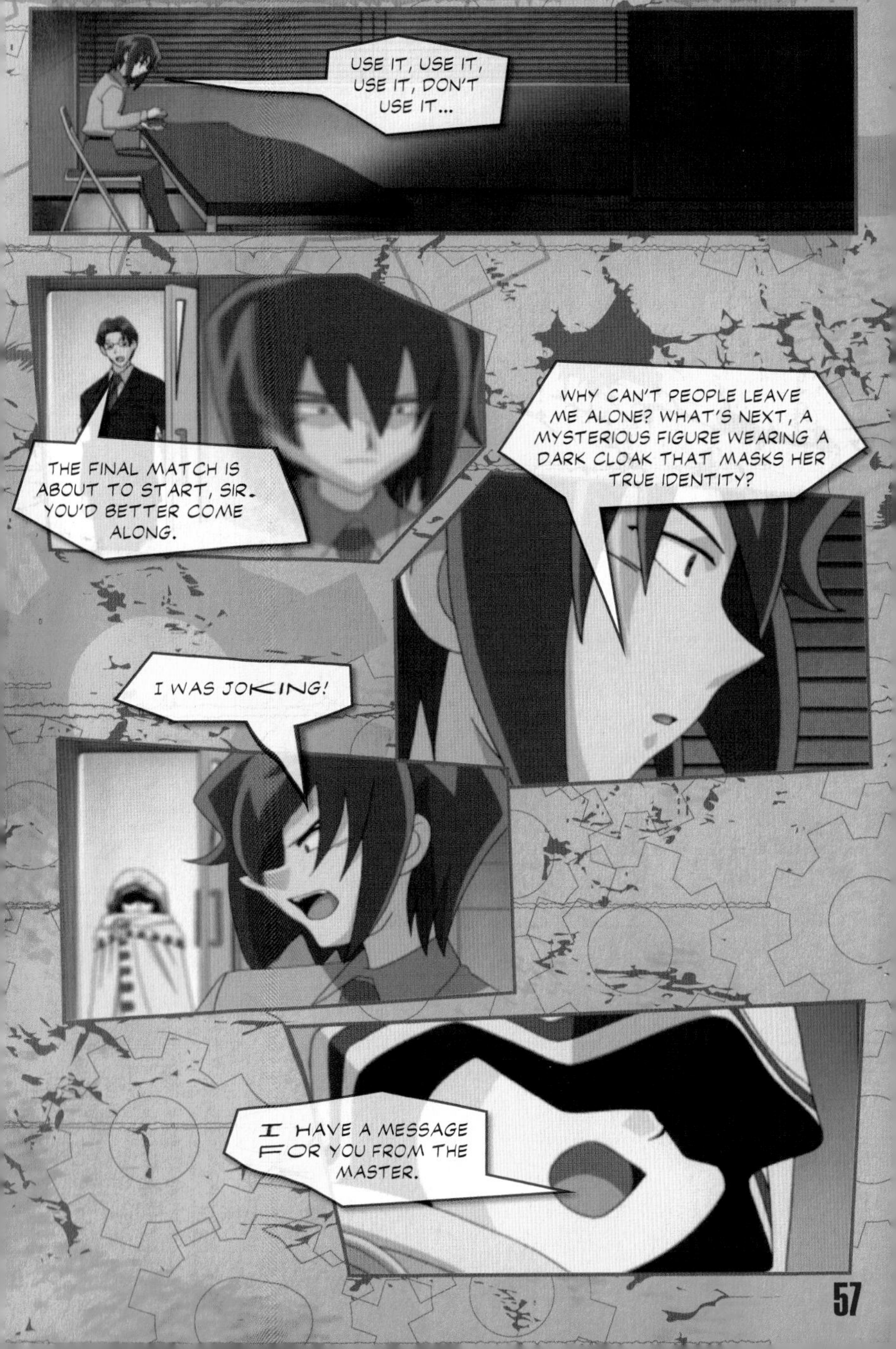
USE IT, USE IT, USE IT, DON'T USE IT...
THE FINAL MATCH IS ABOUT TO START, SIR. YOU'D BETTER COME ALONG.
WHY CAN'T PEOPLE LEAVE ME ALONE? WHAT'S NEXT, A MYSTERIOUS FIGURE WEARING A DARK CLOAK THAT MASKS HER TRUE IDENTITY?
I WAS JOKING!
I HAVE A MESSAGE FOR YOU FROM THE MASTER.

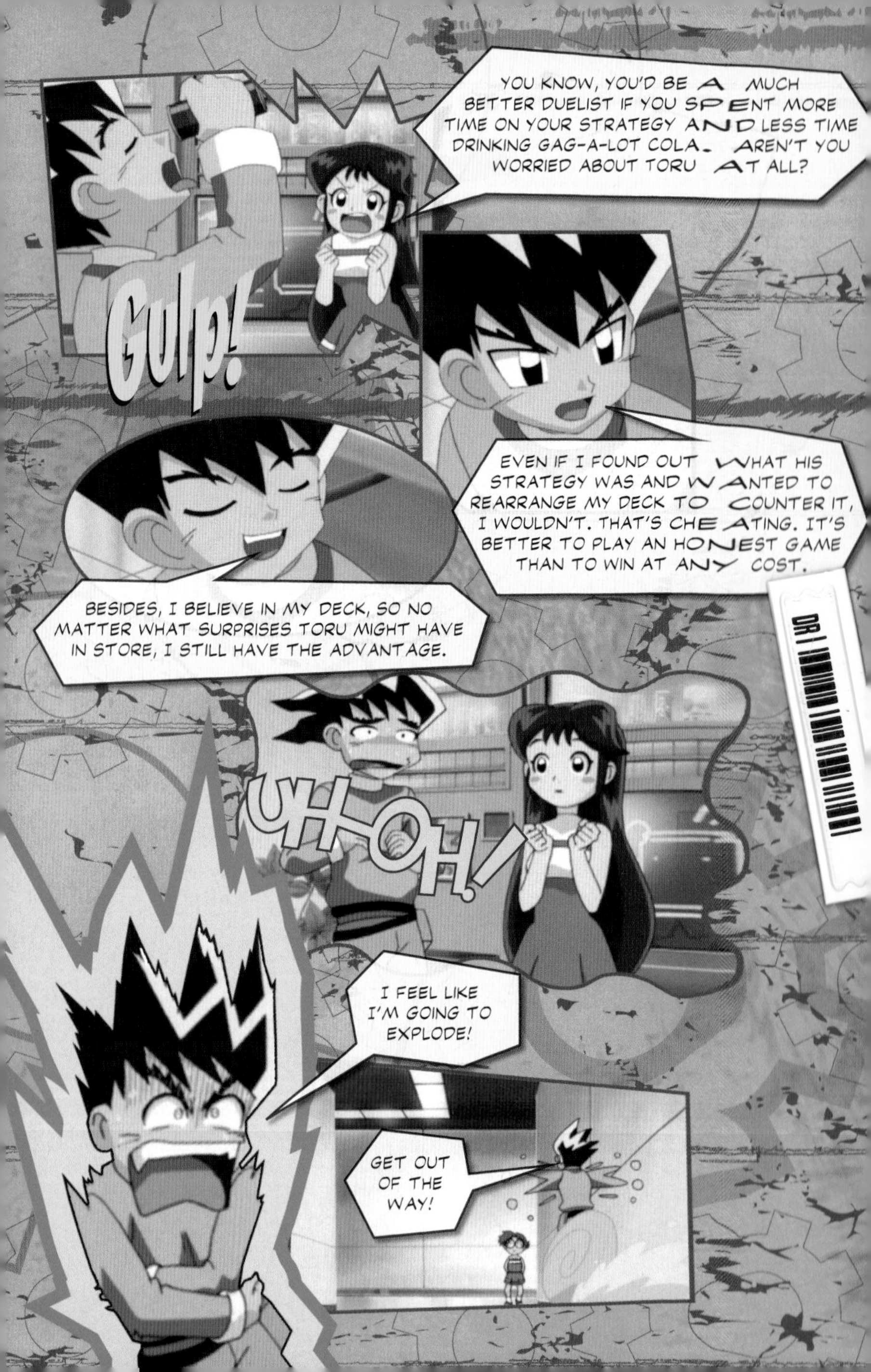
YOU KNOW, YOU'D BE A MUCH BETTER DUELIST IF YOU SPENT MORE TIME ON YOUR STRATEGY AND LESS TIME DRINKING GAG-A-LOT COLA. AREN'T YOU WORRIED ABOUT TORU AT ALL?
Gulp!
EVEN IF I FOUND OUT WHAT HIS STRATEGY WAS AND WANTED TO REARRANGE MY DECK TO COUNTER IT, I WOULDN'T. THAT'S CHEATING. IT'S BETTER TO PLAY AN HONEST GAME THAN TO WIN AT ANY COST.
BESIDES, I BELIEVE IN MY DECK, SO NO MATTER WHAT SURPRISES TORU MIGHT HAVE IN STORE, I STILL HAVE THE ADVANTAGE.
UH-OH!
I FEEL LIKE I'M GOING TO EXPLODE!
GET OUT OF THE WAY!

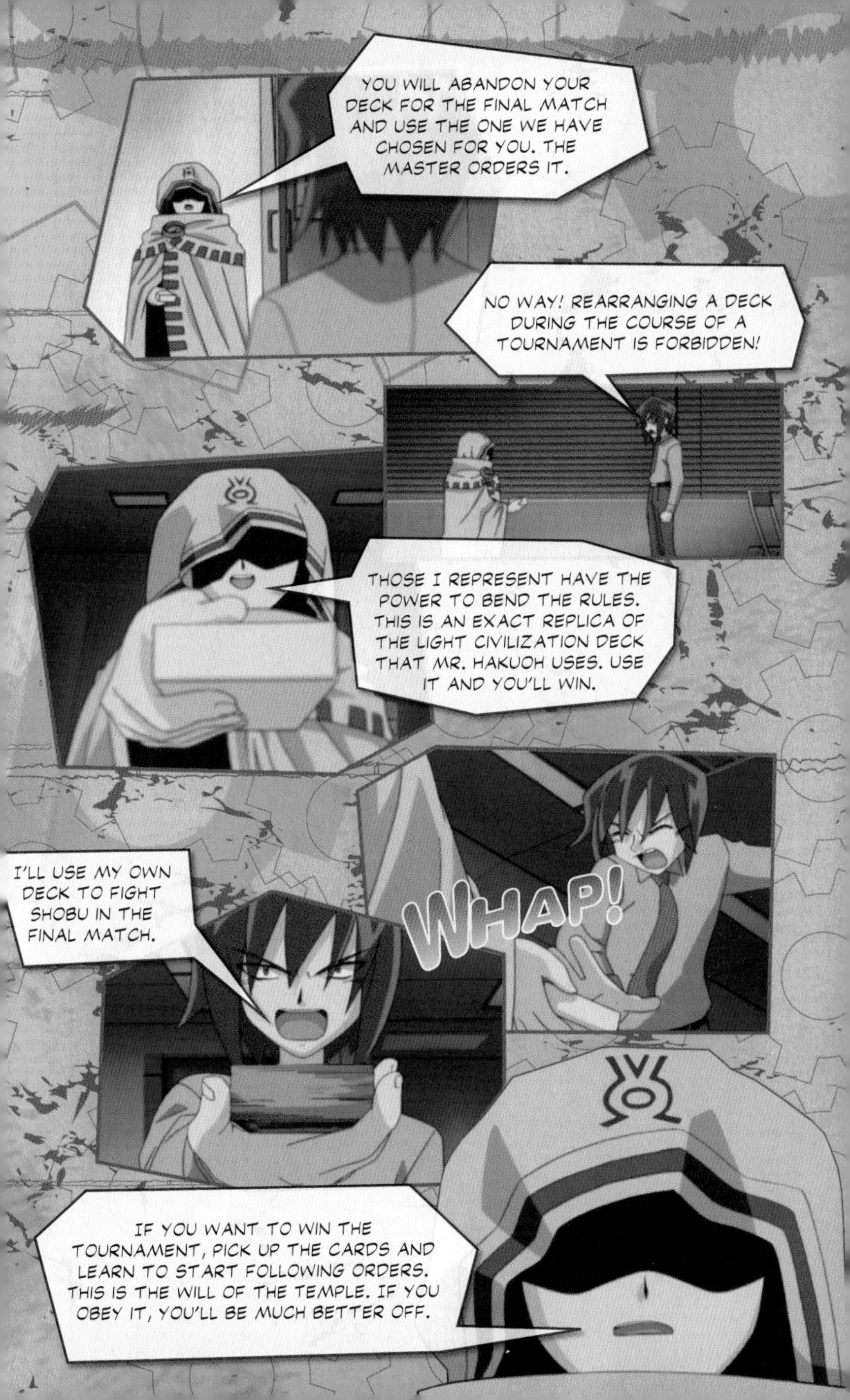
YOU WILL ABANDON YOUR DECK FOR THE FINAL MATCH AND USE THE ONE WE HAVE CHOSEN FOR YOU. THE MASTER ORDERS IT.
NO WAY! REARRANGING A DECK DURING THE COURSE OF A TOURNAMENT IS FORBIDDEN!
THOSE I REPRESENT HAVE THE POWER TO BEND THE RULES. THIS IS AN EXACT REPLICA OF THE LIGHT CIVILIZATION DECK THAT MR. HAKUOH USES. USE IT AND YOU'LL WIN.
WHAP!
I'LL USE MY OWN DECK TO FIGHT SHOBU IN THE FINAL MATCH.
IF YOU WANT TO WIN THE TOURNAMENT, PICK UP THE CARDS AND LEARN TO START FOLLOWING ORDERS. THIS IS THE WILL OF THE TEMPLE. IF YOU OBEY IT, YOU'LL BE MUCH BETTER OFF.

HA! YOU'LL HAVE A TOUGH TIME DUELING WITHOUT THESE, SHOBU.
THOSE CARDS ARE MINE!
Yaaah!
AAAH!
KRUNCH!
WOOSH!

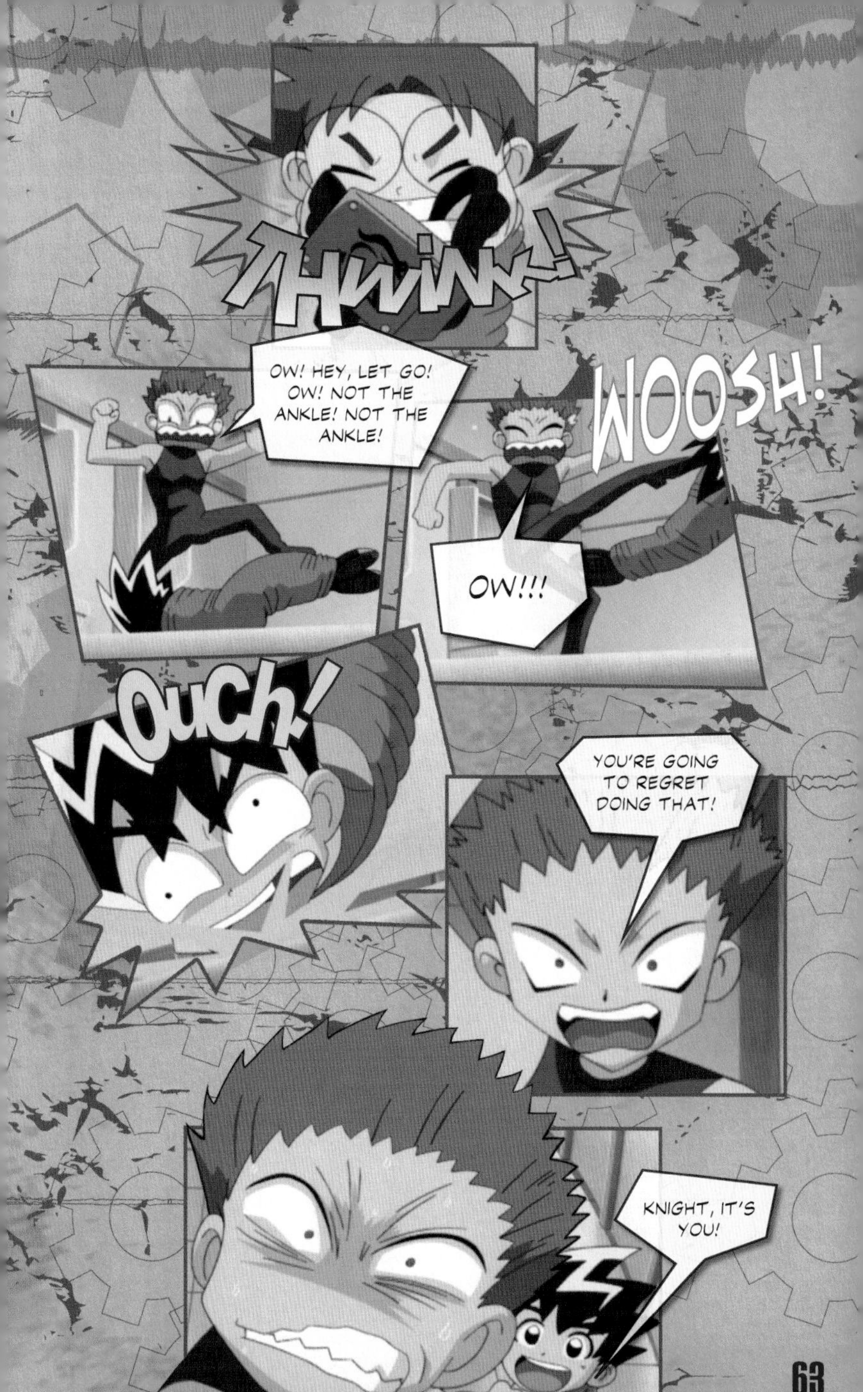
THWINK!
OW! HEY, LET GO! OW! NOT THE ANKLE! NOT THE ANKLE!
WOOSH!
OW!!!
OUCH!
YOU'RE GOING TO REGRET DOING THAT!
KNIGHT, IT'S YOU!

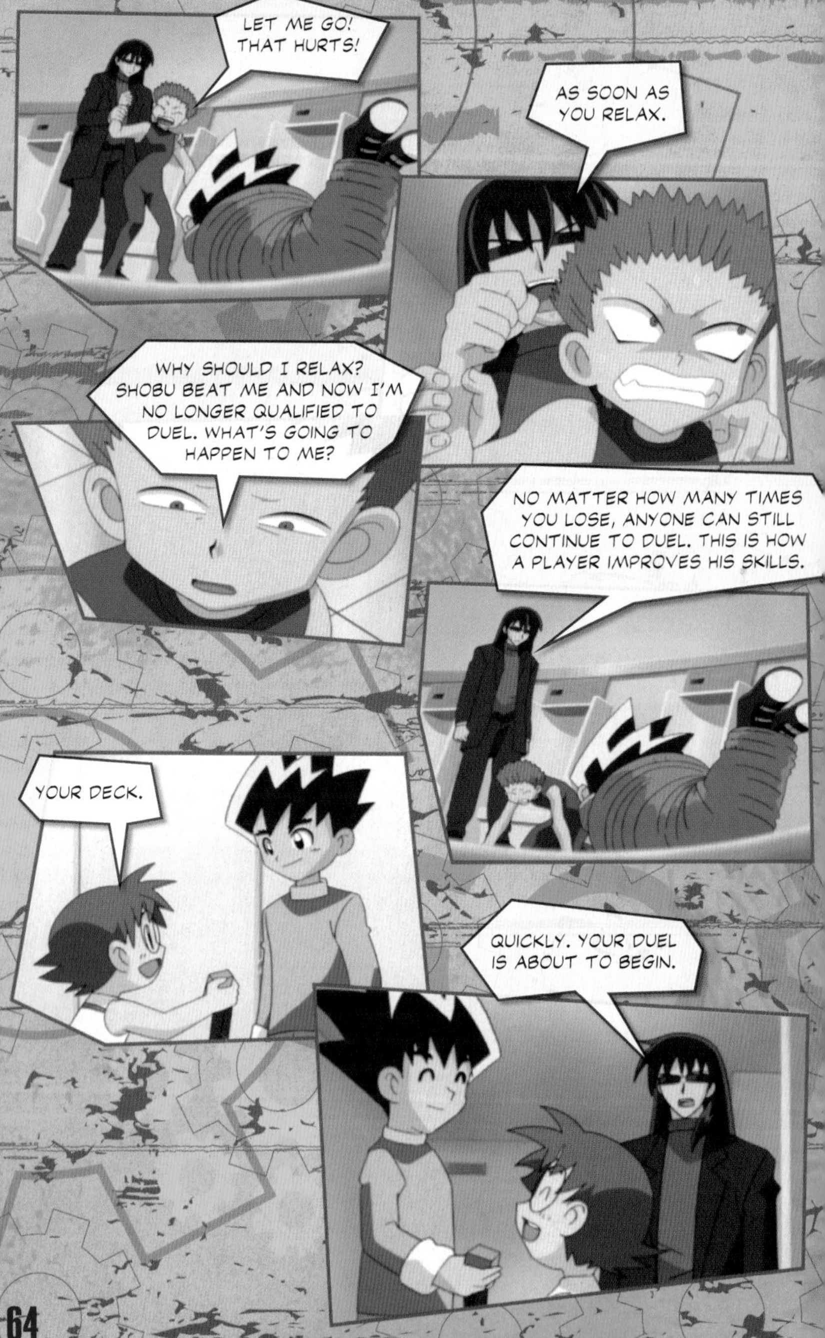
LET ME GO! THAT HURTS!
AS SOON AS YOU RELAX.
WHY SHOULD I RELAX? SHOBU BEAT ME AND NOW I'M NO LONGER QUALIFIED TO DUEL. WHAT'S GOING TO HAPPEN TO ME?
NO MATTER HOW MANY TIMES YOU LOSE, ANYONE CAN STILL CONTINUE TO DUEL. THIS IS HOW A PLAYER IMPROVES HIS SKILLS.
YOUR DECK.
QUICKLY. YOUR DUEL IS ABOUT TO BEGIN.

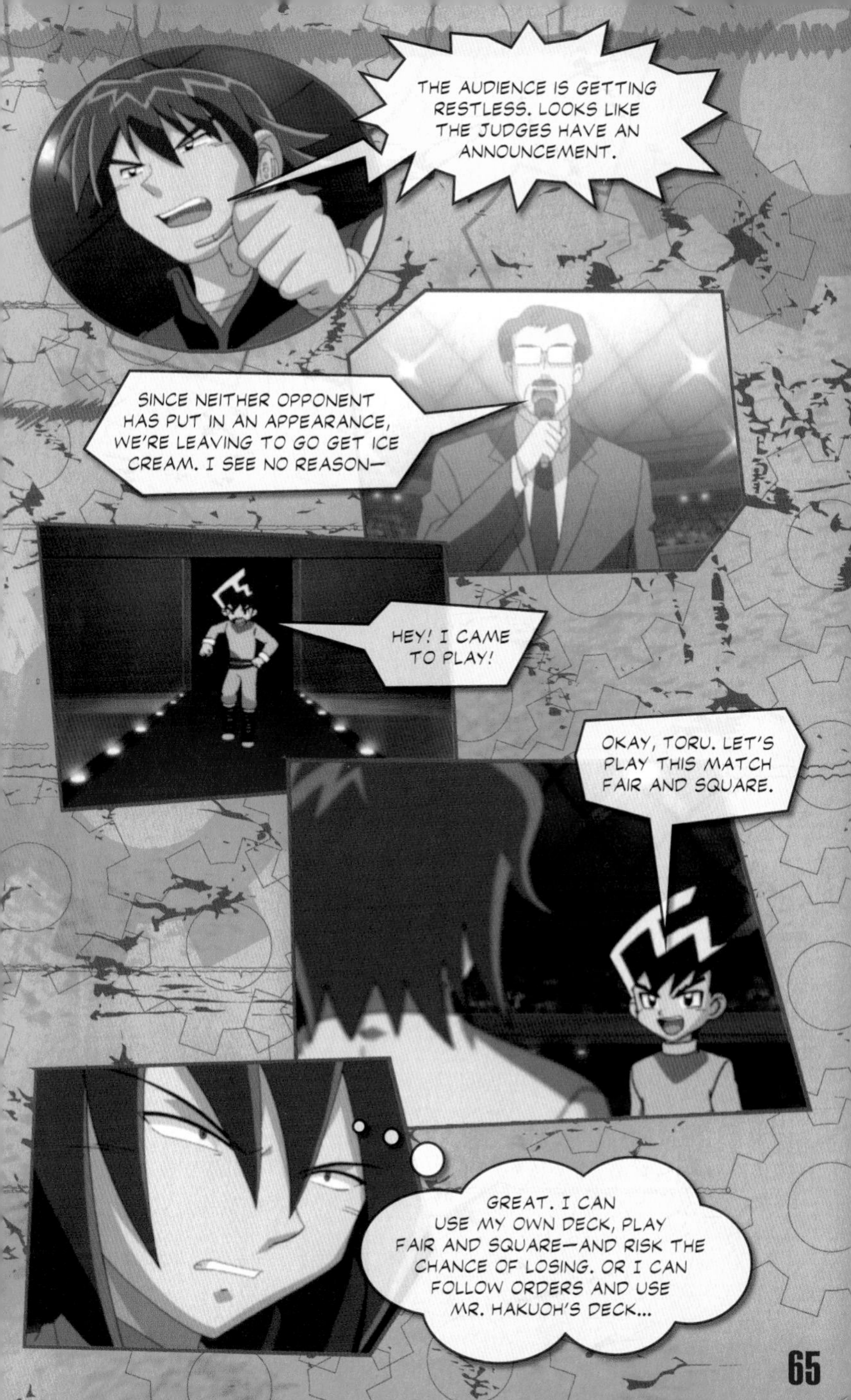
THE AUDIENCE IS GETTING RESTLESS. LOOKS LIKE THE JUDGES HAVE AN ANNOUNCEMENT.
SINCE NEITHER OPPONENT HAS PUT IN AN APPEARANCE, WE'RE LEAVING TO GO GET ICE CREAM. I SEE NO REASON—
HEY! I CAME TO PLAY!
OKAY, TORU. LET'S PLAY THIS MATCH FAIR AND SQUARE.
GREAT. I CAN USE MY OWN DECK, PLAY FAIR AND SQUARE—AND RISK THE CHANCE OF LOSING. OR I CAN FOLLOW ORDERS AND USE MR. HAKUOH'S DECK...

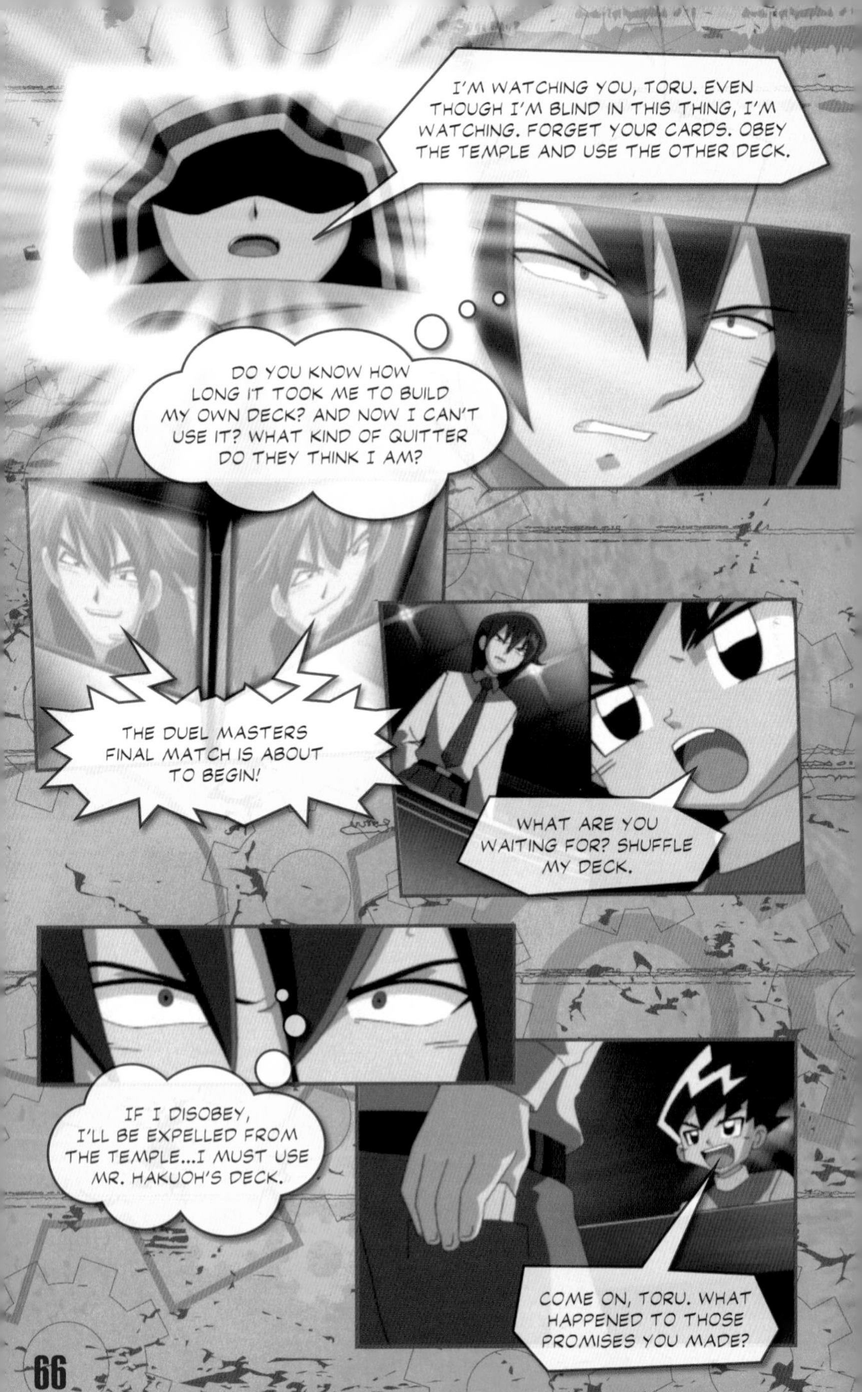
I'M WATCHING YOU, TORU. EVEN THOUGH I'M BLIND IN THIS THING, I'M WATCHING. FORGET YOUR CARDS. OBEY THE TEMPLE AND USE THE OTHER DECK.
DO YOU KNOW HOW LONG IT TOOK ME TO BUILD MY OWN DECK? AND NOW I CAN'T USE IT? WHAT KIND OF QUITTER DO THEY THINK I AM?
THE DUEL MASTERS FINAL MATCH IS ABOUT TO BEGIN!
WHAT ARE YOU WAITING FOR? SHUFFLE MY DECK.
IF I DISOBEY, I'LL BE EXPELLED FROM THE TEMPLE...I MUST USE MR. HAKUOH'S DECK.
COME ON, TORU. WHAT HAPPENED TO THOSE PROMISES YOU MADE?

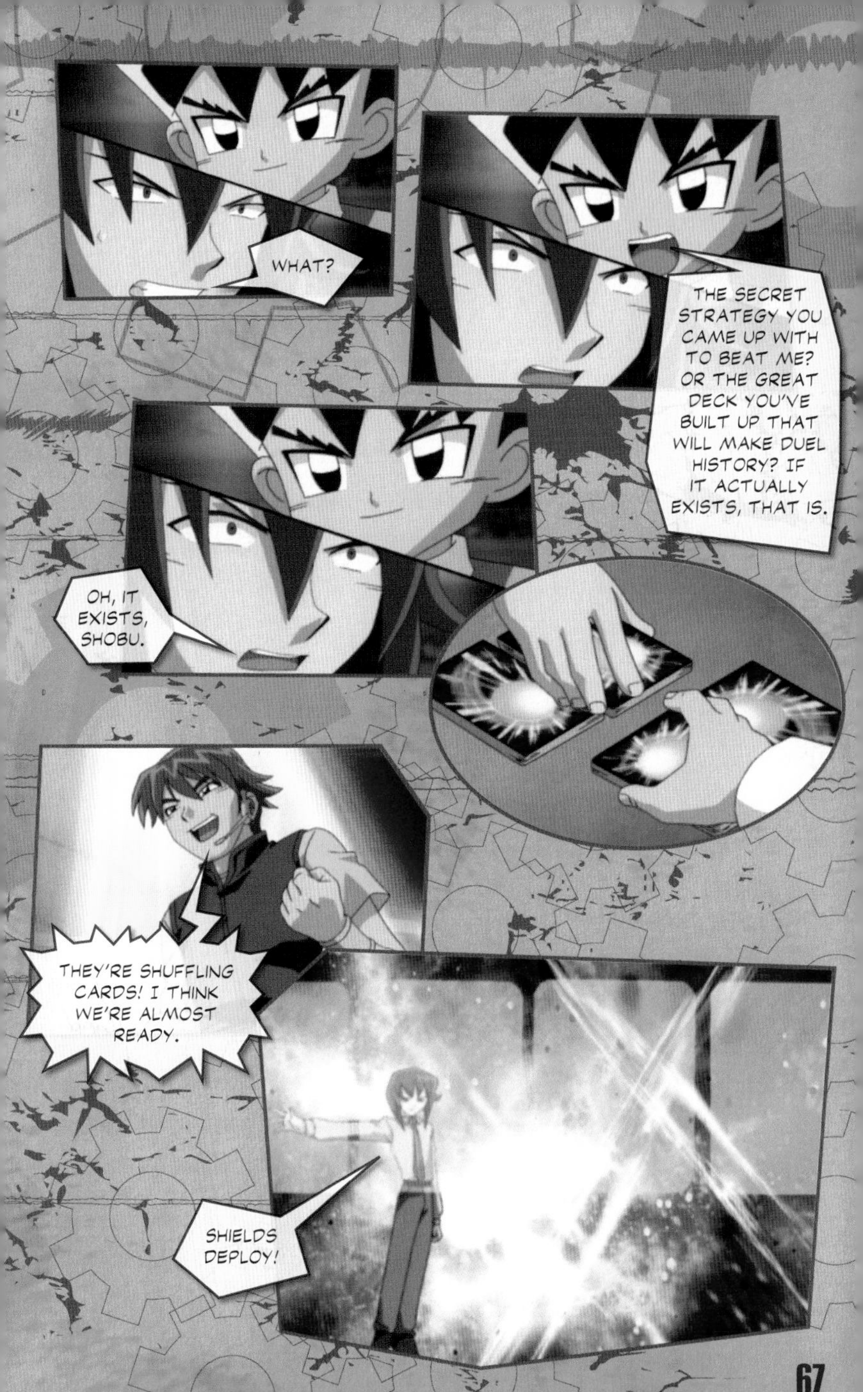
WHAT?
THE SECRET STRATEGY YOU CAME UP WITH TO BEAT ME? OR THE GREAT DECK YOU'VE BUILT UP THAT WILL MAKE DUEL HISTORY? IF IT ACTUALLY EXISTS, THAT IS.
OH, IT EXISTS, SHOBU.
THEY'RE SHUFFLING CARDS! I THINK WE'RE ALMOST READY.
SHIELDS DEPLOY!

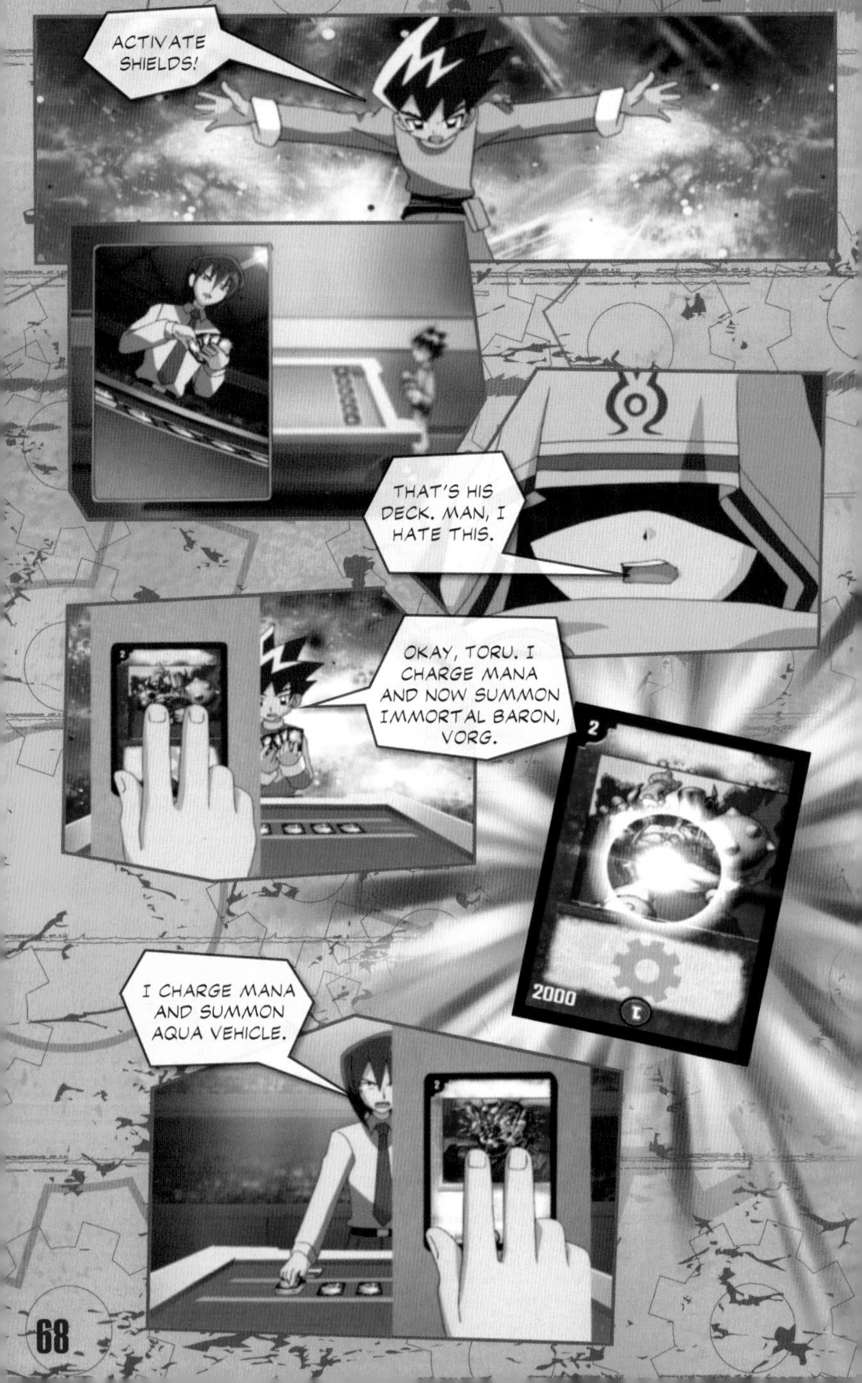
ACTIVATE SHIELDS!
THAT'S HIS DECK. MAN, I HATE THIS.
OKAY, TORU. I CHARGE MANA AND NOW SUMMON IMMORTAL BARON, VORG.
2
2000
I CHARGE MANA AND SUMMON AQUA VEHICLE.

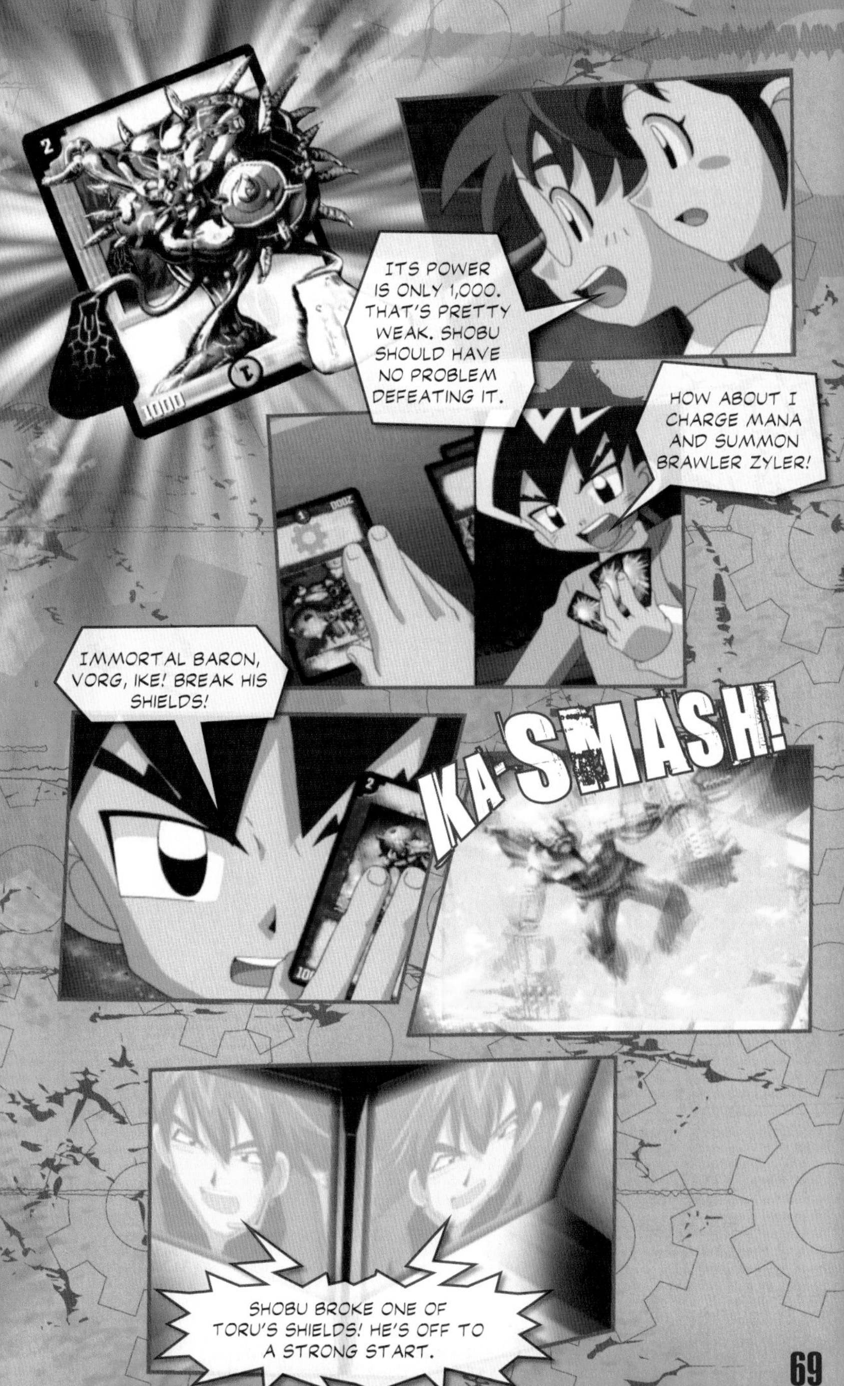
ITS POWER IS ONLY 1,000. THAT'S PRETTY WEAK. SHOBU SHOULD HAVE NO PROBLEM DEFEATING IT.
HOW ABOUT I CHARGE MANA AND SUMMON BRAWLER ZYLER!
IMMORTAL BARON, VORG, IKE! BREAK HIS SHIELDS!
KA-SMASH!
SHOBU BROKE ONE OF TORU'S SHIELDS! HE'S OFF TO A STRONG START.

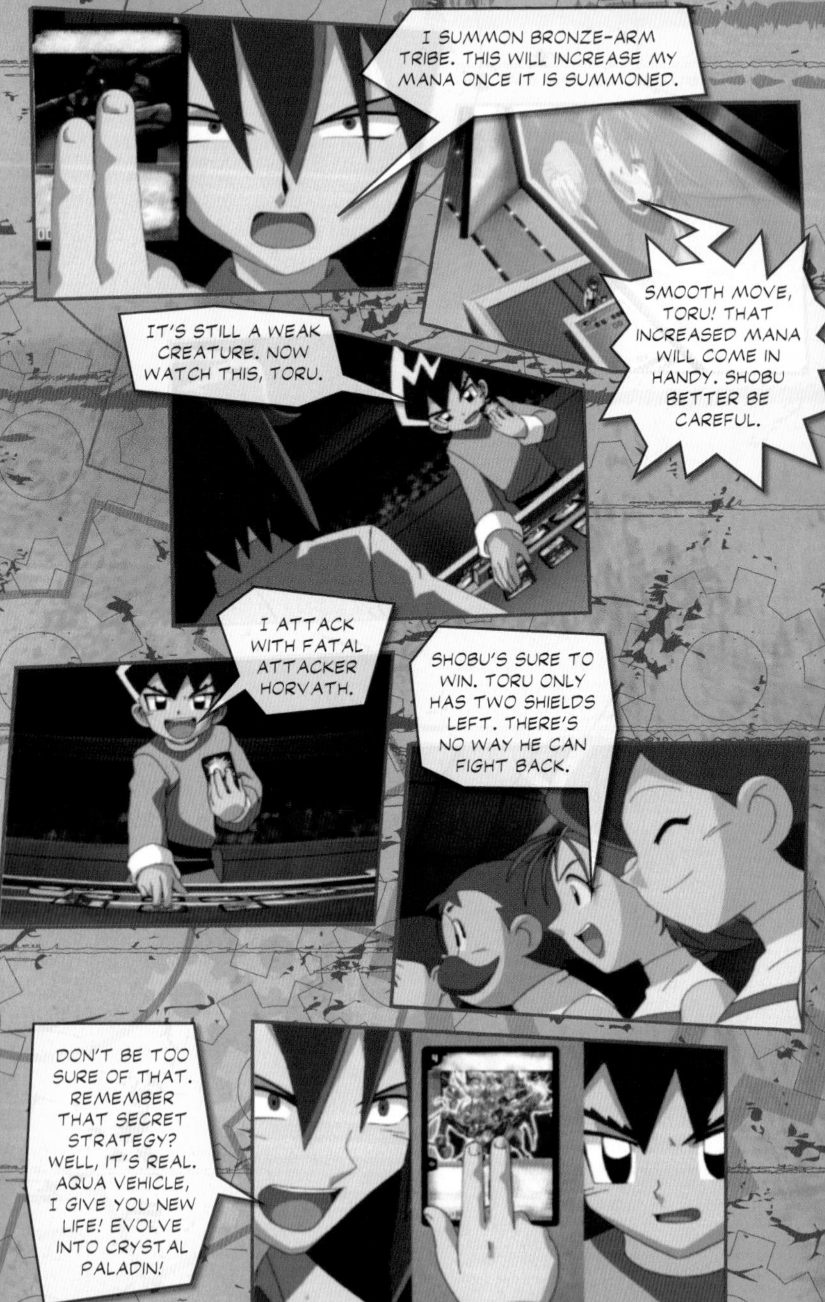
I SUMMON BRONZE-ARM TRIBE. THIS WILL INCREASE MY MANA ONCE IT IS SUMMONED.
SMOOTH MOVE, TORU! THAT INCREASED MANA WILL COME IN HANDY. SHOBU BETTER BE CAREFUL.
IT'S STILL A WEAK CREATURE. NOW WATCH THIS, TORU.
I ATTACK WITH FATAL ATTACKER HORVATH.
SHOBU'S SURE TO WIN. TORU ONLY HAS TWO SHIELDS LEFT. THERE'S NO WAY HE CAN FIGHT BACK.
DON'T BE TOO SURE OF THAT. REMEMBER THAT SECRET STRATEGY? WELL, IT'S REAL. AQUA VEHICLE, I GIVE YOU NEW LIFE! EVOLVE INTO CRYSTAL PALADIN!

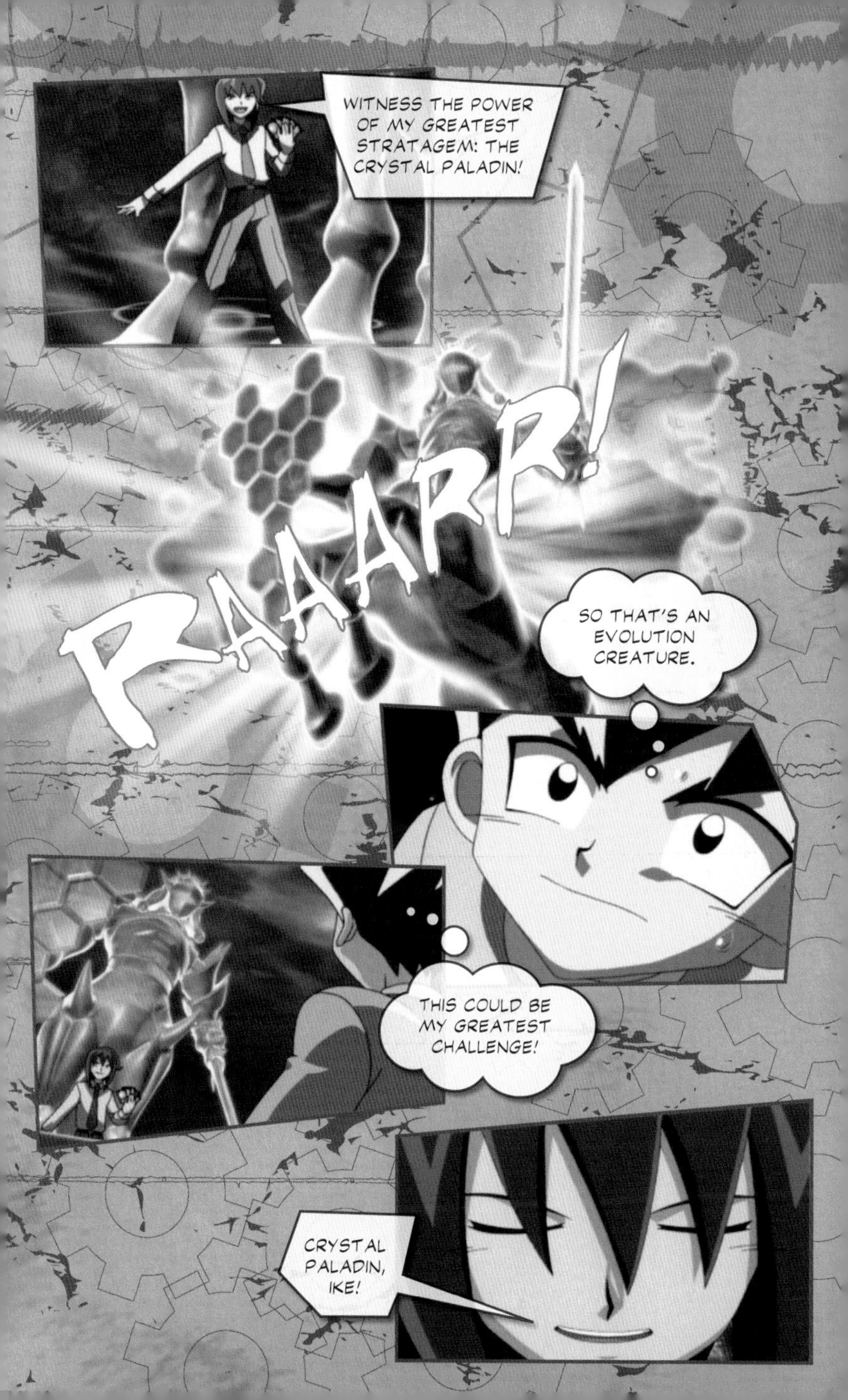
WITNESS THE POWER OF MY GREATEST STRATAGEM: THE CRYSTAL PALADIN!
RAAAARR!
SO THAT'S AN EVOLUTION CREATURE.
THIS COULD BE MY GREATEST CHALLENGE!
CRYSTAL PALADIN, IKE!

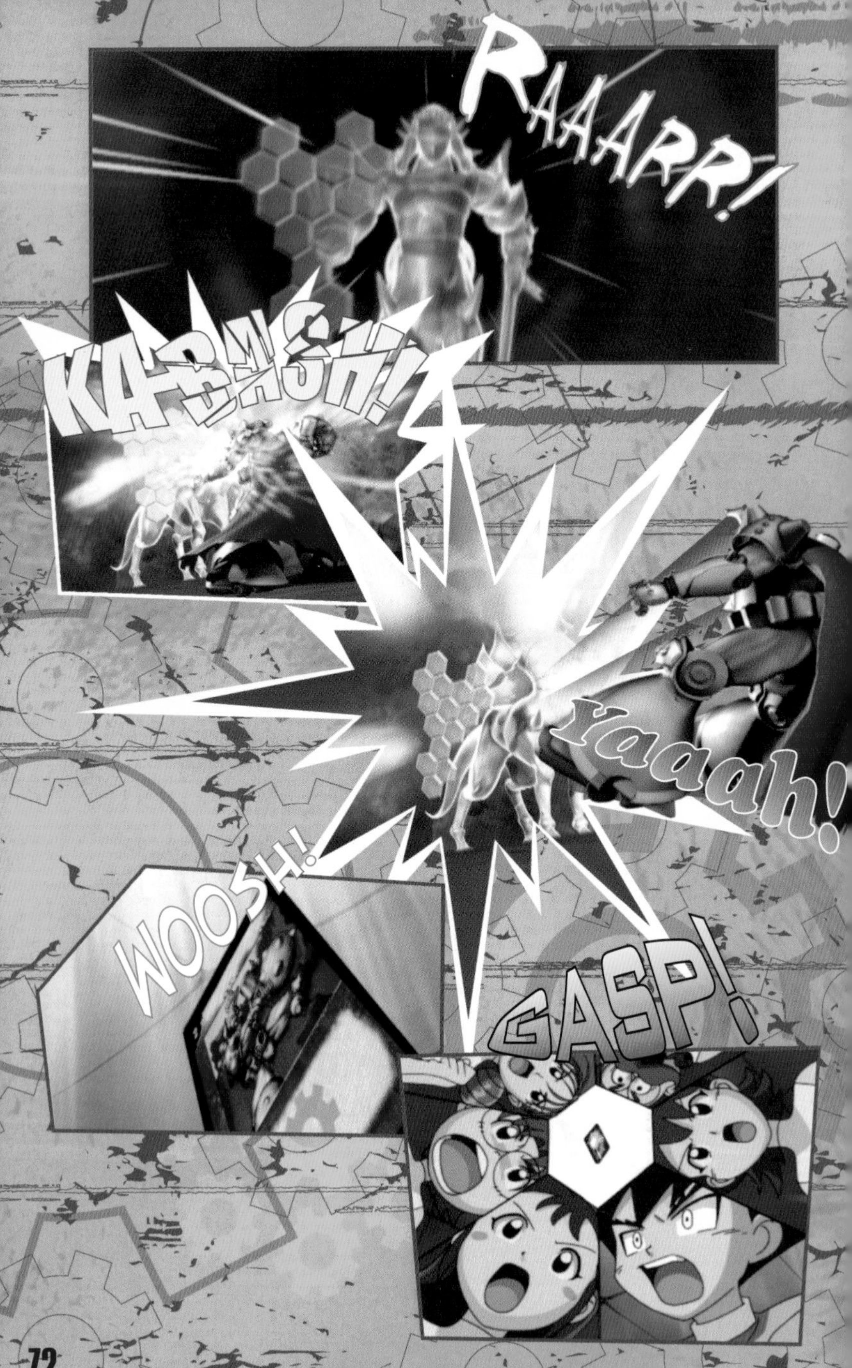
RAAARR!
KABLASH!
Yaaaah!
WOOSH!
GASP!

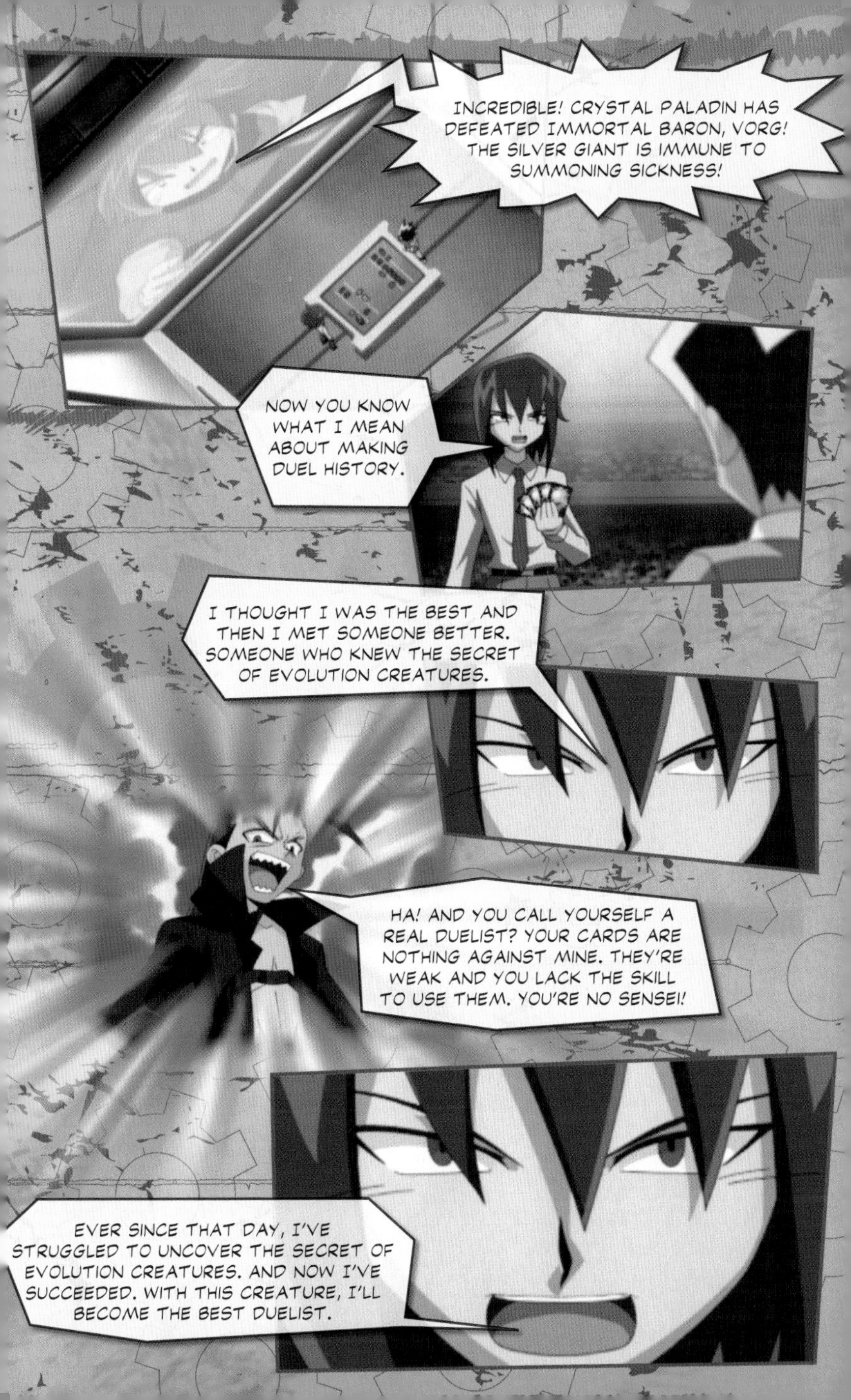
INCREDIBLE! CRYSTAL PALADIN HAS DEFEATED IMMORTAL BARON, VORG! THE SILVER GIANT IS IMMUNE TO SUMMONING SICKNESS!
NOW YOU KNOW WHAT I MEAN ABOUT MAKING DUEL HISTORY.
I THOUGHT I WAS THE BEST AND THEN I MET SOMEONE BETTER. SOMEONE WHO KNEW THE SECRET OF EVOLUTION CREATURES.
HA! AND YOU CALL YOURSELF A REAL DUELIST? YOUR CARDS ARE NOTHING AGAINST MINE. THEY'RE WEAK AND YOU LACK THE SKILL TO USE THEM. YOU'RE NO SENSEI!
EVER SINCE THAT DAY, I'VE STRUGGLED TO UNCOVER THE SECRET OF EVOLUTION CREATURES. AND NOW I'VE SUCCEEDED. WITH THIS CREATURE, I'LL BECOME THE BEST DUELIST.

KZZZOOSH!
KA-SMASH!
ZZZZT!
HOW'D YOU...?!
CRYSTAL PALADIN MEET FATAL ATTACKER HORVATH. I POWERED HIM UP USING MAGMA GAZER. SHOCKING, ISN'T IT?

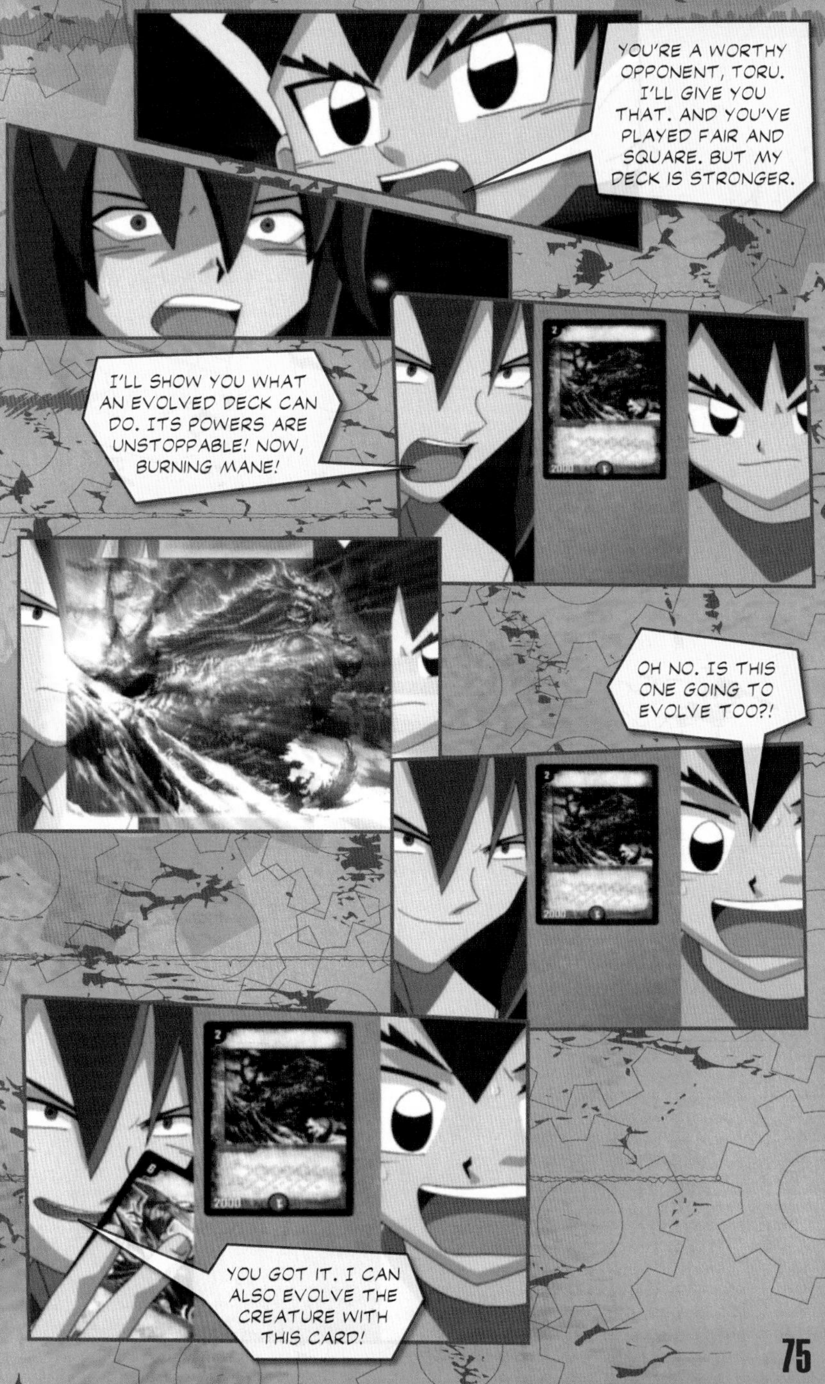
YOU'RE A WORTHY OPPONENT, TORU. I'LL GIVE YOU THAT. AND YOU'VE PLAYED FAIR AND SQUARE. BUT MY DECK IS STRONGER.
I'LL SHOW YOU WHAT AN EVOLVED DECK CAN DO. ITS POWERS ARE UNSTOPPABLE! NOW, BURNING MANE!
OH NO. IS THIS ONE GOING TO EVOLVE TOO?!
YOU GOT IT. I CAN ALSO EVOLVE THE CREATURE WITH THIS CARD!

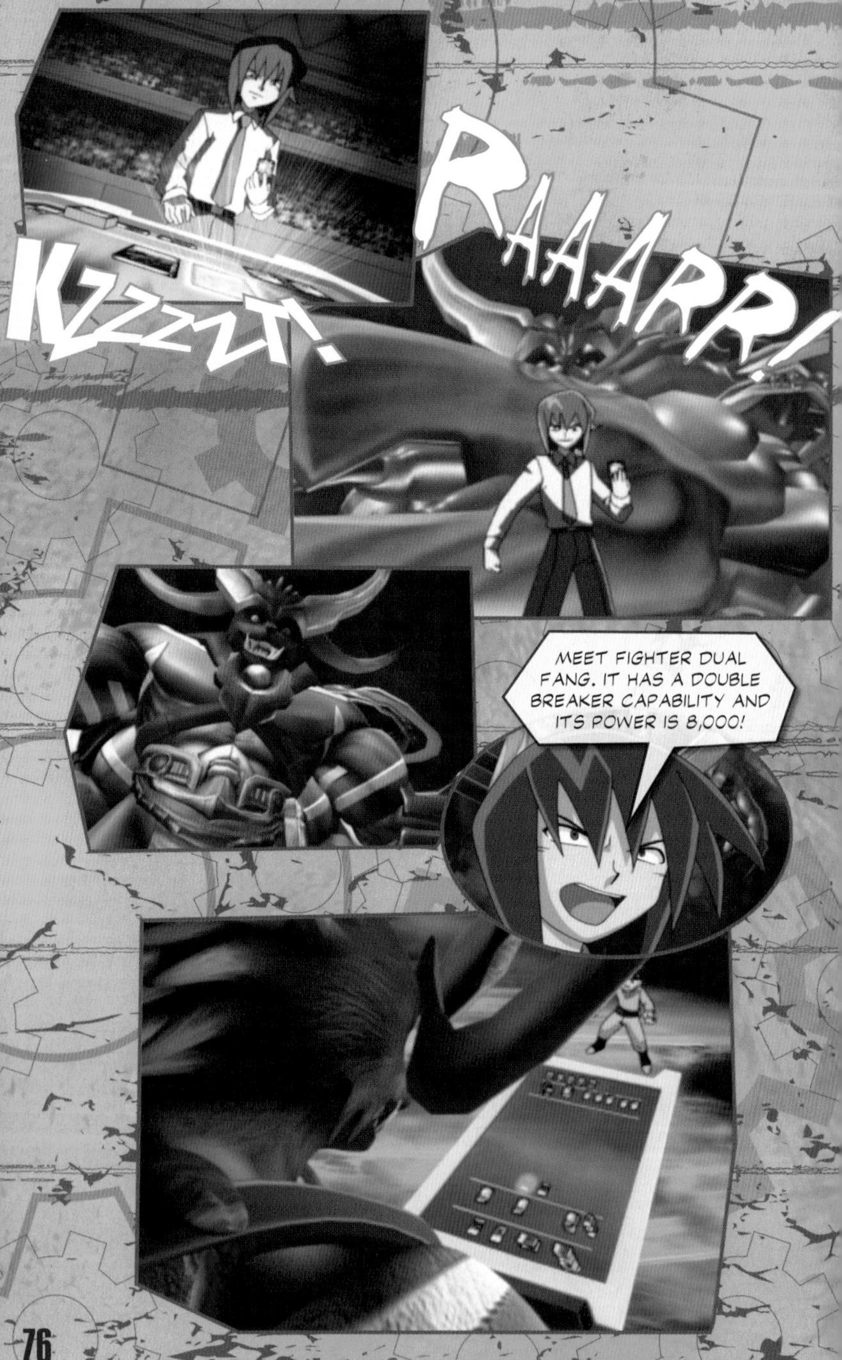
KZZZZT!
RAAAARR!
MEET FIGHTER DUAL FANG. IT HAS A DOUBLE BREAKER CAPABILITY AND ITS POWER IS 8,000!

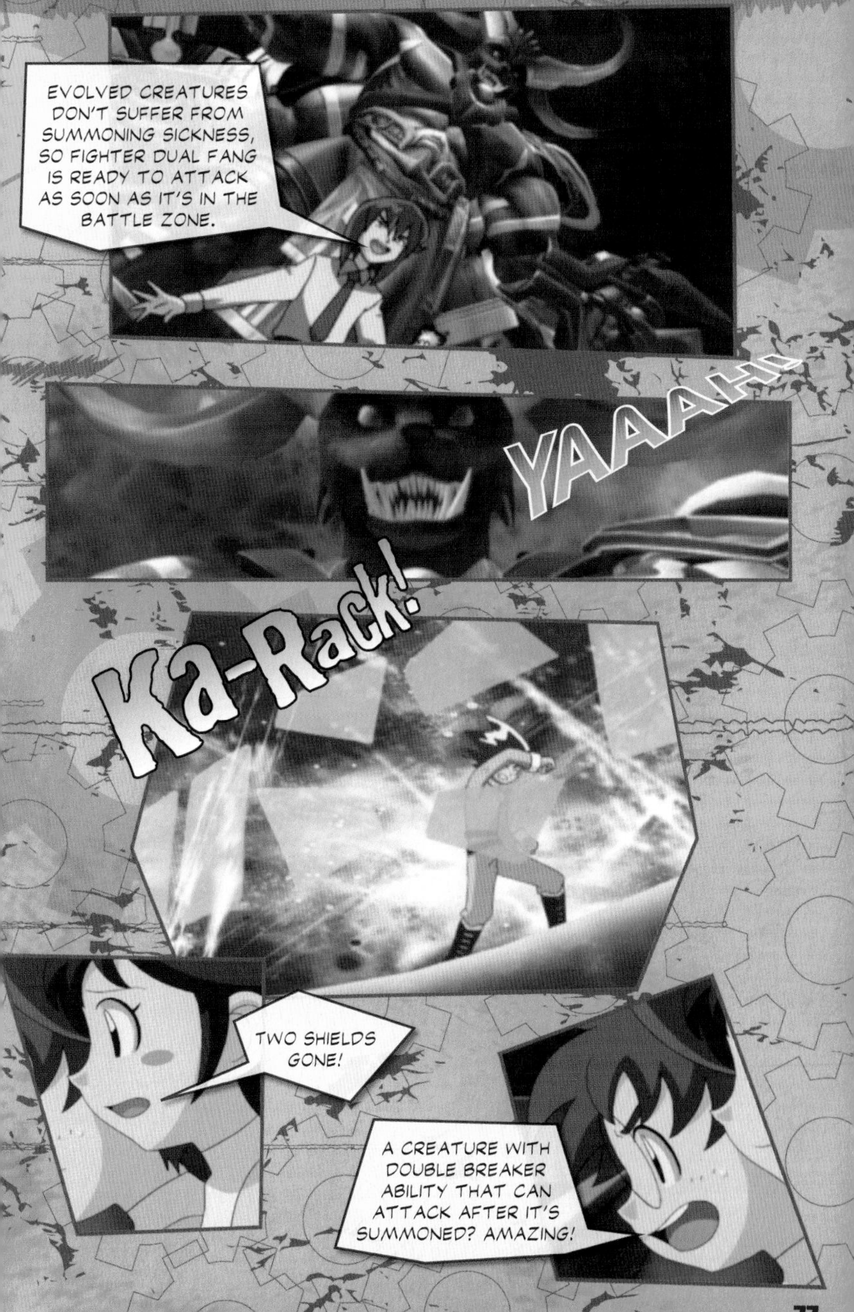
EVOLVED CREATURES DON'T SUFFER FROM SUMMONING SICKNESS, SO FIGHTER DUAL FANG IS READY TO ATTACK AS SOON AS IT'S IN THE BATTLE ZONE.
YAAAAH!
Ka-Rack!
TWO SHIELDS GONE!
A CREATURE WITH DOUBLE BREAKER ABILITY THAT CAN ATTACK AFTER IT'S SUMMONED? AMAZING!

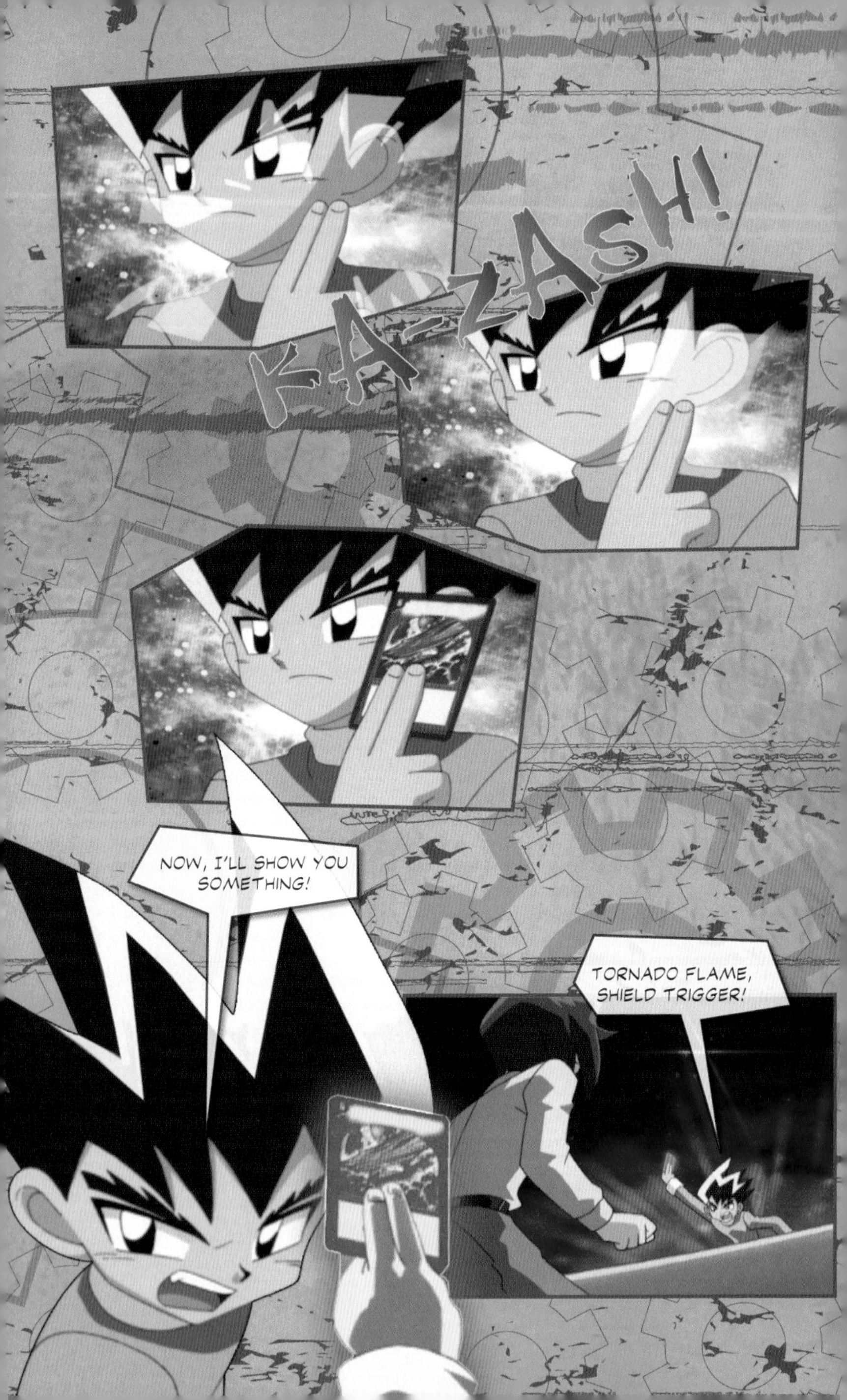
KA-ZASH!
NOW, I'LL SHOW YOU SOMETHING!
TORNADO FLAME, SHIELD TRIGGER!

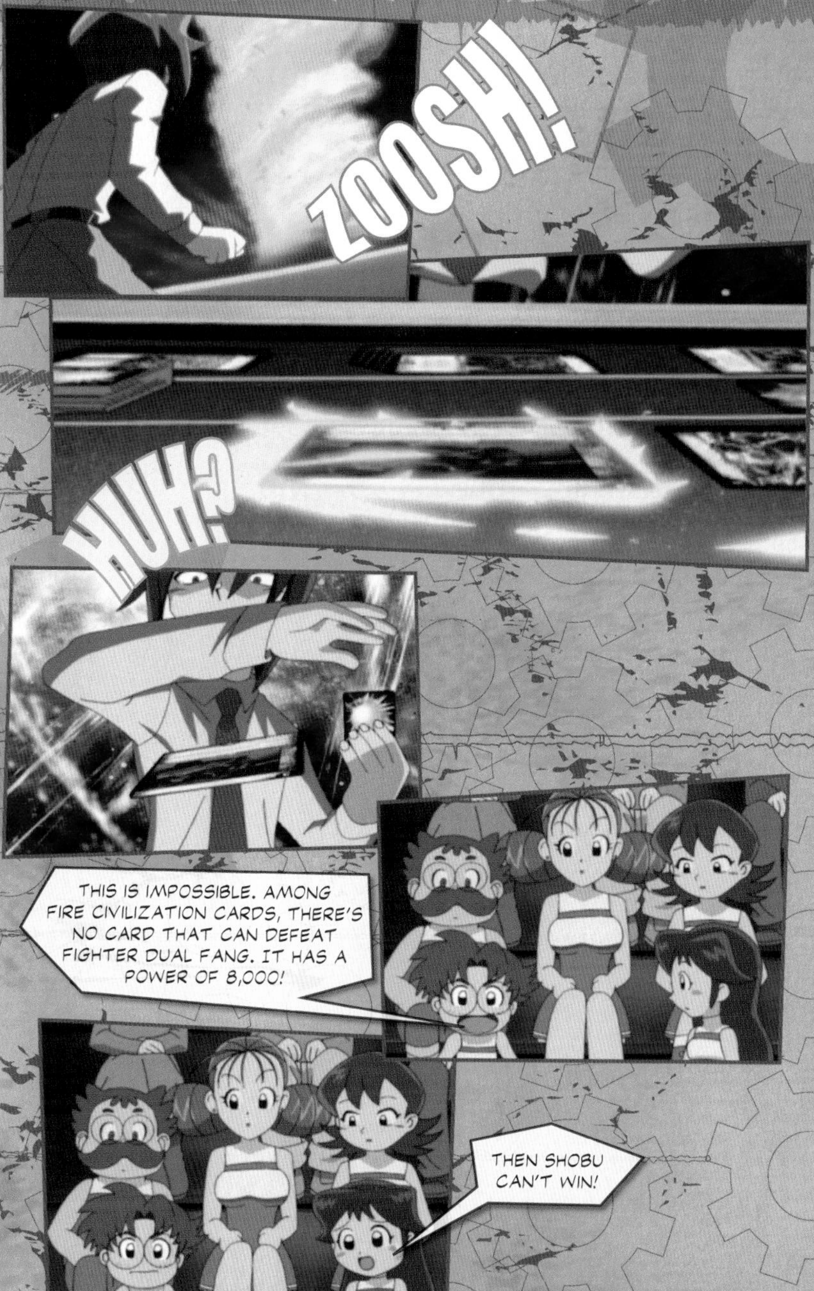
ZOOSH!
HUH?
THIS IS IMPOSSIBLE. AMONG FIRE CIVILIZATION CARDS, THERE'S NO CARD THAT CAN DEFEAT FIGHTER DUAL FANG. IT HAS A POWER OF 8,000!
THEN SHOBU CAN'T WIN!

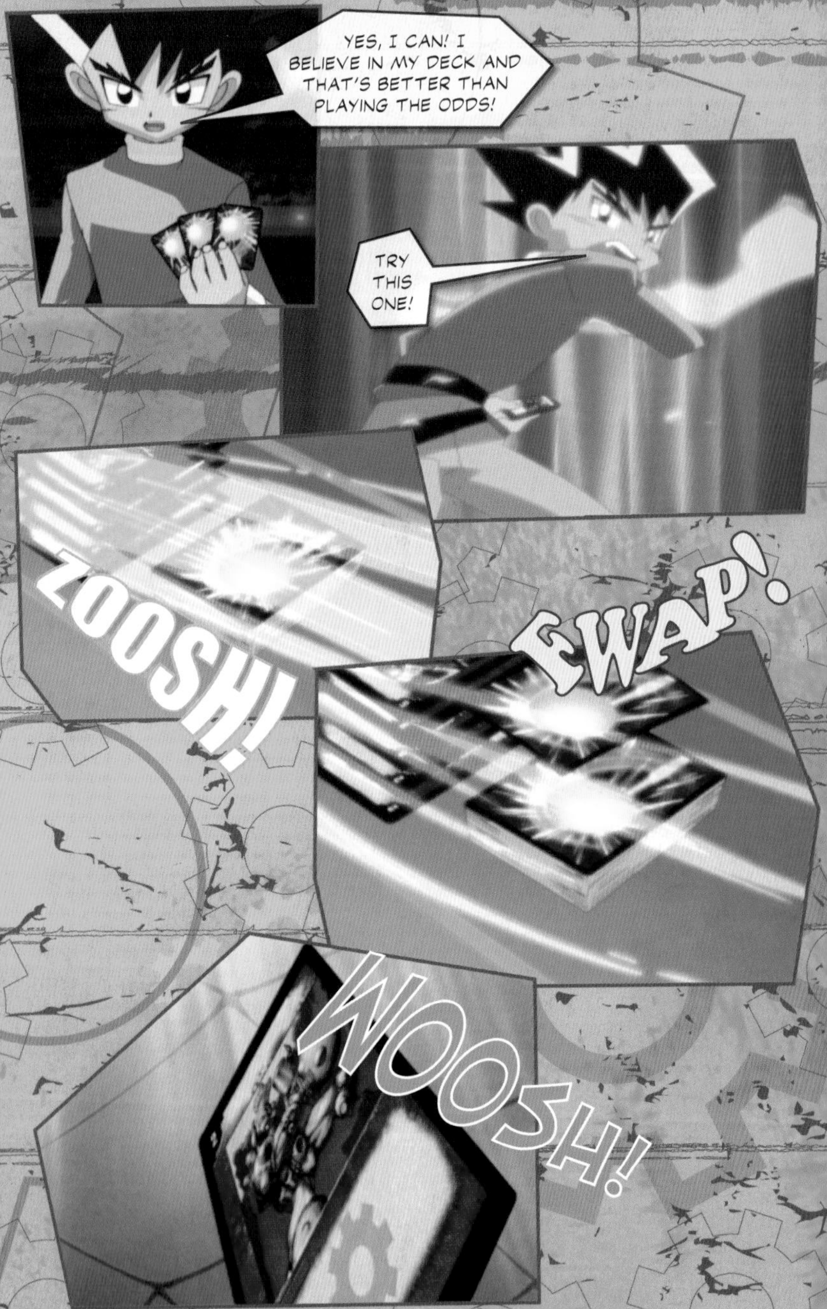
YES, I CAN! I BELIEVE IN MY DECK AND THAT'S BETTER THAN PLAYING THE ODDS!
TRY THIS ONE!
ZOOSH!
FWAP!
WOOSH!

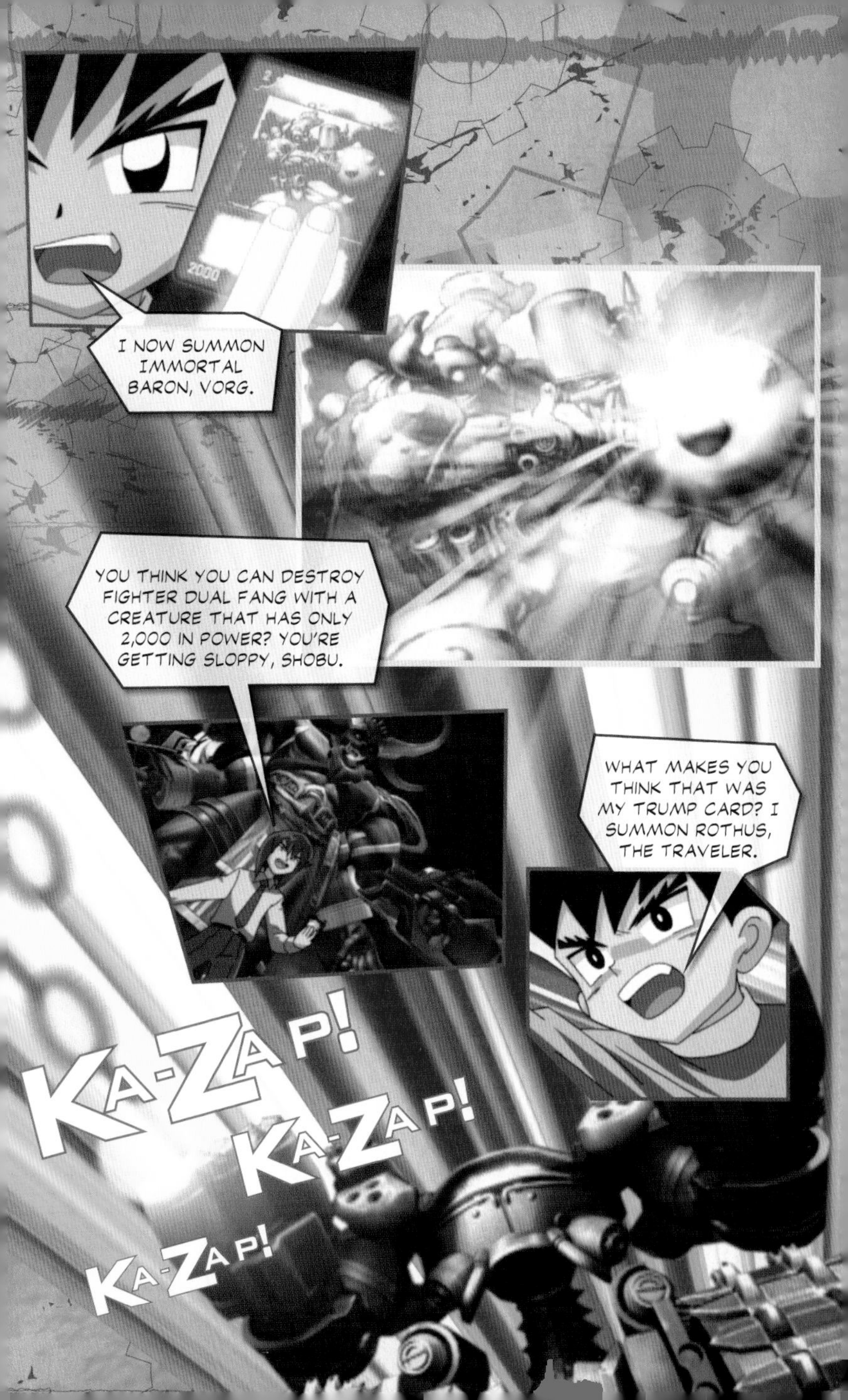
I NOW SUMMON IMMORTAL BARON, VORG.
YOU THINK YOU CAN DESTROY FIGHTER DUAL FANG WITH A CREATURE THAT HAS ONLY 2,000 IN POWER? YOU'RE GETTING SLOPPY, SHOBU.
WHAT MAKES YOU THINK THAT WAS MY TRUMP CARD? I SUMMON ROTHUS, THE TRAVELER.
KA-ZAP!
KA-ZAP!
KA-ZAP!

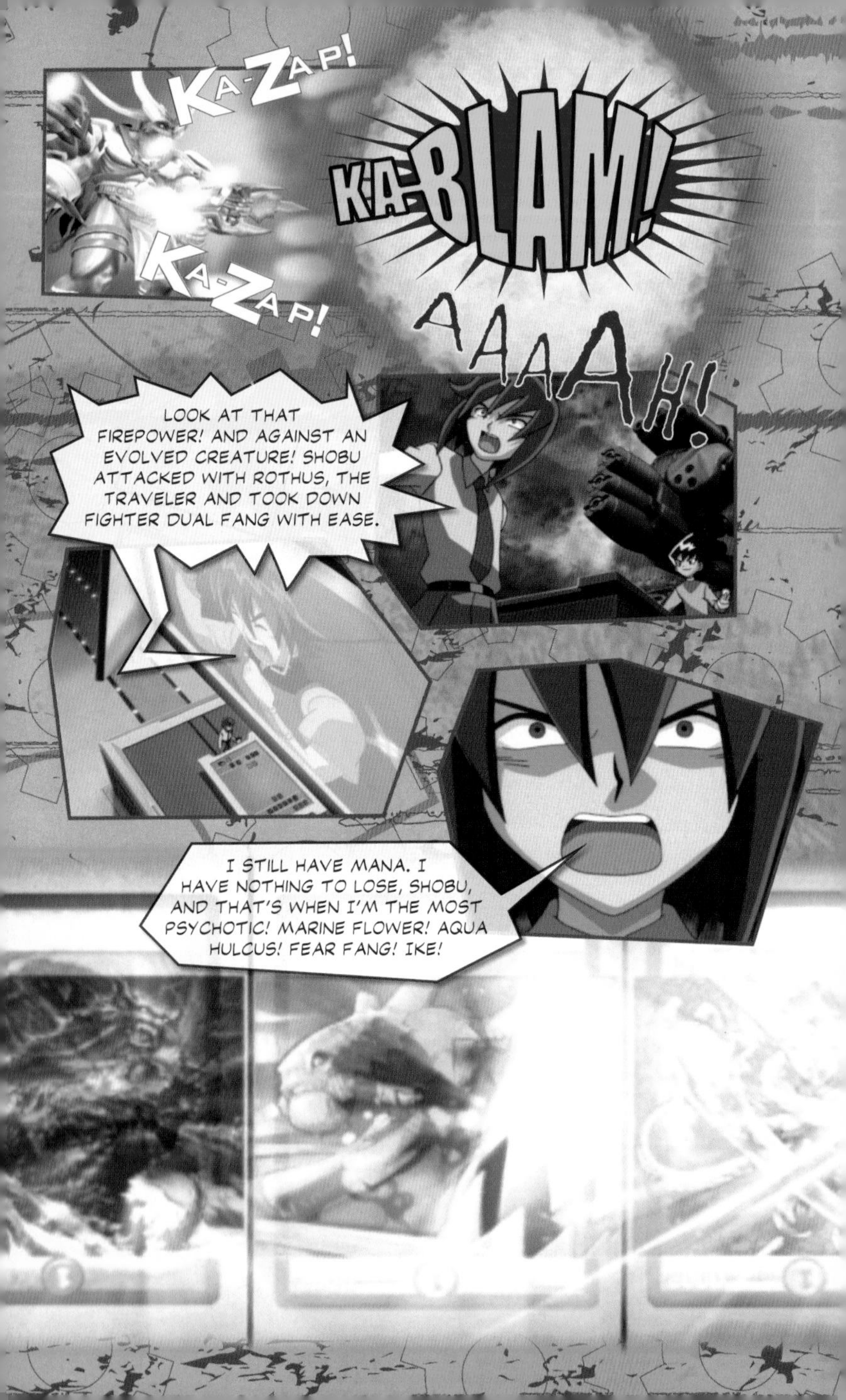
KA-ZAP!
KA-ZAP!
KA-BLAM!
AAAAH!
LOOK AT THAT FIREPOWER! AND AGAINST AN EVOLVED CREATURE! SHOBU ATTACKED WITH ROTHUS, THE TRAVELER AND TOOK DOWN FIGHTER DUAL FANG WITH EASE.
I STILL HAVE MANA. I HAVE NOTHING TO LOSE, SHOBU, AND THAT'S WHEN I'M THE MOST PSYCHOTIC! MARINE FLOWER! AQUA HULCUS! FEAR FANG! IKE!

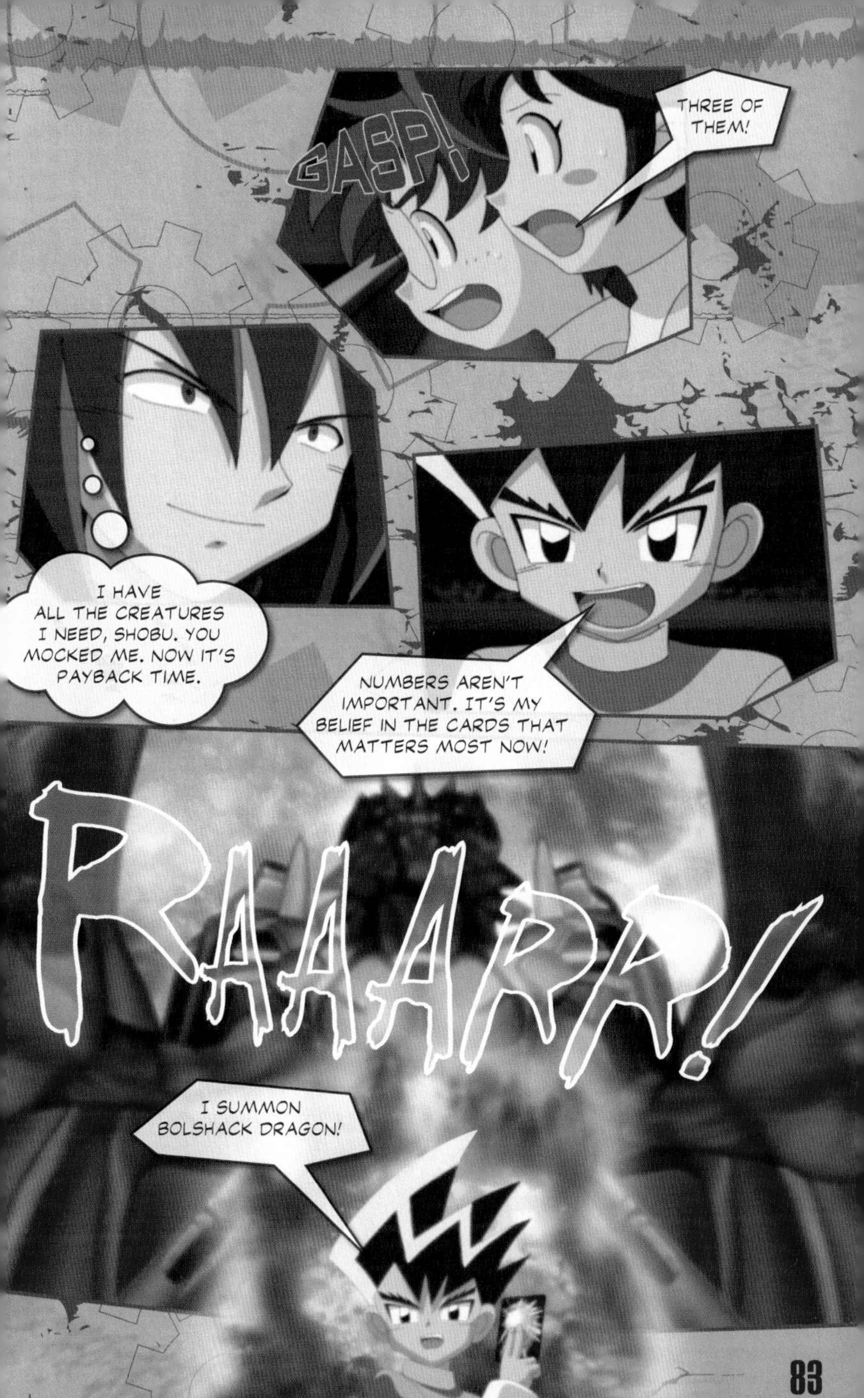
GASP!
THREE OF THEM!
I HAVE ALL THE CREATURES I NEED, SHOBU. YOU MOCKED ME. NOW IT'S PAYBACK TIME.
NUMBERS AREN'T IMPORTANT. IT'S MY BELIEF IN THE CARDS THAT MATTERS MOST NOW!
RAAARR!
I SUMMON BOLSHACK DRAGON!

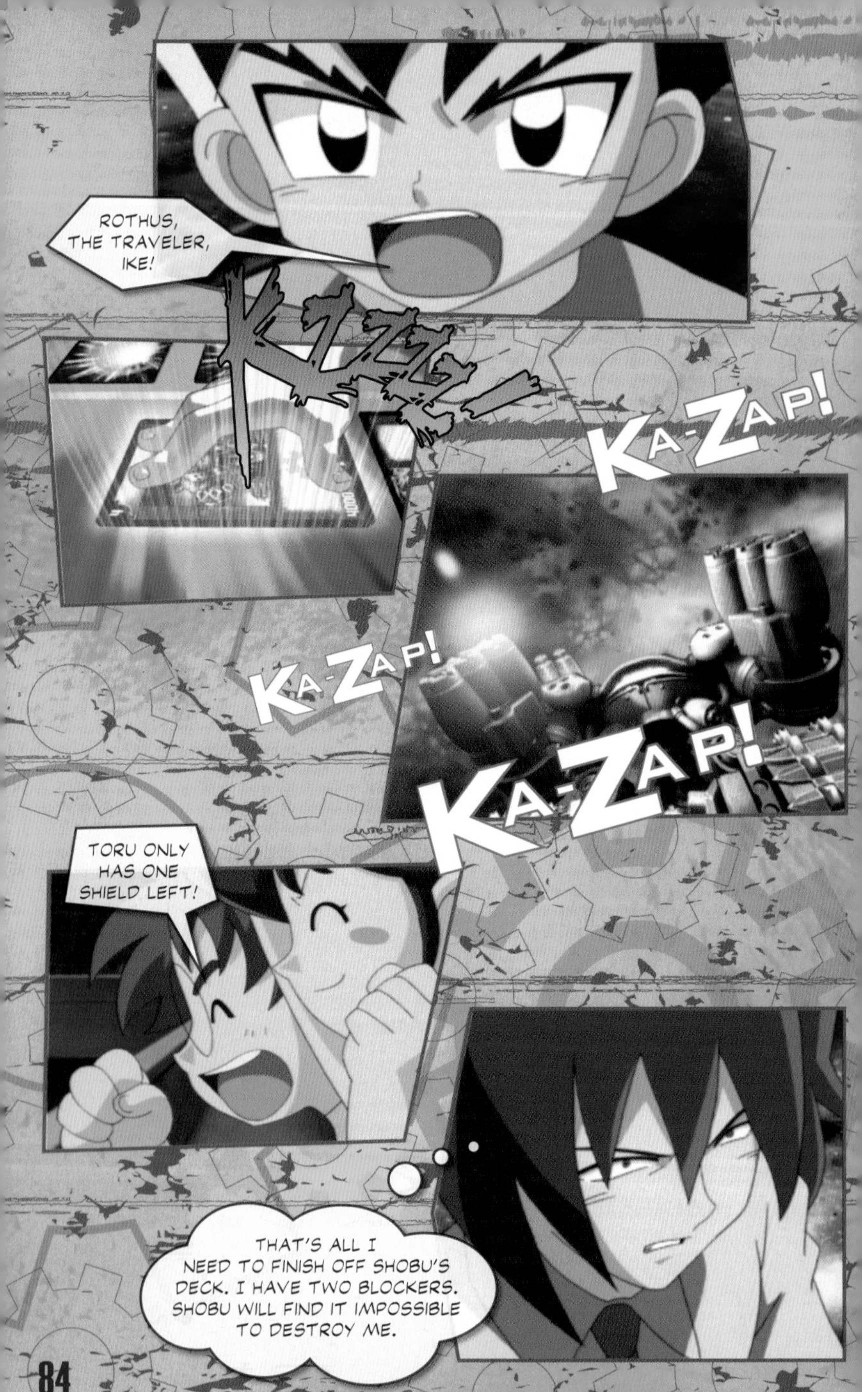
ROTHUS, THE TRAVELER, IKE!
KZZZZT!
KA-ZAP!
KA-ZAP!
KA-ZAP!
TORU ONLY HAS ONE SHIELD LEFT!
THAT'S ALL I NEED TO FINISH OFF SHOBU'S DECK. I HAVE TWO BLOCKERS. SHOBU WILL FIND IT IMPOSSIBLE TO DESTROY ME.

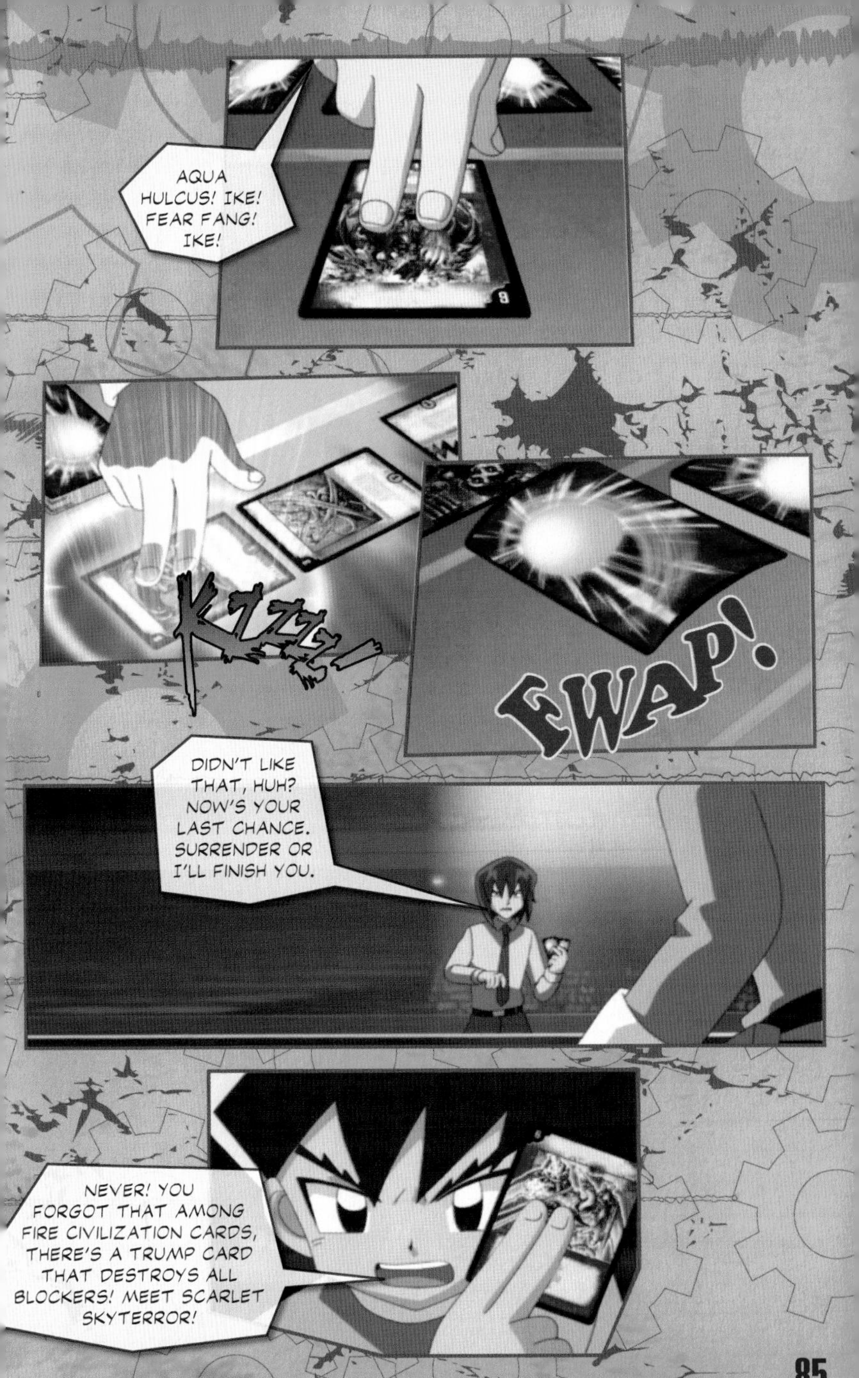
AQUA HULCUS! IKE! FEAR FANG! IKE!
KZZZZ!
FWAP!
DIDN'T LIKE THAT, HUH? NOW'S YOUR LAST CHANCE. SURRENDER OR I'LL FINISH YOU.
NEVER! YOU FORGOT THAT AMONG FIRE CIVILIZATION CARDS, THERE'S A TRUMP CARD THAT DESTROYS ALL BLOCKERS! MEET SCARLET SKYTERROR!

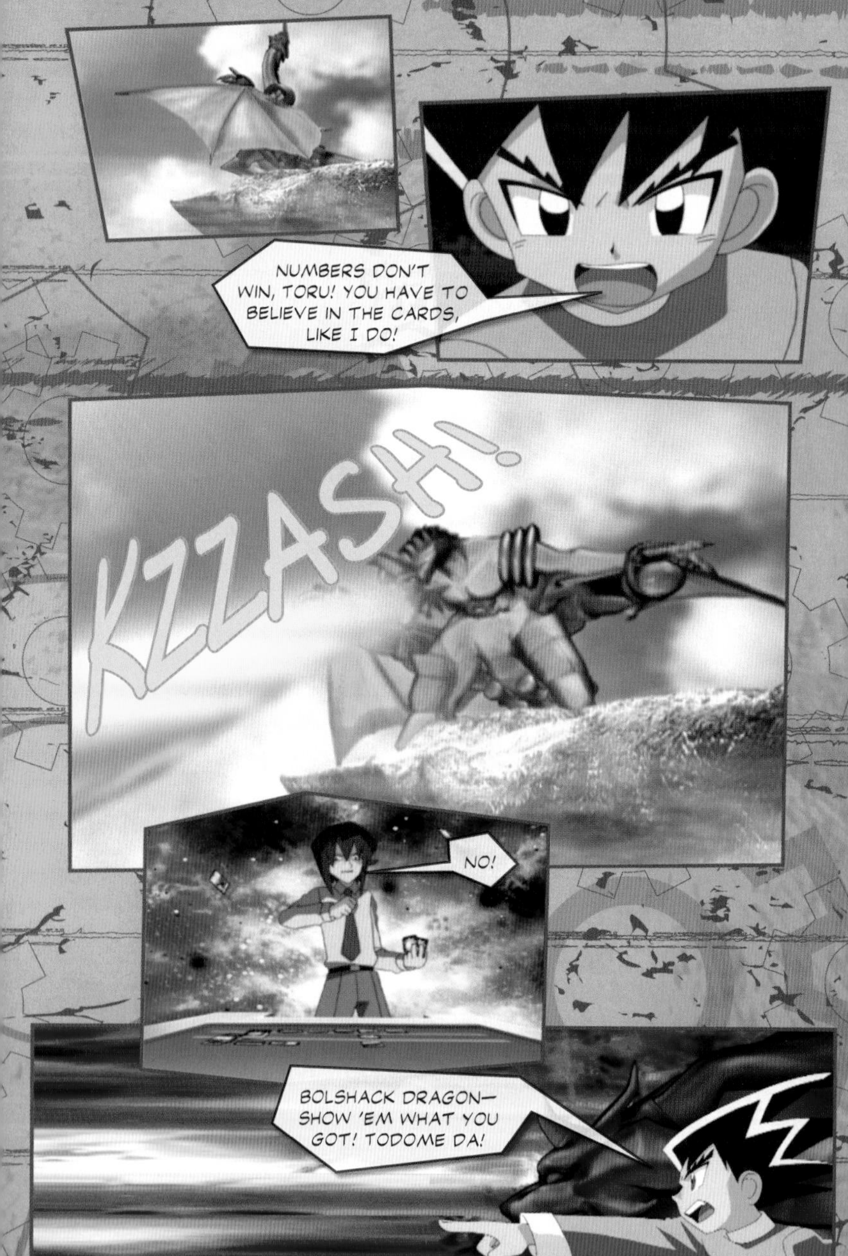
NUMBERS DON'T WIN, TORU! YOU HAVE TO BELIEVE IN THE CARDS, LIKE I DO!
KZZASH!
NO!
BOLSHACK DRAGON— SHOW 'EM WHAT YOU GOT! TODOME DA!

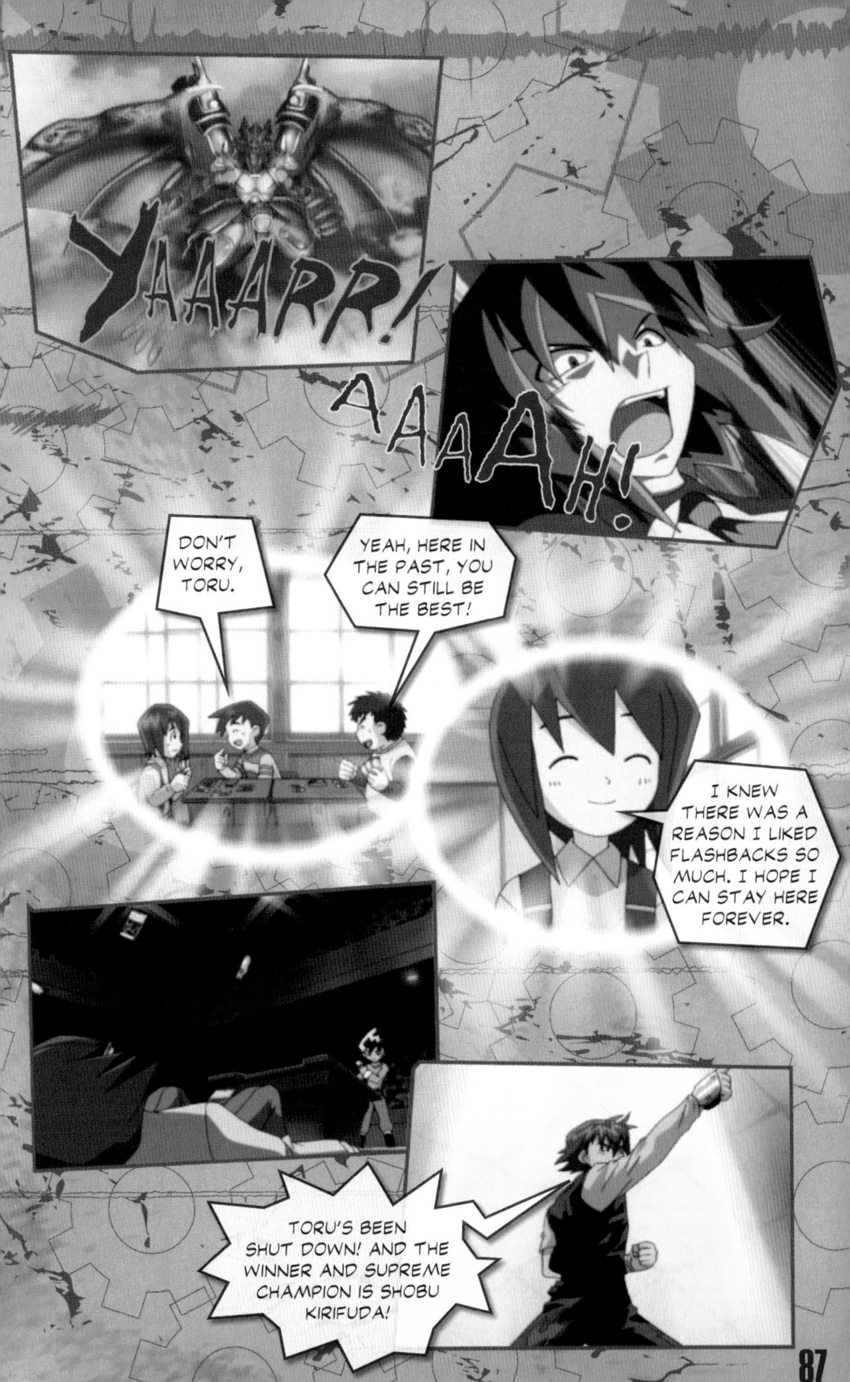
YAAARR!
AAAAH!
DON'T WORRY, TORU.
YEAH, HERE IN THE PAST, YOU CAN STILL BE THE BEST!
I KNEW THERE WAS A REASON I LIKED FLASHBACKS SO MUCH. I HOPE I CAN STAY HERE FOREVER.
TORU'S BEEN SHUT DOWN! AND THE WINNER AND SUPREME CHAMPION IS SHOBU KIRIFUDA!

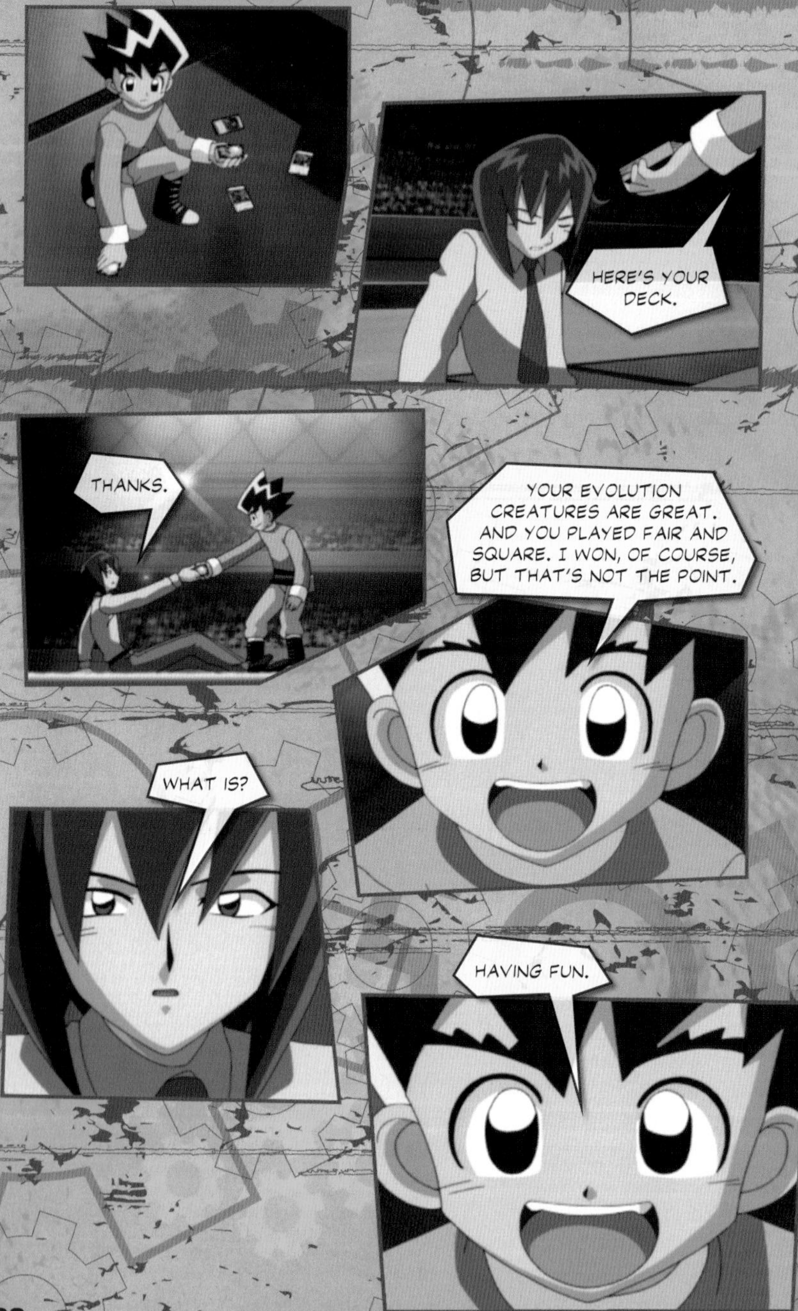
HERE'S YOUR DECK.
THANKS.
YOUR EVOLUTION CREATURES ARE GREAT. AND YOU PLAYED FAIR AND SQUARE. I WON, OF COURSE, BUT THAT'S NOT THE POINT.
WHAT IS?
HAVING FUN.

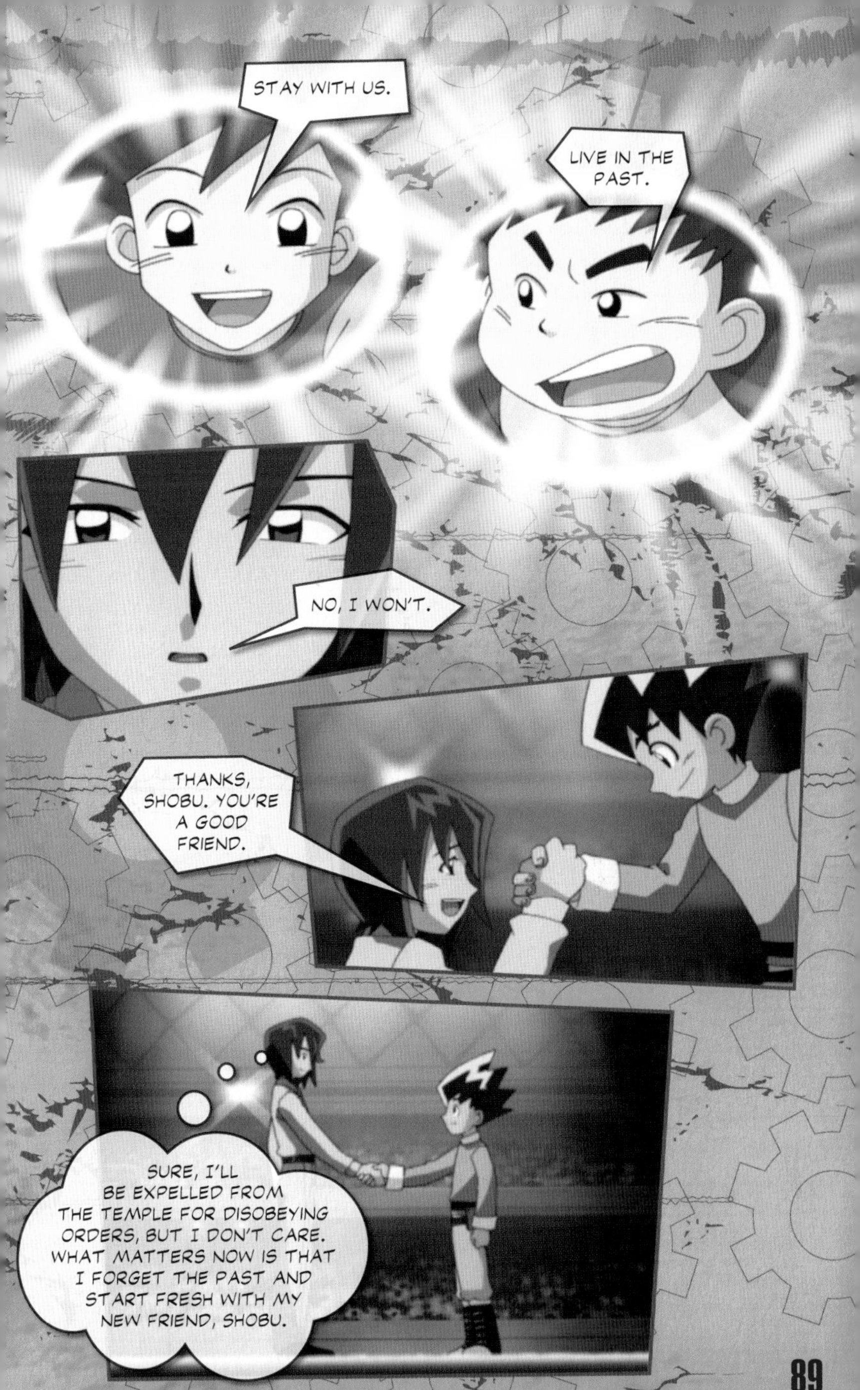
STAY WITH US.
LIVE IN THE PAST.
NO, I WON'T.
THANKS, SHOBU. YOU'RE A GOOD FRIEND.
SURE, I'LL BE EXPELLED FROM THE TEMPLE FOR DISOBEYING ORDERS, BUT I DON'T CARE. WHAT MATTERS NOW IS THAT I FORGET THE PAST AND START FRESH WITH MY NEW FRIEND, SHOBU.

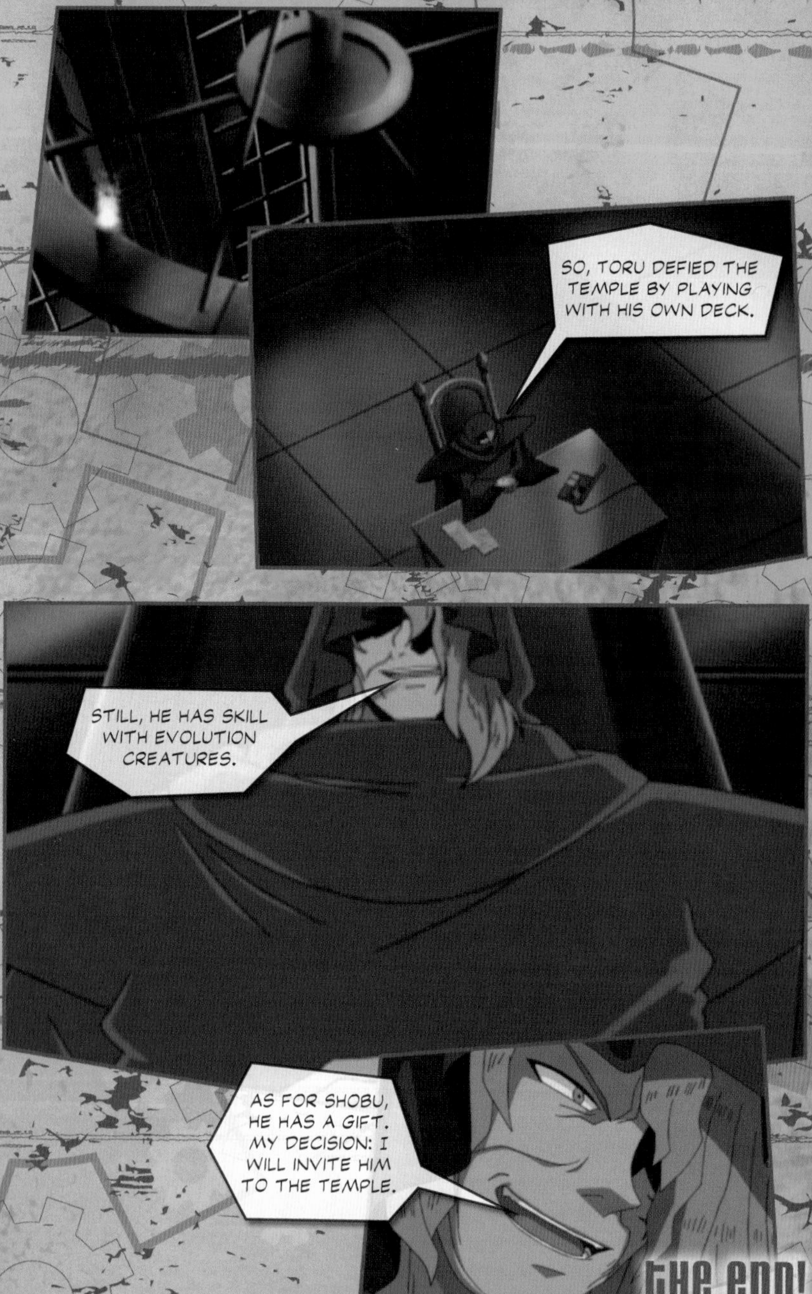
SO, TORU DEFIED THE TEMPLE BY PLAYING WITH HIS OWN DECK.
STILL, HE HAS SKILL WITH EVOLUTION CREATURES.
AS FOR SHOBU, HE HAS A GIFT. MY DECISION: I WILL INVITE HIM TO THE TEMPLE.
THE END!

ALSO AVAILABLE FROM ◎TOKYOPOP®

MANGA

HACK//LEGEND OF THE TWILIGHT
ALICHINO
ANGELIC LAYER
BABY BIRTH
BRAIN POWERED
BRIGADOON
B'TX
CANDIDATE FOR GODDESS, THE
CARDCAPTOR SAKURA
CARDCAPTOR SAKURA - MASTER OF THE CLOW
CHRONICLES OF THE CURSED SWORD
CLAMP SCHOOL DETECTIVES
CLOVER
COMIC PARTY
CORRECTOR YUI
COWBOY BEBOP
COWBOY BEBOP: SHOOTING STAR
CRESCENT MOON
CROSS
CULDCEPT
CYBORG 009
D•N•ANGEL
DEARS
DEMON DIARY
DEMON ORORON, THE
DIGIMON
DIGIMON TAMERS
DIGIMON ZERO TWO
DRAGON HUNTER
DRAGON KNIGHTS
DRAGON VOICE
DREAM SAGA
DUKLYON: CLAMP SCHOOL DEFENDERS
ET CETERA
ETERNITY
FAERIES' LANDING
FLCL
FLOWER OF THE DEEP SLEEP
FORBIDDEN DANCE
FRUITS BASKET
G GUNDAM
GATEKEEPERS
GIRL GOT GAME
GUNDAM SEED ASTRAY
GUNDAM WING
GUNDAM WING: BATTLEFIELD OF PACIFISTS
GUNDAM WING: ENDLESS WALTZ
GUNDAM WING: THE LAST OUTPOST (G-UNIT)
HANDS OFF!

HARLEM BEAT
HYPER RUNE
I.N.V.U.
INITIAL D
INSTANT TEEN: JUST ADD NUTS
JING: KING OF BANDITS
JING: KING OF BANDITS - TWILIGHT TALES
JULINE
KARE KANO
KILL ME, KISS ME
KINDAICHI CASE FILES, THE
KING OF HELL
KODOCHA: SANA'S STAGE
LEGEND OF CHUN HYANG, THE
LOVE OR MONEY
MAGIC KNIGHT RAYEARTH I
MAGIC KNIGHT RAYEARTH II
MAN OF MANY FACES
MARMALADE BOY
MARS
MARS: HORSE WITH NO NAME
MINK
MIRACLE GIRLS
MODEL
MOURYOU KIDEN: LEGEND OF THE NYMPH
NECK AND NECK
ONE
ONE I LOVE, THE
PEACH FUZZ
PEACH GIRL
PEACH GIRL: CHANGE OF HEART
PITA-TEN
PLANET LADDER
PLANETES
PRESIDENT DAD
PRINCESS AI
PSYCHIC ACADEMY
QUEEN'S KNIGHT, THE
RAGNAROK
RAVE MASTER
REALITY CHECK
REBIRTH
REBOUND
RISING STARS OF MANGA
SAILOR MOON
SAINT TAIL
SAMURAI GIRL REAL BOUT HIGH SCHOOL
SEIKAI TRILOGY, THE
SGT. FROG
SHAOLIN SISTERS

09.21.0

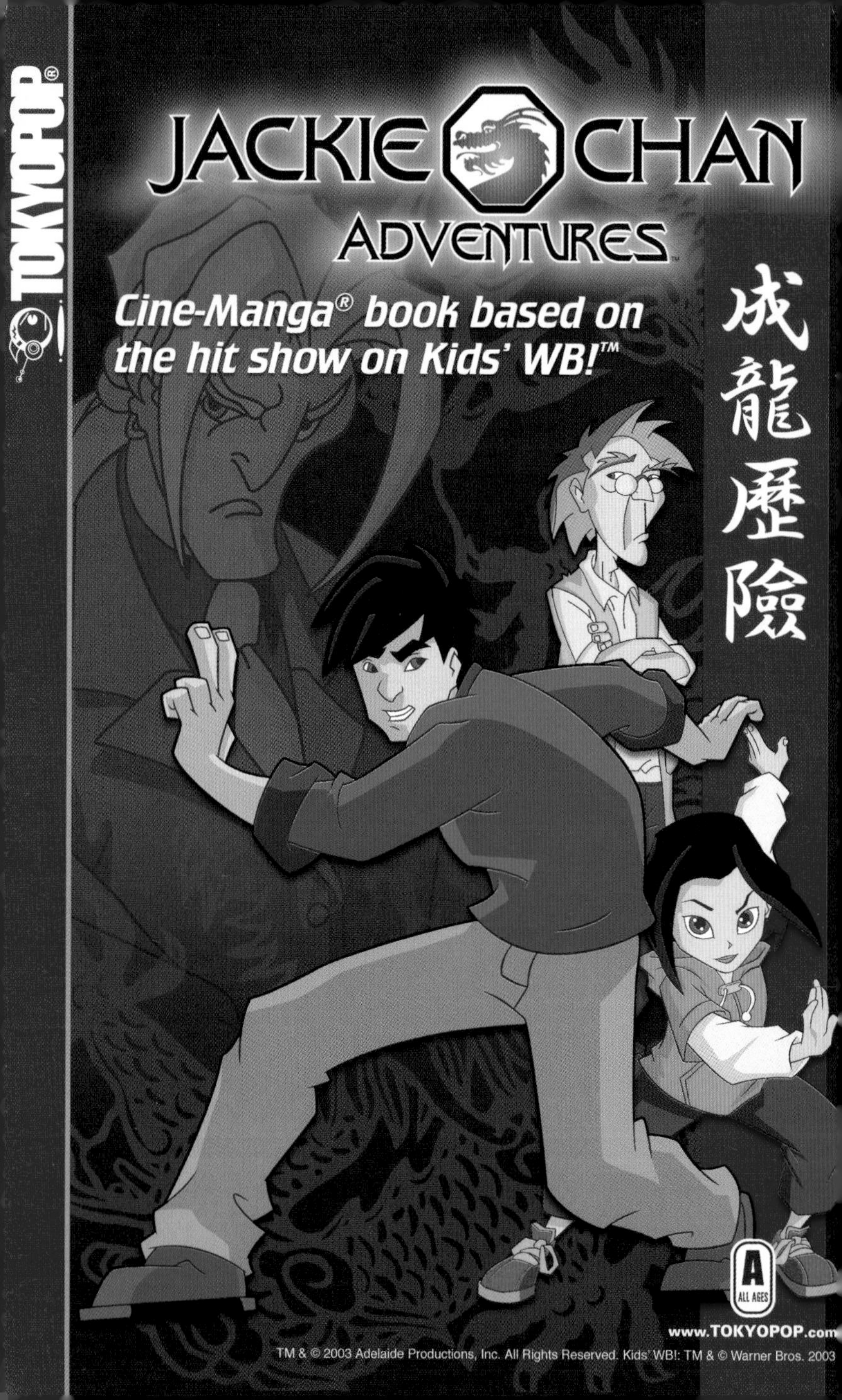
TOKYOPOP®
JACKIE CHAN ADVENTURES™
Cine-Manga® book based on the hit show on Kids' WB!™
成龍歷險
A
ALL AGES
www.TOKYOPOP.com
TM & © 2003 Adelaide Productions, Inc. All Rights Reserved. Kids' WB!: TM & © Warner Bros. 2003

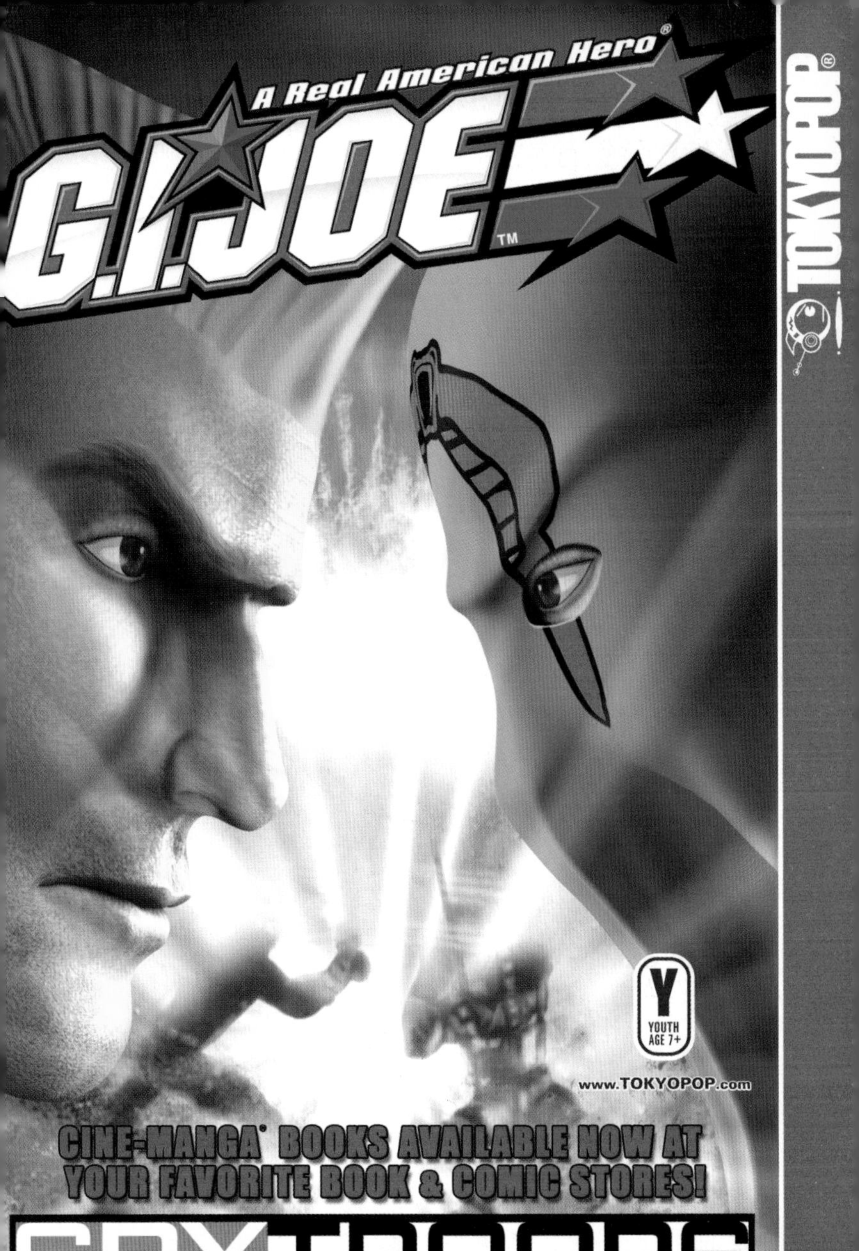

A Real American Hero®
G.I. JOE™
TOKYOPOP®
Y
YOUTH AGE 7+
www.TOKYOPOP.com
CINE-MANGA® BOOKS AVAILABLE NOW AT YOUR FAVORITE BOOK & COMIC STORES!
SPY TROOPS

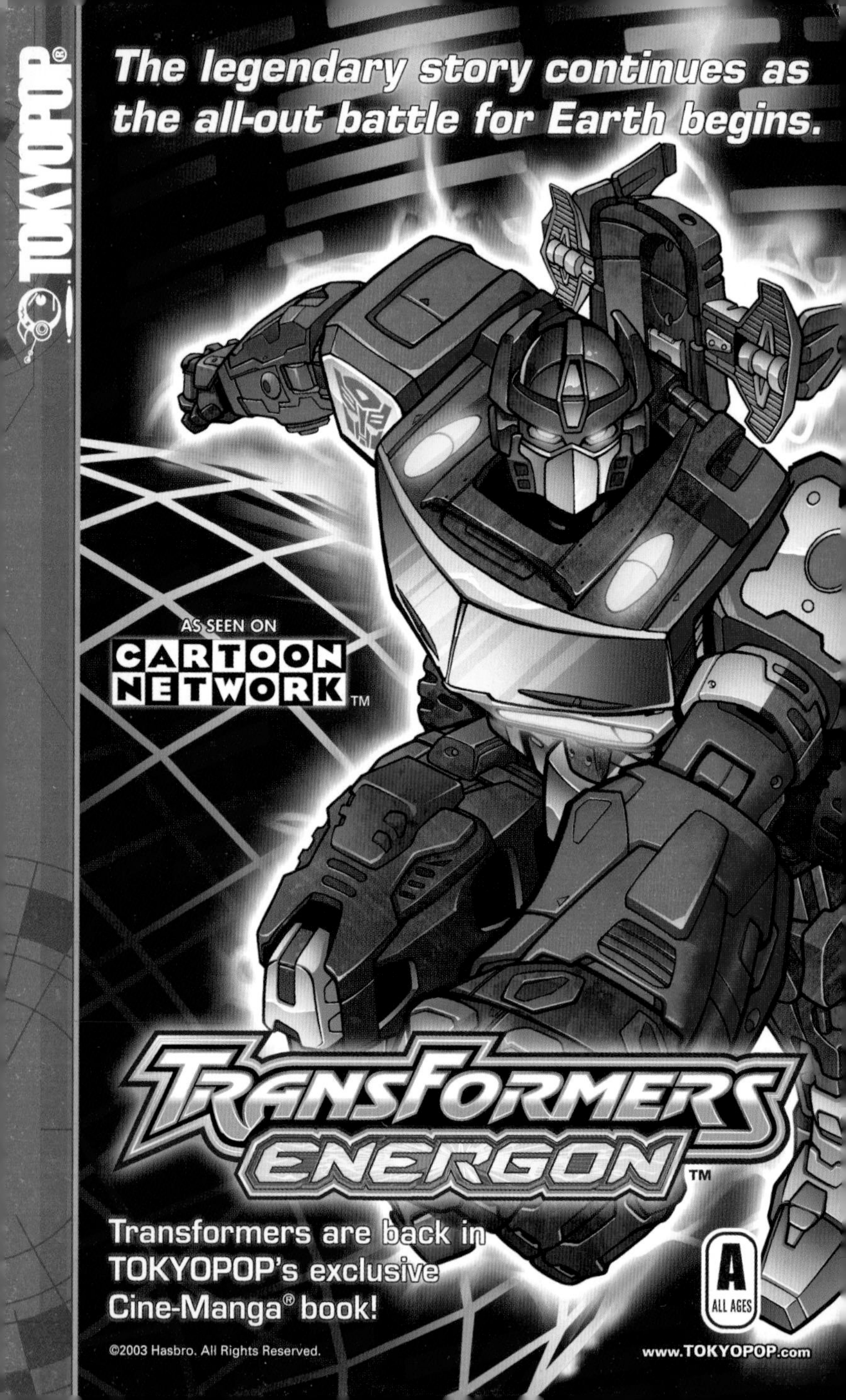
TOKYOPOP
The legendary story continues as the all-out battle for Earth begins.
AS SEEN ON
CARTOON NETWORK™
TRANSFORMERS ENERGON™
Transformers are back in TOKYOPOP's exclusive Cine-Manga® book!
A ALL AGES
©2003 Hasbro. All Rights Reserved.
www.TOKYOPOP.com